P9-CEZ-562

WHITE TIGER
ON SNOW
MOUNTAIN

WHITE TIGER ON SNOW MOUNTAIN

David Gordon

NEW HARVEST
HOUGHTON MIFFLIN HARCOURT
Boston   New York
2014

Some of these stories have appeared, sometimes in different form,
in the *Paris Review, Five Chapters, Fence, Blackbird, Kindle Singles,*
and (in Japanese) *Hayakawa's Mystery Magazine.*

This edition published by special arrangement with Amazon Publishing

Amazon and the Amazon logo are trademarks of
Amazon.com, Inc. or its affiliates.

For information about permission to reproduce selections
from this book, go to www.apub.com.

www.hmhco.com

Library of Congress Cataloging-in-Publication Data
Gordon, David, date.
   [Short stories. Selections]
White tiger on Snow Mountain / David Gordon.
   pages cm
ISBN 978-0-544-34374-0 (hardcover)
I. Title.
PS3607.O5935W55 2014
813'.6 — dc23
2014016714

Printed in the United States of America
DOC 10 9 8 7 6 5 4 3 2 1

To my family and my friends

CONTENTS

WHITE TIGER
ON SNOW
MOUNTAIN

Man-Boob Summer

I was spending some time at my parents' place that summer. I was thirty-eight and out of ideas. I had finished my midlife crisis graduate degree a bit early, and after turning in my thesis, I promptly fell into the utter despair that comes from completing a long, difficult, and entirely pointless project. I was deeply, profoundly in debt, ruined really, and had no idea what I would do next. Also, I'd just been kicked out of the apartment in Soho where I'd been living for several years when my landlady, a ninety-five-year-old artist, finally died. That crumbling little building was like the last ragged fort of Old Bohemia, sandwiched between Louis Vuitton and Victoria's Secret. For decades my landlady had clung on, through Alzheimer's and pneumonia and broken hips, while her relatives and accountant bided their time. When at last she went, only the South American woman who looked after her cried, and a month later the building sold for $12 million. My books and winter clothes went into storage with the dining room set I'd won in my divorce settlement, and I moved across the bridge to New Jersey.

. . .

Immediately, I established a new regimen. I rose at eight, so that my parents wouldn't think I was a bum, and sat at my little desk, really a folding snack table in the guest room, doing the crossword puzzle until they left for work, when I sometimes took a quick nap. They never reproached me, but I wallowed in my failure and liked to imagine the looks on their faces if I got a job in their building buffing the floors. Then I went running. Then lunch. Then down to the pool.

The apartment complex (I wish there was a more graceful term for these minor high-rise city-states) actually had a very nice pool, small but almost empty on the weekdays, and set on the edge of the cliffs overlooking the Hudson and Manhattan Island. On a clear day you could see the individual cars traveling across the bridge and up and down the city's west side, like corpuscles in an IV drip. On a stormy day you could see the weather before it arrived.

That summer I swam, snoozed, and got my first tan ever. I tried to read, but my heart had turned against literature, which I blamed for much of my misfortune. Had I looked at Tolstoy or Stendhal, I think I would have hurled myself off the cliffs. On the other hand, I was afraid that opening a new book by a promising young writer might trigger a homicidal rampage. Would that I had never learned to read! The only safe choice was Simenon's mystery novels about Inspector Maigret, which I consumed one after another, in measured doses, like lithium. Sometimes all you can stand to think about is a guy with a mustache solving a murder.

The only other weekday regulars at the pool were a few lizardy old-timers and this weird Russian family. At least, I thought they were Russian. The leader was an overweight guy with a toupee and a tiny Speedo swimsuit. It was a garish brown-red color, rust really (I mean the toupee here, not the Speedo, which was, get this, white). I kept waiting for it (the toupee) to come off when he swam, but it never did, so maybe it was real after all. It didn't look any faker than his mustache, which turned up at the ends like Poirot's. (I read a few dozen of those Agatha Christie books that summer too.)

The woman (his wife? his daughter?) was blond and stocky, and when I sat submerged in the Jacuzzi, bubbles rumbling around my nose, and she lowered herself in across from me, I saw how her thighs were scored with the plastic pattern of her chair. The marks looked like welts, like someone had whipped her, and even though I knew it was only from sitting and reading *Us* magazine, I instantly felt something sorrowful and wounded about her, like there was always smoke in her eyes, smoke only she could smell, or else she was allergic to something that was there around us but that I was too crude to sense.

Then there was the kid. He was five or six maybe. A real whiner. He was blond and wan, and no matter what he was doing — floating in the man's arms and practice-kicking, jumping into the pool, eating a cookie — he screeched incessantly in this high, petulant squeal that set my teeth on edge. I shouldn't say this, because I'm sure I was a kid like that too, but I couldn't stand the little crybaby.

But the thing I wanted to say, the significant thing, was about the guy's boobs. Yes, they were hairy. However, that isn't the key issue. What I really wanted to mention was that one of them was bigger than the other. I think the left. And I mean dramatically bigger, like several cup sizes. I didn't even notice it at first, he had so much else going on, but one afternoon I just happened to lift my gaze from *Maigret Sets a Trap,* and there he was, rising from the pool, mustache drooping, water streaming through his body hair like rushes along a sandbank, and I saw it, one flat male breast and one pendulous female breast. It was as if something womanly, long buried, was fighting to burst forth, as if the man was riven in two. Although I knew he couldn't see me behind my shades, I felt like he was staring right at me, with a plaintive face, and deliberately showing me his burden and his wound. What could cause such a thing? Cancer? Cholesterol? Love? (Love in the Time of Cholesterol?) The mad thought occurred to me that it might start throbbing wildly, like a cartoon creature in raptures. Teetering on the verge of a freak-out, I quickly looked away.

The other people who were always there were the lifeguards, mainly local teenagers. There were usually two on duty at a time, one sitting in that high chair over the water and one checking for passes as you came in. It had been a very long time since I'd swum in a supervised pool like that, maybe since I was a kid myself, and the change in perspective was dramatic. Before I'd been intimidated, especially by the girl lifeguards: Not only did their sleek bodies, summer-streaked hair, and impossibly tan, impossibly smooth legs disturb me, but they also swam better than me, obviously, and by virtue of that seemed more adult, as if they had been promoted to Woman while I was still a little boy who might get water in his eyes and need to be yanked out, bawling.

Now of course I was old enough to be their father, and for the most part they treated me as such, punching my pass with a thank-you, informing me politely if the pool was about to close. When I said good morning to a burly blond lifeguard with a nest of big back zits (bacne, we called it in my day), and he looked down to avoid my gaze, it suddenly hit me, maybe for the first time: I'm an adult now, and he is the one intimidated by me.

Except for Lisa. Of course, I didn't know her name at first. Remember, they sat up top and the sun was always in my eyes. She was just a slim silhouette, with long dark hair, a life-saver's red one-piece, and one of those macramé things braided around her ankle. But this day was extra hot, and every few pages, I'd jump into the water to cool off. I was the only one swimming, and I realized after a couple of turns that, due no doubt to some insurance rule, each time I got in the pool, she had to put down her book, leave her shade and soda, and climb up the ladder to her post.

"That's OK," I shouted as she sprang from her chair. "Relax."

"No, that's OK," she said. "It's my job."

I dove in, wriggling along the bottom like a tadpole, and popped up at the other end. "Look," I said, "I think it's safe, really," and showed her how the water only came up to my eyes, although I cheated a bit, pushing onto my toes at the deep end. "If I start drowning, just yell, 'Stand up, you idiot!'"

A girlish laugh rang out from the haze of sun I was talking to. "No way. It's my sacred duty to protect you."

"Hey," I asked, "do you think if you had to, you could really lift me out of the pool? You're kind of little. Don't they have some kind of height requirement?"

She stuck her tongue out at me. "Try it and see."

"OK," I said, hoisting myself onto the concrete. Water ran

down my legs and puddled around my feet. I waved a finger in challenge. "Be on your guard. When you least expect it, expect it."

I lay back down in my chair, and from the safety of my sunglasses and book, I looked her over more closely. She wasn't really short at all. In fact, her legs were long and slender, and they kept folding and unfolding, rubbing against each other like cats in the warmth of the sun. She wore a too-big hooded gray sweatshirt, and the bathing suit cut high above her jutting hip bone. And her ass, when she climbed down from her throne and sprawled on her belly to read, was just perfect.

After my landlady died, the thing that really stuck with me was how — what word shall I use? — how lustful she remained right up to the end, long after you'd have thought that her body would have forgotten and her mind slipped free of such base desires, moving on to less worldly matters, or at least more urgent fears like, for instance, death itself. Nope. The very first time I met her, her Alzheimer's was already well advanced, and when her caretaker, Maria, introduced us, she gave me a warm kiss on the cheek. "Of course I know him," she scolded Maria, and then tittered coyly, "very well. And he knows me ... very well." She batted her eyelashes at me.

Maria laughed. "She thinks you are one of her former lovers." Apparently she'd been pretty wild in her time, and bisexual too. She slept with Jane Bowles and Max Ernst and tried to seduce Tennessee Williams, which would have been a real coup, but they ended up just friends. After that, she flirted with me about half the time. When she got her second bout of pneumonia, she even asked me to escort her downstairs to the ambulance. Otherwise, she ignored me completely or asked Maria who I was.

"Maybe I should marry her," I suggested. "Then we'll all live happily ever after."

Maria laughed. "Yes, I'm sure her family would be very pleased."

"Who are they to doubt our love?"

Then Maria told me a story about taking the landlady to a party, when she was already in her late eighties but still able to get around a bit. It was held by one of her old pals, a decrepit composer. When Maria came to pick her up, the old woman's clothes were all mixed up. She didn't have her bra on, and her underwear was backward.

"Did you have sex?" Maria asked her, but she just giggled. It turned out she'd gotten together with one of the other old ladies, who was still naked in a back bedroom, wrapped in a quilt and smoking. Meanwhile, and this is the part that gets me, Maria said she found the host, who was probably ninety himself, sitting and brooding at his piano, plunking chords in a dark fit of jealousy.

"Don't ever fall in love," he told Maria. "It's just poison."

That's when I realized: It never stops, this nonsense. We are fools to the end. On my own deathbed, no doubt, I'll be peeking at the nurse's legs and desperately hoping she smiles at me.

The place where I went running was a few blocks away, along a quiet road of big private homes with a wide, tree-lined median. One morning as I was finishing up, I noticed that a cop had stopped his car along the street and was talking to a black guy at the curb. Figures, I thought as I walked by, one black guy for miles around and of course he picks on him. I went to a nearby tree to stretch, and when I looked up, the cop car had pulled alongside me.

"Excuse me," he yelled. "Can you step over here a minute?"

I felt a rush of free-floating guilt, and a sudden urge to flee, but I walked over, calmly as I could.

"What's going on, Officer?" He was a beefy guy with a round pink face.

"I was just wondering, what were you out here doing today?"

"Me?" I looked around and then down at my shorts and sneakers. "Running."

"Running?"

"Yeah, you know. Jogging. Like for exercise."

"Actually, sir, you were walking when I saw you."

"Well, I finished running and I was cooling off."

"Uh-huh. Do you have any ID?"

"I was running. I don't even have pockets." I showed him my key. "This is all I have. Do you go running with a wallet?"

"No, sir, I do not." He looked me over, narrowing his eyes. "I'm going to tell you why I stopped you. We've had several break-ins in this area recently, and you were acting kind of suspicious."

"Me?"

"One, you were on the grass when most people use the sidewalk."

"But it's better for my feet."

"And you were looking around a lot, like maybe you were looking at houses."

"Well, I probably was. It gets boring running. I always look around. Even when I'm just walking, I tend to look around."

"And I saw you looking at me before when I was talking to the other gentleman."

"Oh yeah?" I wasn't going to explain that one. Finally I gave him my address, or rather my parents' address, and my name and social security number. Then I waited while he checked me over. He stuck his head back out, looking a bit sheepish.

"OK, sorry, sir."

"Everything OK?"

"Yes, sir, hope I didn't bother you, but we've just been having these break-ins. They're really on my back about it."

"No, that's fine. I understand. But I can go now?"

"Oh yeah, for sure, sorry, sir."

"No problem." I realized that he too was much younger than me, not much older than the lifeguard with the back zits, and he now seemed slightly cowed, as if I might get him in trouble. "Thanks," I said.

"No, thank you, sir, and sorry again. It's just they're really busting my ass about these break-ins."

Then as I was walking away, a man came by on a bicycle. He was wearing only bike shorts and sneakers and rode sitting up, with his hands free of the handlebars. He had a broad, smooth chest that looked shaved or waxed and tattoos on both biceps. As he rolled by, lost in his thoughts, an absent expression on his face, his fingers lightly but insistently and unmistakably brushed his nipples, arousing them in slow circles. We made eye contact, and he gave me a frank and innocent look, still teasing his stiff nipples, as if completely unaware of what his own body was doing. Then he sailed away.

When I got to the pool that day, the same lifeguard, the long-legged girl, was sitting at the table by the entrance. Now

I could see what book she was reading — Hart Crane's *Collected Poems.*

"Hey," I said. "Good book."

"Hey there." She laid it facedown. "How's it going?"

"I just got hassled by the cops. I got pulled over for jogging."

"What?" She laughed. "No way."

Then I told her the whole story, leaving out the part about the nipple-biker and how it had reminded me of the Russian with the one big boob, who I saw was right there at that very moment, waist deep in the water, swinging his snively kid or grandkid around in a circle. Lisa laughed at my impression of the cop, and when I handed her my guest pass, instead of punching it, she just gave it back and said, "Don't worry, it's cool."

"Thanks," I said. "What's your name anyway?"

She held up the cursive, golden word that dangled from a chain around her neck. I couldn't make it out.

"What's it say? Tina?"

"Jeez, are you blind?"

So I brushed her hair back out of the way and leaned in closer. She held very still.

"Lisa," I said.

I lay down in my spot, last lounge in the front row, under the umbrella, close to the Plexiglas windscreen, and was dozing into *Maigret's Christmas,* when a tumult in the water jerked me out of my dream. One-Boob was howling like a walrus while his boy choked and gasped. Was he drowning? His thin limbs flailed, and it was hard to see past the splashing. Like everyone else, I instinctively stood (later, I realized I had actually flung my glasses and book across the lawn), but before I could take a step, Bacne, who was on duty, dove in and was lifting the child out. Lisa met him poolside and began CPR. As she knelt and breathed into his little body, her hair forming a private tent for their faces, everyone else clustered around, then got shooed back, then closed in again, cheering happily, as a telltale whine of life went up. The Russians wrapped their yowling child in a towel and carried him off in triumph, while the old folks shook Lisa's hand. One tiny bean-brown lady in a bright pink bikini kissed her on both cheeks. That's when I noticed that I had bitten my own cheek, so hard I tasted blood.

That night was a scorcher, and my parents were getting on my nerves, so after dinner I went back down for a dip. There was still plenty of light. But the pool was packed, and when I saw the splashing crowd, I veered off to walk along the fence. I came across a gap in the wooden posts and, pushing through the bushes, found myself on a small path littered with cigarette butts, crushed beer cans, and, for some reason, feathers, as if a cat had just slaughtered a bird or someone had knifed a pillow. I smelled smoke. It was Lisa, sitting with her legs crossed, puffing away and reading her Hart Crane.

"Psst . . . hey," I whispered through the leaves. "You're under arrest."

She jumped. "Jesus," she said. "You scared me."

"Sorry. Your smoke drew me in like magic."

She held out a pack of Marlboro Lights. "Help yourself."

"No. I quit." I sat beside her, stiffly bending my legs. "Just blow some in my face."

She laughed and put the book down, which I took as an official signal that she wanted to talk to me, but we immediately lapsed into silence, an oddly comfortable silence that I found myself reluctant to break. She smoked, and we stared at the view. It was like a corny postcard: Cliffs and trees, a roll of black road, the wide river hurrying by with a tugboat under its arm. On the far shore, another black line, more bunched greens, and above that the city, spread in squares and spires. And the sun touching here and there: A silver spike, a blinking window, the blazing shield of a car. The spinning, broken blades of the waves. And the bridge.

Her round, tan, smooth knee was just an inch or two from mine, bony, rough, and white. She had lovely hands too, I noticed, as they tapped ashes and toyed with the book. Really they were her best feature, long and finely boned, with a violinist's tapered fingers. I felt like I could stay like that a long time — sitting in that spot and almost touching this girl, who had that book and those fingers and those knees — and keep on not saying anything.

"Great job before," I said. "Saving that kid."

"Oh." She laughed. "I didn't really save him. He just got scared and swallowed some water. It happens all the time."

"Still you should feel good about it. It's more than I did today."

She shrugged and looked straight ahead, but I could see she was smiling.

"How's Hart Crane treating you?" I asked.

She ruffled the pages of the book as if it were her little brother's hair. "Fine. I just started."

"Did you read 'The Bridge'? Sitting here makes me think of it."

"No. Is it about this bridge?"

"The Brooklyn Bridge. I don't think this one was built yet."
She handed me the book. "Read it to me."

"Well, it's really long," I said. "Like forty pages or something." So I read her the "Proem" instead, "To Brooklyn Bridge," a kind of prologue to the epic that was Crane's masterwork. To be honest, I found it rough going. I mean I had this book, buried in a carton somewhere, and I thought of Crane as a favorite, but somehow over the decades my taste had blunted or sharpened or something, and now that thick language stuck in my mouth like peanut butter. I could barely follow it. Even his double-punning name (Hart! Crane!) now seemed like a bad pseudo-Japanese word-picture. But Lisa loved it. She even read it back to me, and that was better.

"Do you write poetry?" I asked her.

She nodded. "But it's not any good. Do you?"

"I used to."

"He killed himself, didn't he?" she asked.

"Yeah. He jumped off a boat." I told her what I knew about his short, wild life, his uncontrollable drinking, his turbulent existence as a gay man in those times, and of course the final leap. I pointed at the open book in her lap. "I think about that jump whenever I hear this line about 'elevators drop us from our day.' And I think of him cruising for sailors when he says, 'Under thy shadow by the piers I waited.' Or, 'We have seen night lifted in thine arms.' You know what his last words were? As he jumped off the steamship?"

She was watching me very closely now. She shook her head.

"'Good-bye, everybody!'"

She laughed abruptly, a short burst, and covered her mouth with her hand.

"It's true," I said. "I think anyway. I read it somewhere."
And then, while I wasn't looking, she kissed me. It really took
me by surprise, and for a second I wasn't sure what had happened. She just kissed my mouth softly and sat back, watching.
Her eyes focused in on mine. I leaned forward and kissed her.

We undressed quickly, peeling off her shoulder straps and
slipping her suit down her legs, pulling off my T-shirt and
trunks. She climbed onto my lap, and we jostled a bit until I
was inside her, and then we just sat there like that for a while,
mouths together, chest to chest, not moving, except for our
breath. She stopped kissing me and spit in her hand, then
reached down in between us, making a serious face. Then she
began to move against me, and grip me harder, and I took her
in my arms and pushed her onto her back as her breathing
raced and she put her nails into my chest and I brushed back
the hair from her eyes. Later, after it was over, we both lay on
my towel and she smoked. Again it was silent, but this time the
quiet felt uneasy, and when I tried to put my arm around her,
she shrugged me off.

"Are you OK?" I asked.

She nodded but continued to face away, smoking methodi-
cally as if burning through this cigarette was a chore she was
determined to complete. I tried to look at the scenery. Then a
scary thought crossed my mind.

"Lisa?" I touched her shoulder. "Listen, was this, you know,
your first time?"

"First time what?"

"You know. Are you, were you, a virgin?"

She frowned at me, with a look that mingled derision and
pity.

"What?" I asked.

"Don't you know anything?"

"What? What do you mean?"

"If you're a virgin, you bleed. And it hurts and the hymen breaks and everything."

"OK, sorry."

"Don't worry." She snorted and put out her cigarette. "You're not the first guy to fuck me. Or the second. And I'm on the pill, so it's fine." She lit another cigarette, clicking her lighter and blowing the smoke out with a sigh. Then she looked back at me, eyes bright. "But I guess you better still worry 'cause I have VD and AIDS."

"What? What're you talking about?" I felt a wave of panic, more nausea than fear.

"I'm just kidding," she said very softly, realizing she'd gone too far.

"What a fucked-up thing to say."

"Sorry. I didn't mean it."

"Jesus."

"Sorry, I said."

"What a fucked-up thing to say."

"Are you mad?"

"Not mad," I said, and it was true; the hollow feeling in my belly was not quite fear or anger. "But I kind of feel now like you jinxed us, you know what I mean? Like it's bad karma. Like a broken mirror or something. You gave us bad luck."

"Sorry," she said again. We both sat there, still naked, and went back to staring at the view. A couple of barges went by. Traffic on the Henry Hudson was heavy, yet the bridge itself was light. It occurred to me that, unlike most vista viewers at that moment, we were actually facing east, away from the sunset, although the moon was nowhere to be seen. But the river's darkness seemed to be swelling, leaching up the banks and into the blackening trees, like their roots were drawing it in. In the city, the shadows of the buildings deepened, as if each were a door slowly opening onto deep corridors and basement stairs. Already the bridge beneath us was fading. Its far side was gone. She flicked her cigarette away in a bright arc, and I thought: This world will manage with no more poems about it. Just one last bored young girl, talked out of her clothes, and by poor old Hart no less.

"Hey," she said, and it was really getting dark now, the bridge was lit and the bugs were out, but she sounded cheerful again, and when I looked closely, she was smiling slyly at me. "Are you sure there isn't anything I can do?" She put her hand on my inner thigh and whispered into my ear. "Isn't there anything special, an act of atonement I can perform, that will get rid of the curse?"

She giggled as I moved her hand farther up my leg. I shrugged. "I don't know."

We Happy Few

They say there are no coincidences, that nothing in this world truly happens by accident. So perhaps, deep down, I really meant to show my penis to my entire class. After all, that one seeming mistake began the adventure that changed my life.

Or maybe I just suck at computers. I only intended to expose myself to one particular student, Sunhi Moon, a twenty-something Korean girl in the English conversation class I taught at a community college in Queens. It's the same old story: a plaid skirt and white knee socks, a few giggles followed by a heated discussion of dangling modifiers and some cutely dropped articles (I mean articles like "the" and "an," not, alas, the aforementioned knee socks or skirt), leading to an increasingly wild, if idiomatically incorrect, iChat affair, ("I wants you into me!"), then to a picture of a slender, rosy, headless body blooming in my in-box one morn, and, finally, my own doomed response, the fatal crotch shot I snapped and, unwittingly, sent to my whole class email list.

Imagine my surprise the next evening, when I showed up to teach and found security waiting. They seized my faculty ID and, fearing lawsuits, dispatched a grief counselor to my class. I signed a paper agreeing to never again set foot on campus and wandered, stunned, into a winter landscape that had switched from day to night behind my back. I raised a silent cry to the moon. O mistress of perverts and fools! The wind howled back and shook the stop signs. The stars, rarely seen, gleamed suddenly like the points of falling knives. I rode back to the city and an AA meeting, where I raised my hand to grand applause. It was the anniversary of my twentieth year clean and sober.

One of the best things about being a sober alcoholic is that, no matter how low you sink, your experience can still help others by letting them forget their own problems and laugh at yours. So my sorry tale that night — freshly fired, nearing eviction, an old single with crumbling molars — won their hearts and hugs, but I prefer to be loved from a distance, anonymously, and after sucking up a little warmth, I left the church basement alone. I was shuffling down the powdered street when a voice stopped me.

"Hey! Wait up!" My interlocutor was a vigorous sixty, pink with specs and a tidy white goatee. Snow melted on his warm, smooth skull. No doubt some sad slob like me, wanting to make friends. I thought of running, but I'd probably slip and bust a hip, so I set my teeth in a smile.

"I like what you shared," he said. "I like your realness."

"Thanks," I said, while my realness was thinking, "Fuck off."

"But it sounds like you need a job. My name is Dr. Tony."

Dr. Tony, or Dr. T, as he claimed to be widely known, was an ex–drug addict and ex-convict turned counselor to the stars, out in LA, of course, where he sold the weak and wealthy something called a sober companion — basically a paid buddy who

hung around and kept you from getting drunk. This was a con-
troversial idea in AA and NA, which frown on profit motives.
And we help only those who seek our help. In Dr. T's business,
often it was a family or board of directors that demanded its
wayward son or CEO be monitored. In effect, the sober companion was a babysitter, trading his dignity and values for three
hundred dollars a day, plus expenses.

"Sounds great," I said. "How do I begin?"

"I actually have a client in mind," Dr. T said, "someone I
think you'll really connect with. Derek Furber. A terrific young
writer."

"Fantastic," I managed to hiss through my frozen grin.

Back in the ancient '80s, when I was just beginning to degen-
erate, I too had been a terrific young writer. My book of short
stories, *Shoot to Kill,* detailing the life of a young art-damaged
junkie in the East Village, sold surprisingly well, and for a short
time I became a literary celebrity, which basically meant free
drinks in a few clubs and free passes at a few girls, all of which
I took. Over the next few years, I shouted on a record with a
punk band (the Scum, first single "Shooting to Kill"), wrote a
screenplay (*Shoot to Kill,* sold but never produced), and tried to
write a play (unfinished, working title *Shoot to Kill*). I want to
emphasize that I did each of these things exactly once. Then,
for a long time, I did nothing. In fact, when I was forced, later,
by rehabs and shrinks and the IRS, to reconstruct my past,
there were whole years I couldn't account for: I nodded on the
couch, in the sunny spot by the window, and petted my girlfriend's cat. I went to the corner bodega for a Snickers. You
think being a punk-rock writer/junkie was thrilling? It was,

briefly. But in the end it was like being a mailman, making my daily rounds, snow or rain, in my torn sneakers and moth-eaten coat, stomach twisting, guzzling Pepto from a bag. In abandoned buildings where the homeless shat. In alleys where kids picked their pimples and fingered their guns. In shooting galleries where, if you died, you got thrown out with the trash.

That was another lifetime. Today I am remarkably healthy, considering. I do yoga (stiffly) and run (slowly). I eat vegetables and fold the laundry. I water my neighbor's plants. I even quit smoking. But I didn't write a word. I tried at first, but I couldn't get started. Then I took a break. Then I decided it didn't matter anyway. The world wasn't weeping for my unwritten books. Now when people ask what I do, I say: "I'm a teacher." Or: "I proofread legal documents." Or: "I hand out jalapeño humus dip at Trader Joe's." I say, to myself, mostly: "I'm alive, motherfucker." What else do you want?

Two days later, I was on a plane to LA. After checking whether I had a driver's license, a social security card, and a criminal record (yes, yes, and yes), Dr. T had briefed me on my mission. Derek Furber was the twenty-five-year-old author of *Down Time,* a fictionalized memoir or memorialized fiction about his life in Beverly Hills, where he sold drugs to his high school friends and their famous parents. He was busted, sentenced to community service, and ended up coaching some team (debate? polo?) of inner-city youth, which rapidly led to his own redemption, a plug from Oprah, and the bestseller list. Now young movie stars were competing to play him in the film, models were competing to play his girlfriend in *Vanity Fair,* and he himself was due, in a week, to accept the Lionheart Award, presented annually for a Work of Literature That Exemplified the Human Spirit and the Power of the Word to Change Lives. The only problem was, he couldn't stop getting high.

According to Dr. T, Furber was bound for disaster. You simply do not go on *Oprah* with your face numb and call her Opera. He'd become so risky that he'd had to sign a contract promising to sober up and prove it on demand by pissing in a cup. If he failed, he'd forfeit his movie deal, the Lionheart, and everything that went with it. He was getting out of Dr. T's fancy Malibu rehab on Monday. My job was to escort him home, through a series of hurdles, and finally to the Lionheart back in New York. Dr. T gave me his book to read on the plane. I fell asleep on page six, during his parents' divorce, somewhere over Pennsylvania.

The exact address of Freedom Ranch, which I am legally obliged to withhold, is known only to a select handful of wealthy screw-ups and a few million Internet users but you take Sunset to the ocean and make a right. I recommend a bright winter day. The fresh hills glittered with dew all about me, and the eucalyptus trees, shedding long peels of droopy bark to show the whiter meat beneath, soothed the worn linings of my New York nose and throat. As the mist burned off, a clear blue heaven expanded above the ocean, which struck me blind for a scary second as I hit the Pacific Coast Highway: countless tiny beads of diamond light jumping across the waves.

I turned up a dusky road and was met by two goons in a golf cart, who told me that I'd be joining "a group encounter already in progress." I could only pray that I wouldn't have to remove my clothes.

The encounter was held under a thatched roof, open to the salt breeze and commanding a five-star view. The group? Well, their haircuts and tans were better than usual, but however impressive the names on the wristbands, it was still a rehab crowd: itchy, scratchy, nervous, patchy, smoking too much and laughing too loud, endlessly rearranging their lighters or cell phones or limbs with the compulsive restlessness of the profoundly uncomfortable. And there, in the lead, was Dr. T himself, the elf who'd appeared in my whirlwind. With his shining dome and the modest muffin overhanging his belt, the man glowed like a burnished good luck charm. No wonder people paid so much to rub against him.

He put his hands together, *shanti* style, and declaimed. "I want now to invite my higher power, the universe, and all of our higher powers to enter my spirit here today and speak through my heart instead of my mouth."

Or other orifice, I thought, while the rest shut their eyes. It is a strange feeling, when everyone around you has closed like sleeping flowers, and you are the one soul on guard. But I was not alone. As I scanned the faces — even the hardest looked vulnerable without their watchtowers — I spotted a wooly head above the flock. Two dark eyes darted between a mop of dark hair and a fashionably fuzzy beard. An ironic charmer's grin found me, as if to say, "Just look at these suckers." I somehow knew, this was Derek F, my new best pal.

My first date with Derek was awkward. I drove back down the coast while he sat silently behind dark sunglasses and filled the car with smoke. Wasn't that considered rude nowadays? I'd become strongly anti-smoking since I quit.

"Sorry, but do you mind putting that out? It's bugging my eyes. Probably dry from the plane or something."

"What? Oh, sorry." He flipped it out the window, a billion-dollar fine in these parts. I cringed, imagining the forest fire raging on the news, but held my tongue. Two reprimands in the first five minutes was not the way to warm a new employer. Which raised the larger issue: Who's the boss?

"First stop is Century City," he said, settling that question. The sun lit the edges of his beard with gold fire, and the glare off his watch stung my eye. "I've got a meeting with my agent."

The agency's headquarters was in a glass fortress with a hole cut in the center, presumably for Will Smith to chopper in, but we left the car with valet parking, still pretty impressive to me. An elevator whispered us up to a vast waiting room that held a few million in art—Day-Glo graffiti splotches, a conceptual hat sculpture that was also a real hat—and an Amazon in a black minisuit clicked over. Her heels, headset, and tight bun made her seem like an angry android, but she smiled at Derek.

"So good to see you. I love the beard. I'll tell Yoel you're here."

"Thanks, Katie," he said, stroking.

She pressed something, and a small, shiny, round man in a black suit popped out of a great big door.

"Hey, bro," he bellowed, hugging Derek, who introduced me, vaguely.

"This is my, um . . . companion."

"Hi," I said. "We can't legally marry yet."

"Ha," Yoel said. "Good one."

"He's a writer too," Derek offered by way of explanation.

"Awesome," Yoel exclaimed. "I'd love to see your stuff." He led Derek back to his vault. Katie turned to me.

"Would you like coffee? Water?"

"Sure," I said. "Thanks, Katie."

"Which one?"

"Coffee. No, water. Well, both actually." I laughed. "I got very dry on the plane."

"I understand." A light on her headset glowed bluely, as if ordering her to vaporize me. "Sparkling or flat?"

"Ever notice," I rattled on, unable to stop, "how euphemistic English is? In French or Spanish, for water with bubbles, they say 'with gas.' 'Con gaseoso.' Americans would rather die than say 'gas.'"

"So you want gas or not?" she asked me, smile deflated, as if she had suddenly realized how much she hated her job. I have that effect on people.

"Yes," I said. "Thanks. Please give me gas."

I sipped espresso. The sun bled out. Katie worked the phone. Derek and Yoel emerged, laughing, and I sprang up, reflexively chuckling too.

"Thanks for waiting," Derek said. "Let's roll."

Yoel waved. "Great meeting you. Don't forget to send me your stuff."

"Right. Thanks. I will."

Katie validated my parking ticket, and we rolled down the elevator and over to Hollywood, where Derek had an apartment in a building full of transients on their way up or down. His place was nice but unloved. The shelves held only a few self-help books. The never-lit candles on the mantel still had their price tags affixed. The one odd note was that the couch cushions were on the floor, propped against the furniture. Throw pillows leaned against the coffee table, and there was even a towel spread over the corner of the desk.

"Do you have a dog?" I asked.

"No, why? Should I?" he yelled from the bedroom. "Do you recommend it?"

"That's not what I meant." I opened the empty fridge. A cleaning crew had scoured the place for drugs and booze as well as mildew.

"I hope you don't think this is stupid," Derek said, returning. "But do you think you could sign this?" He held out a copy of my book.

"Wow," I said, in a whisper.

"I found it in a used bookstore. It's worth a lot on the Internet now. Like fifty bucks or more, with your signature." He seemed to blush under his beard. "Not that I'd ever sell it. I read it when I was fifteen and suicidal. It made me want to be a writer."

I took the small volume in my hand. I hadn't even seen a copy in forever. I turned it around like an artifact, afraid to look at the author's photo.

"I'll be right back," Derek said. "I've got to hit the can."

I sat on a stool at the kitchen counter. What could I write to this smart-ass no-talent upstart who, it turned out, was the only fan I had left? "Dear Derek, Avenge Me!" Or, "Save Yourself, Get Out Now." Or, "Bring Me With You, Please." Or just: "Take the Money and Run."

A few minutes later, Derek came out of the bathroom, and I looked up shyly from the book. I'd written "Keep Up the Good

Fight," forgetting that I hadn't found his work good particularly. But I was reassessing his writing skills as well as his personality: As a general policy, if you like me, I like you too.

"Here you go." I sauntered over, having decided to play the moment casually cool. "I didn't know what to write." I handed him the book and waited for — who knows? A hug, maybe. Instead, he accepted it indifferently, like a ticket stub, and gave me a quizzical look, as though trying to place my face. Then, as if seized by a fury, he lurched backward, twisting the cheap paperback in both hands. His eyes rolled up, white, like a slot machine. Jackpot.

"Hey, are you OK?"

"Yes," he said, then went rigid and fell like a tree, banging his forehead on the padded coffee table. He bounced once and landed on the floor, knocking his skull on the cushions there, then commenced shaking and flopping while foam bubbled from his lips.

"You bastard!" I yelled. My first day on the job, and the client was throwing a seizure. I'd been around enough to know what this was, but not enough to remember if it was fatal. His arms and legs shot out like a puppet's, and his head rattled, tongue wriggling like a fish trying to escape the net. I knew he could choke if he swallowed it, so I wrenched my book from his fist and jammed it between his jaws. He bit down hard, chewing the cover while his eyeballs strained their veins.

Ambulance. I ran to the phone. It was dead. No doubt the bill had gone unpaid while he'd been in rehab. I pulled out my cell. No signal in these hills. I ran back to the body and began searching for his phone. I tore through the pockets and found it: a Ziploc bag of white powder. I fell to my knees, eyes shut.

"Oh God," I prayed, "save this fucking moron."

Then, miraculously, the storm cleared. He was no longer shaking; in fact he was breathing nicely, bubbling snot through his mustache. I felt his pulse. I didn't know what normal was, or how to take a pulse really, but I was fairly sure he had one. Now there was nothing to do but wait and see what kind of brain damage he'd suffered. With a little luck, no one would even notice.

I dropped into the couch, banging my ass bone on the cushionless frame, and caught my breath. Slick with sweat, I realized how scared I'd been, and immediately, as if some wire in my brain had jiggled loose, I wondered where Derek's cigarettes were. Then I noticed the plastic baggie in my hand. What was in there anyway? Speed, coke, dope? Some new drug that only rich and famous people knew about? Whatever it was, it had to be good. The proof lay right at my feet, snoring peacefully. I gazed at the pretty powder sparkling in my palm once more. Then I hauled myself up and I flushed it.

Back in the living room, Derek was groaning. He rolled over, spit out the rare, half-eaten copy of my book, and abruptly puked all over it.

"What happened?" he moaned.

"You had a seizure. I'm guessing it's not the first?"

He nodded, eyes closed. "It's a medical condition." He coughed up a bit more of my writing. "Get me a glass of water."

"Get it yourself." This time I put a cushion on the couch before I sat back down. He stood carefully, as though we were in a rowboat, and felt his pockets.

"What are you looking for?" I asked.

"Nothing. Cigarettes."

"'Cause if you're looking for that baggie, I flushed it."

"What?" He instantly recovered. "Holy shit, why? That was . . . " He paused.

"What? Splenda for your tea? Baby powder for your chapped ass?"

He slumped in a chair. "It was a thousand bucks, for one thing."

"Who gave it to you, your agent?"

"No. It wasn't Yoel."

"No wonder you were both so excited to see my work. You were wasted."

"That was for real. He totally respects you even when he's not wasted."

"Whatever. You know they're going to urine-test you at the studio tomorrow."

"Is that what you're worried about?" He laughed. "I got it covered." He strode into the kitchen and opened the freezer. "What the . . . " Murmuring, he stuck his head in the icy hole, as if there were more room back there. When he pulled it out, he looked scared.

"The bastards stole my urine. I had six bags of clean piss in there."

"Who did?"

"Fucking Dr. T. They said they'd search for drugs and alcohol, OK, fair enough. But why take piss?" He stared at me, hands clutched together, outraged at the injustice. "It's just harmless piss."

"Of course they took it. Why would any normal person be hoarding urine?"

"Oh God, I'm fucked. Oh God, I'm fucked." He kept mumbling this as he ran his hands over his face and through his hair, as if he could erase what he'd done. "I'm so fucking stupid," he said, switching themes. "Why am I so fucking stupid?" He gonged his temple with a closed fist. "Why? Why?"

"Hey, that's enough," I said from the couch. "It's not the end of the world."

"It's not?"

"You're alive. You could have OD'd just now."

"That's true." He sat down again.

"Everything will work out."

"How?" he asked, face splotchy, hair sticking out.

"Maybe it's for the best. You'll get honest, get humble . . ."

"No, that won't work." He snapped his fingers. "I know. You can do it."

"Do what?"

"Piss. You can give me yours. You've been clean a million years. You must piss Evian by now."

"No way," I said. "Forget it."

"Why not?"

"It's illegal. It's immoral. And it's not my problem."

"But it is. You need money, right? You're poor, or why would you be here? If I test dirty tomorrow, you're fired. I'll talk to Yoel. I bet he can get your book reprinted . . ."

Anyhow, he went on like that, and eventually I relented. What did I care? It was just a job. But I did have one condition:

"You have to stay clean. Totally clean. I won't lie about that to anyone."

Derek raised his hand, as if pledging to the flag. "I promise."

I laughed. "Your promises aren't worth shit."

"True," he allowed. "So what do we do?"

"Take me to your nearest sex shop."

"What?"

"You know, a store that sells sex toys. Hollywood is full of them."

He frowned. "Like gay or straight? Because I'm straight."

"Fine. Take me to a straight one."

"Listen, when I said I'd do anything, I meant almost anything."

"Hey, Lionheart," I said, starting to enjoy this new career. "Just between us straight dudes, do you want my piss or not?"

And so, we paid a visit to Kinky Planet, where I selected a pair of handcuffs, some leg restraints, and, just because I was having fun and Derek was paying, one of those ball gags with the dildo attached to the front. It was pink and wobbly and looked like something you'd wear to a Halloween party at Caligula's. It made Derek's eyes go wide, and I figured it was wise to keep him guessing. I let him change into sweats before cuffing him, ankle and wrist, to his bed.

"Ow, that's tight."

"Quit whining. I got the fur-lined ones, you baby."

"What if there's a fire?"

"Hey!" I shook the dildo gag in his face, and the pink tuber bounced off his nose. "Another peep and you get this."

He quieted down after that. I turned out his light and went to the couch, where I spent the next two hours on Derek's laptop, fighting the urge to write Sunhi. I sent two lines: "I'm in LA working. I miss you." Too bad I didn't have another set of cuffs for myself. Then I curled up with Derek's memoir. I was out by page thirteen.

The next morning, before Derek's meeting at Warner Bros., I filled a jelly jar with fresh, pure urine and held it between my legs to keep it body temperature on the ride over. We were met by another black-clad assistant and a nurse, who sent Derek to the restroom with a specimen bottle while we waited expectantly like relatives at a difficult delivery. He emerged triumphant. Then I consumed more free coffee and water while the young author decided which world-famous actor reminded him most of himself.

Next I watched him get a haircut and beard shaping. Then we met his trainer, and I read the paper while they squatted and thrust. It was a pleasant enough way to earn three hundred bucks and, feeling magnanimous, I agreed to hit the 101 Coffee Shop for fried chicken and black-and-white milkshakes before strapping him in for the night. As soon as our food arrived, he started to rebutter me.

"I know this sounds like a bunch of crap now, but your book really did change my life."

I stuffed my mouth with fries and gravy. "You're right, it does sound like crap."

"Anyway, I fully intend to buy another copy, no matter how hard it is to find. I still remember that story where you shoplifted Burroughs and Ginsberg and everyone. It was like a reading list to me. I got every book. Except I paid."

So had I. The story was based on an incident I had witnessed, when a clerk at St. Mark's Books caught a punk kid stealing but let him go because his taste was so good. In my story the clerk, an old-time beatnik, befriends the kid and turns him on to dope.

"I actually read Kerouac first," I said, "and immediately ran away to hop a freight train, but the cops brought me home. Then I started on Burroughs. I read *Junky* and ran right out to cop dope."

"Me too." Derek laughed. "I couldn't wait to try heroin."

"I took the bus to Avenue B and got ripped off."

"I got ripped off in Hollywood, trying to buy acid after I read *The Electric Kool-Aid Acid Test*."

"Me too. In Washington Square." I hadn't thought of it in ages. "I bought a Disney sticker and licked it."

"I paid twenty bucks for a piece of gum."

"What about *Cain's Book*?" I asked him.

"Great. Though being a junkie on a tugboat sounds nauseating. What about *Basketball Diaries*?"

"I loved it. Though I didn't love his poems."

We went on to discuss *Fear and Loathing in Las Vegas*, *Jesus' Son*, and *Confessions of an English Opium Eater*, dipping too into the whiskey-logged volumes of that fine old American firm Hemingway, Fitzgerald, Faulkner and Wolfe.

"And Bukowski!"

"Right, the Poet-King of Beers."

What was it, this subterranean river that flowed between addiction and literature, those two measureless seas? And which was the costlier habit? Did I inspire young Derek, up in his bedroom, to start writing or to start sniffing glue? I remembered another story, this one unwritten but true: I no longer owned a single one of those books. I'd sold them all to buy drugs.

Derek and I drove home in a stupor, burping contentedly, and he seemed almost comforted when I locked him to his bed and said good night. Then I checked my email, and there it was:

Thank you for a letter. I am happy to receive. Miss you too ☹

You are in LA writing the movie? Excite! See you maybe soon ☺

Sunhi

I was so excite I had to read twenty pages of Derek's book before I fell asleep.

We sat side by side on the plane. The Lionheart ceremony was tomorrow, when I'd toast his success with one last cup of pee. Although it should have been a victory lap, our mood was a bit melancholic. Derek confessed that he felt safer with me around to tuck him in and keep him in line with dildos. For my part, though I'd made a decent chunk of money, I still saw a vast, hopeless void ahead. Except for one bright spot: Sunhi.

I'd answered her last email, sidestepping the question about my screenwriting job, and mentioned how I'd be staying at a swanky hotel in Manhattan. To my delight, she agreed to visit that midnight.

We put up at the Pierre. Afraid of losing my charge so close to home, I didn't even visit my apartment. The suite was far larger anyway, with a view of Central Park, and I had my own room. It was as if I were visiting some other, finer city, also by chance called New York.

Lionheart folks came and went. Derek's suit was tried on and adjusted. We ordered room service, and I perched on the couch, mooning for Sunhi in my head while I forget which *Star Wars* movie played on the grand TV. At last, after an intergalactic millennium, Derek yawned.

"Better get some sleep," I told him. "Big day tomorrow."

"But it's only dinnertime in LA."

"Still, you don't want to be jet-lagged. Biggest day of your life."

"Really? I assumed you thought it was bullshit."

"Well, yeah, but big bullshit, you know. The biggest."

A few light-years later, I bundled a happy lion off to dreamland. "Hey," he said, as I buckled his ankle restraint, "I want to be serious for a second."

"Uh-huh." I pulled the blanket up to his chin.

"I know this is all a lie and you don't respect my work and I don't give a shit about staying sober, but still I want to say thanks. I couldn't have done it without you."

"It's not a total lie. That book's inspiring lots of people to change, even if you're not one of them. You still wrote it."

"Yeah, that's true. Good night."

"Good night." I gently shut the door. Then I slathered my armpits with deodorant, brushed my teeth, and trimmed my ear hair. I was drawing back the drapes, to impress Sunhi with the view from "my" suite, when there came a gentle tapping on the door. I checked my warm but raffish smile in the mirror and opened up. My visitor punched me in the gut.

My eyes crossed in pain, but as I clutched my burning belly and gasped, like a drowning man, for air, I ascertained the following: My visitor was indeed young and Asian, but he was not Sunhi Moon. He was a big, muscular, and very angry dude in a Marine Corps T-shirt.

"Surprise, you old perv," he called in perfect Americanese, and struck me again on the nose. I felt a sickening crunch, like tasting a bone in your chicken salad, and a flower of pain bloomed across my world. I fell on the floor, which was thickly carpeted, and felt much better.

"Who are you?" I asked the floor, softly, as my blood seeped in.

"Not who you expected, huh, asshole? I'm Tony Moon, Sunhi's cousin. She told me all about you."

"Oh." Satisfied, I shut my eyes. Tony admired the view.

"Some place you got, for a teacher. This a two-bedroom or what?"

I was smiling into the carpet, amused that this knucklehead didn't even know we were in a hotel, when I realized where he was headed. "No!" I moaned, loudly, or thought I did.

"What the fuck is this?" Tony yelled. "You a homo too?"

"Help! Help!" I heard Derek trilling in panic.

I began heroically to crawl. "Don't go in there. That's my retarded little brother's room." I climbed to my feet in time to greet Tony as he stormed out, waving a fur-lined pair of cuffs and the dildo ball gag.

"What the hell were you going to do to my cousin?" His fist slammed my temple, or perhaps a freak lightning burst entered the hotel and split my skull, but either way, the entire city went dark.

· · ·

I woke up the next day on the bathroom floor, my wrists cuffed to a sink pipe and the ball gag in my mouth. As I lay on the tile, facing a wall-length mirror, the dildo that jutted from my face jiggled and hopped like Pinocchio's nose, mocking me gleefully.

"Help . . ." I heard Derek whispering hoarsely.

"Glurg bur vip glurg," I answered.

"Who's there?" I could hear him thrashing about like a trapped rabbit.

It took me three hours to unscrew the pipe, while our cell phones both rang ceaselessly. Finally it came free, releasing a faceful of old stinkwater. I pulled off the ball gag and stumbled in to Derek. His eyes were wild with fear.

"Call the cops," he burbled. "We were robbed by a Chinese gang."

"Well, not quite."

I explained. He was not pleased. But considering his own indiscretions, he agreed that the cops, the Lionheart people, and Dr. T were all best left uninformed. Besides, there was barely time to clean up and get to the ceremony. Derek fetched his suit, and I went to the minibar to ice my nose and lip. I looked like a cartoon of myself.

"Oh God, no," he called again. For a second, I thought Tony was back with his platoon, but I found Derek alone in his undies.

"What?"

"He took my laptop. My Lionheart speech was on there."

"I'm sure if you calm down you'll remember. There was this time I got high and accidentally erased . . ."

"You don't understand. I didn't write it."

"What?"

He sat on the couch, looking into his hands. "I didn't wa̶
you know. A ghostwriter did it. I didn't even write the book."

"Oh." I sat beside him. We shared an exhausted silence. I
knew he was afraid of my judgment, but for the first time since
we'd met, I felt none. Even as a phony and a cheat, Derek had
managed to provide a grateful world some hope and comfort.
What, in my twenty years, had I given?

"Find some paper and a pen," I said. "I'll write your speech."

The Lionheart went off smoothly, or so it seemed from the
echoes of laughter and applause. With my ward safely delivered backstage, I'd decided to ride out the ceremony in the bar.
I was not conspicuous. This was a writerly gathering after all,
and drinks were free; I was shoulder to shoulder with thirsty
literati. I elbowed in beside a long-haired old man in a shabby
overcoat, and before I knew what I was saying, almost as a joke,
I called out, to no one really, "Double shot of bourbon, quick."

I was shocked. This is how it happens, I thought, just like
the stories I'd heard. You lose your way. You forget. And then,
without knowing it, you sleepwalk into a nightmare from which
no one is promised to awake. I saw that my hands were trembling, and I gripped the bar. I noticed that the old man next to
me was doing the same thing, clutching the marble with white
knuckles, although not, in his case, just for moral support. Then
I realized who he was. A poet. Very great.

"Raymond Torquette," I said.

He turned, the dank gray locks parting to reveal an eagle
beak, sunken cheeks, overgrown white brows, and way, way
back there the black eyes that had glowered from the book covers of my youth. "What?" he asked.

I held out a hand to shake. He didn't let go of the bar. "I just want to say that it is a great honor to meet you. Your work has meant a lot to me."

"Then buy me a damned drink," he said, in the lordly growl I'd heard in recordings. "I'm broke, and the damned bartender won't serve me."

I was about to say the drinks were free, but then I noticed the empty glasses on the bar, and the stains on his shirt, and the torn front pocket flapping open, as though for quick access to his heart, and I understood why the bartender had cut him off. A drink landed in front of me, dark whiskey swelling the rim of a thick glass. "Bourbon double," the bartender said. My nose tingled. I took a deep sniff and pushed it toward Torquette.

"Here."

He brightened. "Hey, thanks," he said. The two shivering hands went up slowly and closed around the glass like a wounded bird. He bent to meet the drink and sucked it up, tilting back to let it slide on down. I could imagine the warmth spreading through him, like golden fire, like rough honey, like love. I even felt a bit better myself. Then I smelled urine and noticed the puddle at the great poet's feet.

I got Ray Torquette to the men's room, put him in a stall, and tipped the attendant twenty bucks. Then I went to find Derek in the ballroom, surrounded by admirers.

"Listen," I whispered. "Ray Torquette passed out. I'm taking him home."

"Ray Torquette? He's here? I'm coming."

He made his excuses and met me out front, where I was strolling with my arm around Torquette, asking him where he lived and getting only burps and muttered goddamns. Derek hailed a cab, and we propped the gray eminence between us.

"Where to?" the cabbie asked, and Torquette, from some kind of reflex, called out an Upper West Side address. We cut through the park in silence.

"I can't believe this is Ray Torquette," Derek said as the noble head lolled on his shoulder. "I used to recite his poems with my eyes closed, like prayers."

"I know," I said. "I remember the first time I read *Burnt Edges,* I wanted to cry. Not because it was sad, because it was just so good. He made me want to be better. To write better. That's the best compliment I can give."

"Yeah," Derek said. "It is."

The taxi stopped at a crumbling SRO. We hauled Torquette up in the elevator and found his key, the only thing his pockets contained besides wads of linen napkins embroidered with a lion's head. His room was appalling. Roaches scattered when we flicked on the single bulb. The thin foam mattress was covered in rubber sheets.

We didn't say much, Derek and I. What would we say? We got him into bed and rode the elevator back down. I shook his hand.

"Thanks," I said. "And congratulations, you did it."

"Whatever." He shrugged. "We did it."

"Anyway, you're free. Go celebrate. But I need a meeting." I turned to leave.

"Hey, wait," he called. "Can I come?"

We went downtown to Midnight Madness, a meeting summed up by its name, and sat on folding chairs and drank rank coffee.

We heard a bunch of losers describe their downfalls, and we laughed and laughed. Then we held hands and prayed, each to his own strange god.

Derek asked me to sponsor him, and he stayed sober for a few months, calling every day, going to meetings. Then he stopped, but I saw in a magazine that a huge movie star had signed on to play him. I also read on the Internet that he bumped up from models to supermodels. In August, Ray Torquette died of cirrhosis. The *Times* did a roundup of comments by famous writers, and Derek's quote was especially moving: "He made me want to be better. To write better. That's the best compliment I can give." The movie came out, and I saw him on *Charlie Rose* and *David Letterman* and even back on *Oprah,* where he cried about being high the last time and she hugged him and the audience cheered. He signed a new deal, for a memoir called *The Prevaricator's Lament*. Then he OD'd in a hotel room in Maui and died.

Meanwhile, I got another job, teaching writing in a men's prison, where I had no problem resisting the urge to expose myself. It was scary at first, but the students loved it, and one or two could write. After a great deal of urging from friends, I also sent a couple of new stories to Yoel, Derek's agent, like he'd asked. A month later, I got a response. He'd had his assistant read them and, unfortunately, my stories were "not for us." I was disappointed, of course, but he was right. It's not for them. It's for us.

What I've Been Trying
to Do All This Time

The Argentinean girl first contacted me via the mail. Well, not me, exactly. Oddly, the letter was addressed to "The Estate or Rights Holder of . . ." and then my name. Inside, the salutation declared, "Dear Sir or Madam" (were there female Davids in Argentina?), then went on to explain:

> "I am a university student here in Buenos Aires (similar to your All-American Co-Eds) studying North American Post-Modern Culture, and I am writing my thesis on David Gordon and am hoping to arrive to New York for researching soon."

I was taken aback, to say the least. It's true, I am a writer, and I would consider my work to be postmodern in some respects (although modern in others), but the fact is, I've never really published anything, yet, and as far as I know, no one has even read my novels, which sit, unfinished, in my bottom drawer, so I found it a bit hard to see how I could be the subject of a thesis. Still, out of curiosity and, I suppose, vanity and even, I admit, a kind of desperate, magical hope that she was somehow aware of my work, I wrote to the email address she provided.

She wrote back immediately, but it seemed there was some cultural confusion since she now addressed me as my own "Representation" (or was this postmodern?) and suggested we talk further via Skype.

So I went online, downloaded Skype, and dialed her up. Moments later, via the miracle of digital technology (I think), a vision appeared of a pale oval face, high forehead, and small red mouth, dark hair so black my screen read it as a kind of purple puddle. Black eyes like giant drops of blue ink.

"Hi!" I shouted, waving, since I still couldn't grasp the distance between us. "I'm David Gordon!"

She jumped, as if a continent weren't far enough, and her expression was, if this is even possible, a mixture of wonder and horror.

"You are alive!" she gasped. "I thought you are dead for a long time now."

"Me? No. I'm alive. For a long time now."

"I see . . ." She seemed disturbed by the news, frowning and biting her lip most fetchingly. "This could be a problem for my research. I have describe you as a deceased figure."

"Sorry," I said. "But I have been tired lately. Maybe if you just wait a little longer."

Now she laughed, a dazzling display: dimples, sparkling eyes, that one heartbreakingly crooked tooth. "No, no, is OK! I think you better live. Anyway, I like your blue eyes."

"Really? Thanks." I'd forgotten what a selling point that could be among the darker-eyed nations. I stroked my chin thoughtfully, trying to call attention to what I felt was my other main feature, the sprouting new beard, which my mother and the cashier at the deli both found very manly. "I'm sorry, though, that I didn't have time to shave." I said. "I look so scruffy."

"No." She shrugged. "Is not so big. Is OK normal for a Jew, I think, right? Here we don't have so many Jew with big scruffy. Mine is too little."

"Which is?" I asked. The conversation was getting away from me.

She tapped her tiny freckled curve of a nose. "The scruffy. Is how you say Yiddish, right?"

"Oh, I think that's schnoz, if it's even Yiddish. Or Italian? You think that I have a big schnozollah?"

She shrugged again. "No, a small salad maybe. Or a boiled egg."

In any case, it came out that her research was into cultural and literary "Marginalism," and I apparently qualified, dead or alive. In a move that her professors found brilliant for one so young, and that had earned her a grant to travel to New York, she had evolved past the early postmodern fascination with footnotes to focus her research on acknowledgments pages. By digitally digging in the data mines via methods that boggled my late-twentieth-century brain, she had somehow discovered the following intertextual facts, which I myself had completely forgotten:

1) I was thanked, along with a few other people, in the acknowledgments to *Walter Benjamin's Grave*, a collection of essays by anthropologist Michael Taussig. As it happens, Mick was my landlord at the time. After a random chat in

the kitchen about Bataille, he handed me some pages and asked me to look at them. I offered a few comments, and to my amazement, he returned a couple of hours later having incorporated my thoughts, then kindly and needlessly thanked me in his book. Frankly, I can't even recall what I said.

2) I was also thanked by another roommate: My old friend Paul Grant (known to some of us as Bud) translated a book by Serge Daney, the former editor of *Cahiers du cinéma,* dead now from AIDS. I read the manuscript at one point and caught a few grammar goofs, maybe.

3) Weirdest of all, and requiring the least actual effort, I was thanked on the back of a Bad Religion record. When I was living in LA, I gave my friend Brett Gurewitz, who is a big chess freak, a copy of Nabokov's book of chess problems and the novel *The Defense,* which inspired Brett to write a song (not about me). Finding this reference, an academic coup, was apparently pure luck: Her brothers were old-school punk fans.

While it was hard for me to see anything much in this pattern except that I had odd friends, a lot of extra time, and no stable housing, to Leticia (that was her name, the Argentinean girl) this made me a significant "unimportant" figure. She'd written an article about me, she said, for a key journal, and I was already very popular in intellectual and artistic circles in Buenos Aires, as, she was sure, in New York.

"Not so much," I said. "You'd be surprised."

She frowned at this. "Perhaps they don't understand what you're trying to do."

"Perhaps," I agreed, hoping that when she arrived in New York she'd finally help me understand — perhaps while cradling my head in her lap, stroking my burning forehead with her long, cool, tapered fingers and whispering in her warm, soothing accent — just what, for all these years, I've actually been trying to do.

Leticia arrived a week later. I'd shaved by then and spent the rest of my time in my room, doing sit-ups and other painful exercises that the Internet said would trim my midriff and harden up my core. We met at a Chinese place downtown, where they sit you at gigantic round tables with strangers and plop your food on a lazy susan in the middle, like eating on a carousel. A round family of four bears — dad, mom, bro, and sis — chewed spareribs in silence and stared unabashedly at our meeting/date.

In person Leticia was lighter: Her hair was still black, but her eyes were now a chestnut brown shot with gold. Her skin was very fair, paler than mine and freckled. I was surprised. The Latinas I knew had darker complexions.

"Yes, I am from the South America, but it is far south, even below your south. So far south that we are upside down from you, everything is opposite, and it is winter."

She swabbed her pancake with plum sauce and deftly added several slices of pinkish duck before folding it all into a slim envelope with those long violinist fingers. They were so long they seemed to have an extra knuckle, and they wavered as she talked, writing in elegant script.

"Well, I hope that now that you've met me, you're not still sorry I'm alive."

"No, not at all!" She furrowed her long forehead. "It is still very good for my thesis; plus you are a very sympathetic man who I am pleasured to meet."

"Thanks." It was, I had already noticed, part of her charm that she had no sense of humor at all, at least not in English. She would have made a great straight-lady back in the golden age of cinema, with her unflappable seriousness and black-on-white beauty. Still, thinking that I was at least getting somewhere, I licked the duck sauce from my fingers, rotated the shrimp, which were floating dangerously close to the bear family, and drew, from a plastic Duane Reade bag, my piece of resistance.

"I brought you something. A surprise," I said, laying the frayed and rubber-banded cardboard box between us. "This is my novel. No one else has read the whole thing." Not for lack of trying, I could have added, but having finally found a real fan, I decided not to let the legions of rejecting agents, publishers, teachers, and girlfriends cloud her sunnier southern judgment. Who knows? Perhaps in the land of Cortázar, where poets filled *fútbol* stadiums and public insurance paid for psychoanalysis, readers would be brave enough to understand my tragically experimental novel, *Psoriasis.*

She paused. While her narrowed fingertips tapped her beautifully greasy lower lip, she stared at the box without touching it. "Mmmm . . . no. I think I will not." She picked her sticks back up and chose another shrimp. "It is outside of my scope of research for you. Plus" — and here she smiled a little — "what if I don't like? It is a bit of when you imagine kissing someone and then it tastes bad, no?"

"No. I mean yes." I chuckled lightly and slid the box back into the bag, just as the lazy susan slid beyond my reach. She snatched the last shrimp resting on the little island of spicy salt. I settled for the remains of broccoli and washed it down with a tiny cup of dark and bitter tea. With both my literary and romantic aspirations dashed, I found myself at a loss for conversation.

"You know," I said, "my friend wrote a novel that takes place in Buenos Aires."

"Yes? Who is this?"

"Her name's Rivka Galchen."

She reached out and gripped my wrist, as if I were steadying her on a boat, or she were heading down some stairs, in high heels, a little drunk, after midnight. "Rivka Galchen the Canadian writer?"

"Yes . . . I suppose so. She lives here, though, in New York."

"But she is a very famous one! You really know her well?"

"Yes, yes, we are very close friends," I elaborated, seizing on this new impressive connection and hoping she'd touch me again. "We talk all the time." I felt like I was lying, although I was not, a common hazard when one is just generally full of shit. So I kept rambling on, tossing out random facts (Did you know she went to medical school? Her hair is dark and long like yours!), as if trying to convince her of something there was no reasonable reason to doubt, except for my own dubious motives. The check arrived, and Leticia didn't budge. I would have guessed it was the interviewer's pleasure, but perhaps not on her side of the world. I put down all the money I had. Smiling, she escorted me out.

"So tell me more about Galchen."

"Well . . ." I searched my mind for more tidbits. "Actually this is funny. You know that '20 Under 40' thing in *The New Yorker*?"

"But of course. Galchen is one of these to watch!"

"Well, I'm a character in her story. Isn't that funny?"

"What?" She stopped me in the middle of the street. It was a narrow Chinatown lane, a crooked path through the tilting buildings in the ancient part of town. The crowd swept ceaselessly around us, like the current parting for a rock, softly shoving. The look on her face was very serious, as if I'd revealed a dire medical condition. "You are inside the story?"

"Yeah. I mean not really. It's kind of her little joke. Her narrator has a friend named David who shows up to borrow money for his teeth. I've never borrowed money from her, at least not yet. Though I admit she's offered. It's also true I've had a lot of dental work, mostly because of my childhood illnesses, you know when you have high fevers you don't get the normal enamel, but I mean they're very healthy now and clean and look OK . . ."

"Please . . ."

I trailed off. She had leaned into my shirtfront, and her long hands were splayed against my chest, as if she were trying to peer into a window. "Please, I have never met a really fictional character before." Her small face gazed up at mine, eyes glowing. "You are like a phantom," she said as her nails pressed through to my skin. "Please," she said, "kiss me," and I did. I folded my arms around her, and our mouths met, and we hung like that for a long time, eyes shut and lost in the darkness. I felt the surging, endless crowd brushing past me and kept one hand on my empty wallet. I tasted spicy salt on her lips. She whispered wetly in my ear: "*Imago, imago,* my phantom . . ."

As soon as Leticia left my bed the next morning for the library, I rushed to meet Rivka at the Hungarian Pastry Shop and tell her the whole story. "That sounds wonderful," she said, nibbling a single macaroon. She has the smallest handwriting and the tiniest bites of anyone I know. I made a mental note to tell Leticia this over dinner that night. She sipped her tea and smiled. "Maybe you'll end up in Buenos Aires, living in noble literary exile like Gombrowicz."

"I hope not. Gombrowicz almost starved. Actually I remember a guy that Bud and Pascale introduced me to. He was doing research on how, while Gombrowicz was in exile in Argentina during the war, he was desperately poor but still too snobby to associate with the other Polish émigrés. But apparently there's some suggestion he used to hang around the docks, consorting with lowlifes and hustling for his bread."

"Aw, see, that is just like you," Rivka said. I scowled. She still had like 97 percent of her cookie left. I had consumed my three in three stuffed mouthfuls. "Anyway," she said, "I'm honored that my little story played a supporting role."

"Your story is the hero of my story," I told her. "That's what did it. And let's face it, this is the only way I'll ever get in *The New Yorker.* Though I did have to deflect that business about the teeth. And she didn't even want to read my book."

"Which book?"

"The new one. *Psoriasis.* It's depressing. I'm still a nobody, even to the girl I'm sleeping with."

"Yes, but a beautiful nobody. She just wants you as she found you. You don't even have to impress her or be anybody. You're just her dream. I think that's wonderful."

"I guess."

Anyway, what did it matter? Leticia was a dream girl, and if her fetish was having sex with a fictional nobody, I wasn't about to object. In fact, she was already looking into setting up some speaking engagements for me in BA, and said it was quite possible she could arrange a fellowship so that I could spend six months there. I could fly down in the fall, when it was turning cold up here. It would be their spring, and in that upside-down world I'd be a well-known and respectable phantom with a beautiful lover. Here I had been a nobody forever, and it didn't seem to do me any good at all.

When I got home from the pastry shop, I could see that she'd been crying. Her battered suitcase was packed.

"What's going on?" I asked. "What's wrong? Bad news from home?" I reached out to comfort her, and she recoiled.

"Don't touch me," she hissed. "Don't you ever touch me again."

"What? What is it? What's wrong?"

She gave me a vile look, then turned her gaze to the window. "When Galchen said in her story that you were a writer of the magazine *Hustler,* I think this is a magazine of literary cowboys who sing poems, like we have in my country. But then I was carrying forward with my research into you and I found this." She pointed at my computer.

Now it so happens that, back in my leaner and hungrier days, I wrote a good deal of porn, all of it long forgotten. Apparently, however, thanks to the wonders of the Internet, Leticia had located some of the particularly nasty "true" stories I'd produced, mostly under the pen name MFA (Master of Fine Ass).

"But that's just fiction," I told her. I even laughed at the absurdity of it. "I made it up for money. It's not real. Not like us."

"Real? We are not real." She had tears in her eyes. "This is the real you. A monster."

"But this is crazy," I said, pleading now. "What about us? What about our trip?"

She pointed a long claw at me. "If you ever come to Buenos Aires, one of my brother will cut your throat."

She left. I hung by the open door, floating more or less in the same spot as when I'd first seen her letter. The only sign that the whole affair had ever really happened was the sad pair of damp brown socks I found later, dangling limply from my shower curtain rod. I called poor Rivka again, and she made soothing remarks but didn't really seem all that surprised. I suppose it was never that realistic to begin with. Or perhaps she suspected it was all a delusion.

It was not until late that night that curiosity (and curiosity about ourselves is the worst kind) overcame depression and I found myself using the "history" function on my computer's browser to re-search Leticia's research into me. I came across some old stories, and I had to admit, Leticia had a point. They made disturbing reading. I almost said they were disturbing to reread, but in truth, I didn't even recall writing them. It had, after all, been ages, another life, another city, a whole marriage ago.

As I read these absurd ramblings of a seemingly depraved and disordered mind, what I remembered was sitting at my desk during my lunch break, often with my shirt and tie off so as not to drip mustard on my dry-cleanables, squinting at a set of slides I'd been handed moments before, trying to concoct some vaguely plausible narrative or motive for what the bodies in the pictures were getting up to and still get out for a quick smoke before 1 p.m. A tableau featuring two aproned girls, a dude in a chef's hat, and a cornucopia of veggies became "Bottom Feeders," and a story about two competing female pool sharks and an audience of, for some reason, nude men was called "Eight Balls in the Side Pocket." None of this rang a bell, though I confess the fable "Good Pet, Bad Bitch" did remind me of the cages I saw when, as I child, I went to adopt a puppy and had nightmares for months after. Was that the key? Scrolling through the links, I found my own work reused over the years, without royalties, for murky foreign sites like *Asian Auction, Whores de France,* and, most grimly of all, *Ass Atlas of Romania.*

My ex-wife had despised those writings, refusing to read them and wondering aloud about the spiritual damage they caused while also complaining about how little they paid. As for myself, well, they really had nothing to do with my "self." My real, primal motive had not been lust but fear, fear of the mailman and the phone and whatever bad news they might bring. I also wrote ad copy for a yoga center, edited grant proposals for a choreographer, and proofread legal documents: That didn't make me a dancing Buddhist lawyer.

But isn't this always the case with writing, even the most supposedly personal? Nothing ever turns out as I intend. Nothing I wrote yesterday looks familiar. I can hardly believe it's my handwriting in the morning or unscramble what I scribbled when I dreamed that big idea the night before. And like dream work, fiction takes the bits of real life and its concerns, both grand and petty, recent and ancient, remakes them, and presents the results as a clueless puzzle that only leads us deeper into the dark.

Shortly after I penned those gems, my wife left me for someone who she said better understood her needs. I moved to New York, quit smoking, burned through several aborted careers, and produced a pile of fiction that I called by my name but that seemed as inscrutable as Romanian porn. What the hell was I talking about anyway? But that night, for the first time in a long, long time, perusing "Confessions of a Bi-Babysitter" and "Yanna: Milkmaid at the Stud Farm," I actually found my own work sort of compelling.

It seemed I wasn't the only one. As I pored through the evidence, I detected a second set of fingerprints. Someone named, or screen-named, "delayeddelights" had repeatedly searched for, posted about, and responded to "me." Like a towered princess in a distant galaxy, delayeddelights had even sent a number of distress calls out into the universe, wondering where I, or he, was. Finally, past midnight, and years out of date, MFA sent back a hello. I stood guard over the dark screen for a while, watching the far horizon for a response, then had cookies and iced mint tea. I was busy flossing when her light flickered on and she asked, with a parenthetical, side-ways smile, if I'd like to chat.

As it turned out, delayeddelights was a 20s F living in Wburg, where she was a student and a part-time dog-walker. She'd been in high school when she first discovered my work, a middle-class kid lost in the vast suburban reaches of Long Island, strug-

gling with some sticky young feelings and ancient pitch-black
urges she couldn't talk about with her off-line, real-time peers.
Angelic in the photo she sent — blond, slender, freckled, laughing in the sunshine with a puppy — she apparently had the mind
of a middle-aged pervert, as she visited and revisited my most
far-flung creations, declaring "brilliant" and "so fucking hot"
the sterile fantasies I had composed one-handed while gob-
bling my tuna sandwich.

"I thought I was crazy," she told me on the phone. "I thought
I was the only person in the world who had these feelings. I'd
give my math teacher what I thought were like smoldering
looks — he was fat and ugly, but the pool of older men was really
limited — and he just looked at me like I was nuts." Her voice
was bright and clear and somehow more troubling for being so
straightforward. "I'd drop hints to my friends, like did you ever
hear about people doing this or that, but when they got grossed
out, I'd pretend to be kidding and be like, yeah, isn't that weird,
while inside I was dying. Then I saw your stories. They were
exactly like my fantasies, but better even, things I'd never imagined. I got so excited it was like I had a fever. Then later I'd feel
guilty. I'd think, who does this guy think he is, and get mad and
report you and demand you be taken down. Then I'd go read it
again. I got older and I moved to Brooklyn and went to college
and met some guys, but I was always comparing them to you.
Or like I imagined you. You were like my secret. And now here
you are. The dirtiest man ever."

"Thank you," I said. "I think." I told her what my ex-wife
and Leticia had thought.

"They didn't understand you," she assured me.

"They didn't? I was afraid that they did."

"Or maybe they're really reading them right now. I bet there's hundreds of women, all over, who read your words in secret." She said she'd found Leticia's previous articles online and emailed me the link to a six-month-old academic journal. There was a photo of me, with the caption "Personaje ficticio difunta": Dead Fictional Person.

"But I love the beard," delayeddelights told me. "I like you scruffy." She hesitated. A puppy yelped in the background. "Do you think, maybe, we should finally meet? Talk or whatever? Have a drink? We can do whatever you want."

Should I go? It was late. I was already in my pajamas. How would a guy like MFA dress, anyway? In a mask and cape? I was tempted to ask her to wait and then call Rivka, but there wasn't time. "I don't even know what I want," I told her truthfully.

"That's all right," she said. "I do."

I could hear the excitement quivering in her voice. I imagined her body pressed against mine, fierce little heart beating like a bird. The one thing I knew for sure was that I would ruin it somehow. I would lose it all. I agreed.

"Hurry," she said. "I love your writing! Take a cab. I'll split it."

"No problem," I declared, counting my singles, "I got it." I told her about my experimental *Psoriasis* and offered to bring the manuscript.

She thought about it. "That's OK. Maybe another time."

O dirty love! O dawn! O darkness! The heartbreak of this world is that it could be so perfect, if not for me. And then, like a phantom, like a dark master of the finest arts, like a ghost-writer from the invisible world, I set out to cross that river and touch the unknown shore.

Su Li-Zhen

On a rainy day in April, my ex-girlfriend Nina called me for help.

"What kind of help?" I assumed it would be money or lifting things.

"Research," she said. "I need to look up something and you're the biggest brainiac I know."

"Am not."

"Are so. You're all quotey and everything." She was teasing me for the bookish references that compulsively peppered my speech. Frankly, it hadn't to do with brains so much as a lack of outside stimuli. I've spent my life in a room, reading. All I had to report at dinner is what Genet or Nabokov said that day. Nina's own favorite authors were a heady brew: Ayn Rand, Rumi, and Aleister Crowley.

"What's this about anyway?" I asked.

"I have to track down my ex-lover."

"What?" I was a bit incredulous.

"Don't be jealous. He's my lover from a former life."

· · ·

Nina was an odd girl. I won't go into our whole relationship; I'll just say that we fascinated each other in a way only possible for those with absolutely nothing in common, like an anteater and a flamingo meeting at the waterhole. I remember the one Christmas Eve we shared. She dragged me to church with the rest of her brightly blond clan, sang about Jesus with unnerving gusto, then gave me a framed nude photo of herself as a gift. She was a ballad-singing, break-dancing, DJ-ing actress-model-dancer whose great ambition was to be a pop star or appear in a sitcom. She got by on the occasional overseas toothpaste ad while moonlighting at a midtown massage parlor where, dressed in a bikini, she oiled up and rubbed down tense businessmen for $250 a pop, as it were, plus tip. I pictured a kind of human car wash where tiny elven girls pumped and polished the hoary carcasses of old husbands, detailing them like the fat, sleek vehicles they drove home. Although a dozen years her senior, I was still the youngest and poorest boyfriend Nina had ever had.

Early on she complained that I didn't treat her with the "reverence" and "worshipful attitude" she'd come to expect. Apparently, other reviewers had praised her lavishly as "a once-in-a-lifetime experience." Letting her so much as touch her wallet when accompanying her in a shop was "a major faux pas," which, frankly, made her feel embarrassed for me. I could only laugh. She fell pretty short in the old-fashioned girlfriend department herself: When I was sick in bed for a week, she didn't bring me soup or even visit. She admitted it hadn't so much as crossed her mind. She'd never risk losing her voice. Maybe we were both no good.

Still, like I said, I sit in a room reading, and to see her DJ before a crowd of jumping kids or performing her Qi Gong exercises in the morning, swinging her arms and bouncing up and down in her underwear — well, it was like a breath of life. What she saw in me, who knows? The truth is, in the end, she even started cooking for me, awful concoctions that I wolfed gamely while, suspicious but happy, she slopped seconds onto my plate.

Nina had once lived in Taipei, years before. She'd been recruited as the white member of a multicolored girl-pop group, recorded one minor hit, and been the lover of a Chinese gangster. Or maybe not a gangster. A guy who owned bars and lent money but supposedly didn't involve himself with drugs or violence, the line between businessman and criminal being perhaps a bit blurrier there than here. Perhaps. Anyway, we visited together, and I fell in love with the place. It was like the dream where you don't know if it's the future or the past: Streets full of thousands of scooters, and everyone in those facemasks and helmets. Alleys crammed with stands selling dumplings and papaya milk and candied tomatoes. Girls with umbrellas hiding from the sun. Old men in pajamas chewing *bing-lang* and spitting red juice. Sweet teenagers on dates lining up for tripe.

It was ghost month. The day we arrived, the news showed the opening of the gates to hell. People put out offerings of incense and flowers for their ancestors, but also instant ramen noodles and Oreos and Cokes. They came out of office buildings with bundles of ghost money, red and gold, and set it on fire in the street. We took afternoon naps while it poured and wore things that I at least would never wear at home: red robes, sleeveless undershirts, slippers in the street. At dinner, blindly, we felt for each other beneath the table. We raced back to our tiny rooftop room, with the laundry dripping from the one barred window and neon fish swimming through the drowned streets below. Dressed like a princess in imitation silk, hair pinned high with lacquered sticks, she stepped out into the hall and then reentered our room, where I lay in the dark, pretending to be one of her clients, waving a fat wad of New Taiwan dollars and waiting for the robe to fall.

We returned to New York, and that autumn, things began to change between Nina and me, as if the spell had been broken, although who had cast it on whom, I don't know.

Maybe it was because we were so obviously ill suited that our breakup, while not without sadness, was bloodless, even friendly, and we kept in touch. Or she did, always being the one to call and suggest a meeting. But I always agreed. After all, she was extremely attractive, with big shiny eyes and the light bones of a dancer, small waist, compact torso, long arms and legs. Whenever we got together for coffee or a movie, I ended up trying to squeeze her and she usually acceded.

I'd agreed to meet Nina and discuss her research project, and was waiting in front of the Hungarian, my usual coffee shop, when she popped out of a Porsche SUV (I didn't know they existed either) driven by a sleeveless muscleman in a ponytail.

"New bodyguard?" I asked.

"Music producer," she said. "He likes my stuff."

"I'll bet." I noticed that she didn't mind kissing me on the mouth while he could see. "Hey," I said as we went inside, "that's my sweatshirt." It was a gray hoodie, much too big, that made her look like a monk.

"I found it." She sat cross-legged on the chair and shook her light hair from the hood. "Anyway, I can't give it back right now. I'm not wearing anything underneath."

This was enough to fill my mind with possible squeezings, so I let it go for the moment. We ordered and I asked, "Now what's this about ex-lovers and a former life?"

It had all begun at her acting school. Of course. It turns out one of her teachers was a channeler on the side.

"Channeler? Like a medium or something?"

"It's kind of like that," she said. "She's amazing. This girl in the school was auditioning for the Usher movie. So my teacher went into the future and cleaned the room where the auditions were going to be, and she got the part."

"What's Usher?"

"He's only like the hugest pop star, but of course you wouldn't know."

Actually, it sounded familiar. The movie had tanked, and I'd seen it on sale at the video store.

"This lady is amazing," Nina went on. "She's really just one of those spiritually enlightened souls you meet sometimes."

"I've never met any," I said.

"That's because you're not open. If you're open, they find you."

"If she's got such powers, how come she doesn't just spend all day helping cancer kids or spreading world peace? How could she charge money? Or waste her talent helping some actress get a part in a crappy movie? Why is it more spiritual for her to get the part than another girl? Spiritual to me is Gandhi or Martin Luther King or something. Everything else is just a magic trick."

She looked at me pityingly. "You're such a hater," she said.

Then, spooning up hot cocoa, she told me about the weekend workshop this channeling teacher gave. It involved rolling on the floor to various kinds of music, African drumming, Balinese gamelan gonging, Sufi chanting, each associated with a different chakra. Also they would "call in" colors. I asked what that meant.

"You know, like you call in blue. Or you call in red."

"Like you try to feel blueness or something?"

"Kind of."

"Was this naked?" The whole thing sounded both ridiculous and perverse, but not in a good way, and I knew her acting classes occasionally involved running around naked and crying.

"No, of course not. It figures you would ask that." She shook her head sadly. "It was transformative. And after the workshop, Betsy—that's the teacher—said I had a lot of spirits around me, a lot of energy emanating."

"Of course," I said. "That's how they sucker you in."

Nina ignored me. "Then she said that the images she was getting were Chinese. That I had been Chinese in a past life and that's why I was drawn back to Taiwan. And she even mentioned this." She reached into her collar and pulled a necklace out from under my sweatshirt. It was a small jade dragon curled on itself, with a yin-yang symbol in the center and little holes for eyes. "She said it was something I wore in my previous incarnation."

"But I bought you that," I pointed out.

"I know. I always said you should develop your psychic abilities. You have a lot of spiritual energy around you too. I bet you could see spirits if you were open to them. You're just so closed off."

"OK, OK," I said. "Get to the part about the lover."

"Fine," she said, emptying her mug and starting on my cheesecake. Here's more or less what she said: In a prior existence, back before the Second World War, Nina had been a courtesan named Su Li-Zhen, renowned in the pleasure quarter of Taipei for her singing and dancing as well as her great beauty. Su Li-Zhen fell in love with Liu Ping, the son of a wealthy merchant, but his parents refused to even consider a marriage with a fallen woman. The young lovers fled to New York, but Liu Ping's family hired detectives who tracked them to a cheap hotel in Chinatown. In despair, they committed suicide, swearing to meet in the next life. It was in finding this reincarnated love that Nina wanted my assistance.

"But wouldn't he be in Taiwan?" I asked.

"No. Betsy said he's been reborn in New York. That's why there's so much energy around it. But he could be anyone."

"Maybe that's him," I said. A very fat, very furry fellow in very short shorts was strolling by the window, singing along with his headphones. In New York, traditionally, that's one of the first signs of spring. "Or him." I pointed to a pigeon that was pecking at some filth on the curb. "Look, he's trying to signal you. Hi, Nina!"

"Are you jealous?" she asked. "Is that why you're so resistant to this? Because it's not like a romantic thing for me. It's a spiritual connection. I have to find this person so that Su Li-Zhen's spirit can rest in peace."

"I thought you were Su Li-Zhen. Her spirit is in you."

"Are you going to help me or not?"

"OK, OK. I'll help."

. . .

And so the hunt began. We placed personal ads in the news-papers, including the Chinese ones, and posted messages on Craigslist: "Su Li-Zhen Seeks Liu Ping," "Searching for Lost Love," and so forth. She got a fair number of responses, ranging from the innocuous (people looking for old schoolmates) to the creepy (an Asian-themed porn peddler), but none relevant. We wandered Chinatown, going into any old buildings that we thought might once have been hotels, visiting fortune-tellers, and lighting incense in little storefront temples. I even came up with an idea: We placed the dragon amulet on a copy machine and then taped its picture all over town with a phone number underneath. But everyone who called thought it was for kung fu lessons or an underground rave club. The whole thing was inane, I know, but it was fun. We ate lots of dumplings, and I found a store that sold rare kung fu films and Hong Kong gang-ster movies that hadn't been released in the United States. It rained interminably, and we spent a lot of time under my um-brella or staring out restaurant windows, past glazed ducks on hooks, watching the traffic and drinking tea. Sometimes, in a doorway, we'd kiss. I even wondered, briefly, if Nina hadn't just cooked up this whole story as a way of getting back with me. But that wasn't her style. When we were a couple, she had al-ways been pretty direct. Once she asked me straight out if I was in love with her yet. I couldn't say that I was. For some reason, at the time, my honesty seemed more important than her hap-piness. Now I wonder if that was just arrogance. Or fear. What harm could a little yes have done? Another time she called me the Tin Man.

"Is he the one with no brain?" I asked. "No, wait, hey! The Tin Man has no heart. That's mean."

She blushed. "I didn't mean heartless. It's just that you're so armored. There's no way to get inside." I forgave her with a kiss, but I knew what she meant. She meant what she said, like everyone does, whether they know it or not.

Finally, I did the obvious thing: I looked Liu Ping up in the phone book. I would never have occurred to me to search for a dead man's phone number, but I was looking for something else, a knife sharpener, I think, and on a whim I flipped to P, hoping to find a relative, and there it was, a single listing. It even gave an address, not in Chinatown but on the Upper West Side, a few blocks from the coffee shop.

I called. The phone was picked up on the first ring, but whoever it was said nothing. I heard only labored breathing.

"Hello?" I said. "Is this Mr. Liu Ping?"

I sensed it was a man's breath, but for all I knew, it might have been a dog. It just continued, a plaintive wheeze, without any waver or rise that could be taken as recognition. Then he hung up. I looked at the phone in my hand, at the spoon and coffee mug before me, at the bodies passing by outside the window, watery and quivering in the warped glass, and for no good reason, a chill went through me and I was brushed by an intimation of the truth: One day none of this will remain.

I tried calling back later and again the next day, but no one answered, and finally, I just walked by. It was a run-down residential hotel, once a common sight, back before the neighborhood went over the top. It had a saggy awning and a few bedraggled tenants sitting on folding chairs out front. The bulletproof-glassed reception desk was unmanned, so I went straight to the elevator. As it shut, I caught, from somewhere down the hall, the unmistakable perfume of cooking heroin.

I found 7402. It had a dented metal door, with the number just painted on. Paint drooped from the hinges, and there was a painted-over mezuzah on the frame. I hesitated a moment before knocking. Till now, this had all been a lark, to me at least, or at most a courtship game, a reason to eat noodles and hold hands with Nina. But once I knocked, things would change, one way or the other. The moment I found Liu Ping in the phone book, I had a clue, and the romantic comedy became a mystery, and mysteries demand to be solved. I knocked.

A young black man opened the door.

"Hello? Can I help you?" He was soft-spoken and strong, dressed in a white ribbed T-shirt and tight jeans. Liu Ping's lover?

"I was looking for Liu Ping. Is this his residence?"

"It is."

"Could I possibly speak with him?"

He shrugged. "It's possible, but it's not likely. That man hasn't said a word in years. What do you want with him?"

"I'm a detective," I said, to the surprise of us both.

"A cop?"

"No, no. More just like a researcher. I'm helping someone who thinks she may be — may have — a common relative. Maybe his uncle or grandfather."

"I don't know about that, but this man has no family. And any father or grandfather is long gone. He's eighty-nine years old himself. And he's got Alzheimer's and lung cancer and cirrhosis, and that's just the highlights."

"Eighty-nine?" Seeing the confusion on my face, as I tried to add and then subtract in my head, he stepped aside and let me enter the dim kitchenette. The counters were covered with prescription bottles, and there was a pyramid of toilet paper rolls stacked on the little table.

"I'm his home health aide Durel," he said. "I've been taking care of Mr. Ping a year now, and you're the first visit he's had." In the room behind him, I could see ratty flowered carpeting and faded wallpaper with a different, clashing bloom. There was a broken-down easy chair pulled up to a TV, and in a dark alcove beyond that, I saw part of a hospital bed. I could hear that same breathing as on the phone. Even up close it sounded like it had come from far away, like a faint breeze off the river that just barely brushes your curtains.

"What about family back in Taiwan?" I asked.

"Not that I know of. No mail, no phone calls. Excuse me." Durel grabbed a roll of paper and what looked like a plastic bicycle pump and hurried around the corner into the alcove. I realized that the breeze had stopped. He's dead, I thought, and held my own breath for a few agonizing seconds. Then Liu Ping started up again, exactly like before. His breathing had a wistful air, as if he were merely sighing. Relieved, I started nosing around the kitchenette. It was painted the same beige as the door, and the linoleum was yet another horrendous floral print. I saw a file beside the sink and opened it up. I don't know where I got the nerve. Maybe from pretending to be a detective.

I flipped past the medical information to a section entitled "Personal." By "DOB" it said only "1915?" The place of birth was "Taipei, Formosa." Then it said, "Arrive US Customs: December 19, 1935." I heard Durel approaching and shut the file.

"Sorry," he said, walking in. "His lungs fill with mucus." I stepped aside sprightly as he put the spattered pump in the sink.

"And he never talks?"

"I don't think he speaks English. Anyway, if he did, he forgot it. Just like he forgot everything. Even his name. Now he can't even remember how to swallow."

I left the apartment in a state of somber excitement, or perhaps melancholy elation: I had found Liu Ping. What that meant, I didn't know, but whoever Liu Ping was, that was him. Plus I'd found another clue. I went to the library to track it.

I found nothing in the major dailies of the day, the *Times,* the *Tribune,* the *Daily News,* but after hours in front of a microfilm machine, I dug down to a layer of long-defunct tabloids focused on celebrity gossip and the police blotter. One weekly, the *New York Speculator,* seemed in the winter of 1935 to be particularly obsessed with ethnic crime. I slid through page after page of black-and-white drama, knifings in Harlem nightclubs and mafiosi with their hats over their faces, and then I saw it: The headline read, "Chinatown's Poisonous Den: Deadly Love Pact or Harlot's Shocking Revenge?" The photo showed a broken-down hotel with a Chinese sign, maybe even one we'd passed before. The story related how, in the middle of the night, hotel guests heard one Mr. Liu Ping, age 20, moaning for help in the hall, where he was discovered crawling on his hands and knees. Miss Su Li-Zhen, 19, was found dead in the room.

She had overdosed on raw opium and cut her wrists. Mr. Liu Ping had also eaten opium, but had thrown it up and managed to survive. Witnesses and cops figured this had been a suicide pact that only one party had the guts to go through with. But Liu Ping's family attorney offered a different take: Liu Ping had broken off his affair with Su Li-Zhen, a prostitute, and told her of his intention to return home. She had then poisoned him with opium-laced wine before taking her own life.

I left the library and called Nina. We had a date to meet back downtown, but I asked her to come to the coffee shop instead: I did it, I told her. Case closed.

"What?" Nina was outraged. "He's alive? In his own body?"

"Sort of."

"He didn't kill himself? Bastard!" She snatched the printout of the article from my hand and ferociously scanned it. She smacked the table and waved the paper at me. "First of all, I'm not a prostitute."

"I didn't say you were."

"I was a courtesan."

"Right."

She read the rest and slammed the table again. "And I did not try to murder him. We were supposed to die together, for love. That coward. That asshole. I can't believe he let me die. And here I am looking for him in the next life, like a fool."

"Well . . ." I decided to keep silent. She stood up.

"I have to see him."

"No, Nina, wait." I followed her out. "It's no use, I told you. He can't even swallow. He's dying."

"Good," Nina said, hailing a taxi. "He should have died sixty-nine years ago. With me."

I tried reasoning with her in the cab, but she just worked herself up even more, eventually turning on me, if only because I was there: I was, she declared, secretly pleased at this outcome. I had never believed her and had been snidely playing along, mocking her the whole time in my pompous, bookish way. I was completely closed off to spiritual ideas and emotionally shut down as well. I did think she was a prostitute. I had never loved her at all.

"Who do you think you are anyway?" she demanded.

I shrugged. "I don't know. No one."

It must have been Durel's day off because when we got to 7402 and Nina banged on the door, a small, round Latina lady answered.

"Yes? Can I help you?"

"Liu Ping!" Nina shouted and ran past her.

"Sorry," I said, "she's family," which was ludicrous. Nina looked like the pep squad captain in a cable movie about All-American cheerleaders. We followed to the alcove where Liu Ping lay dying. He was definitely dying — that anyone could see. His shriveled head seemed no bigger than my palm, the features all folded into each other, like a fist. His body was just sticks and plaid pajamas. There was really almost nothing left of him, some skin, a few white hairs, two stunningly beautiful brown hands, and that slow breath like a wind from the other side. Instinctively we all stopped, Nina, the lady, and I. We stopped and stared, in awe, at the dark majesty of death. Then

Nina started to berate Liu Ping in fluent Mandarin, screeching and waving her arms. And the lady started yelling in Spanish. So I yelled too, in English, for everyone to stop yelling.

That's when Liu Ping awoke. Just like that, two of the crumples in his face parted, revealing two wet brown stones. We all shut up and went back to staring, while his eyes swam around, as if landing from outer space. When they focused on Nina, they widened crazily, showing their whites. Suddenly, he sat up, pointing a tremulous finger. Nina froze. The nurse gasped. Liu Ping began to speak, in a rasping, dust-choked voice, unused and abandoned for years.

"Su Li-Zhen," he croaked. "Su Li-Zhen."

Then he died. Or he started to anyway. He started to finish dying. He fell back into the pillow, and his eyes rolled back, and his throat began to gurgle. I pulled out my cell phone and dialed 911, but the nurse was on the phone already, talking while she loaded a syringe. That's when I realized Nina was gone. The nurse squeezed my arm.

"Please," she said. "Help him."

"What should I do?"

"He shirt."

While she readied the shot, I struggled with his pajama buttons, firing one into the wall. Finally, I got his top open, and there it was, tattooed on his sad, emaciated wreck of a chest, crossed with the lumpy scar of a lung repair: a dragon wrapped around a yin-yang symbol, with glinting, narrow eyes. I was so busy gaping, I got caught off guard when Liu Ping lurched forward and grabbed my sleeve, yanking me toward him with surprising strength. I panicked and began to wrestle with the poor old man, as if he were trying to pull me down with him into the grave. He clutched at my shirt, and I realized he wanted my pen, a felt-tip marker clipped in the pocket. I watched in fascination while he grabbed it and, with desperate haste, scratched something onto the back of my hand, tracing the figure until the paramedics pushed me aside.

I waited in the kitchenette while the medics and the Spanish lady worked, but it was no use. I went downstairs and called Nina. She didn't pick up, so I left a message on her voice mail. I thought about Durel getting the news the same way or maybe showing up for work tomorrow. I hoped my name didn't come up. Then I walked down Broadway, cradling my marked hand, and found a Kinko's. I xeroxed it, adjusting the contrast until it was clear.

Then I went home.

Over the next couple of weeks, I called Nina several more times, and just when I figured out that she was avoiding me, I got a message. She was in Miami with her producer, recording an album. She'd be back in a month or maybe two.

Meanwhile, my own life, such as it was, demanded my attention, and I went back to my routine, running, reading, sitting in the coffee shop and staring out at space. But I did continue to visit Chinatown, to frequent the restaurants we'd found, and, in particular, to shop at the video store, where one day I purchased a DVD of a 1987 film called *Rouge*. Now, I generally prefer action movies to love stories, but this film starred two of my favorites, Leslie Cheung and Anita Mui. A star since child-hood, and said to be the longtime lover of Jackie Chan, Anita Mui recorded forty albums and acted in dozens of films, several with her dear friend Leslie Cheung. Cheung starred in John Woo's *A Better Tomorrow* I and II as well as the early Wong Kar-wai films — an action hero, pop music heartthrob, and perhaps the first openly gay movie star of his magnitude.

Anyway, I took it home and watched it. The story was iden-tical to Nina's in almost every respect, but set in 1930s Hong Kong rather than Taipei and New York: Anita Mui plays a woe-fully beautiful courtesan who falls in love with equally beautiful and charming rich boy Cheung. His parents interfere. She kills herself; he does not. In the 1980s, she returns as a spirit and en-lists the help of a couple, two reporters, in tracking down her supposedly reincarnated love. They find that he is still alive, of course, a broken man, addicted to opium and working as an extra at a film studio. I recall one image in particular: At the studio, when the still young and beautiful but dead Anita con-fronts the living but decrepit and soulless Leslie, in the back-ground an actor, who is playing a supernatural hero in the film they are making, is swung back and forth on a cable from a crane, waving a sword at nothing, again and again.

The film has no villains. The modern couple is simply too busy, too self-involved for that kind of melodramatic romance, in which the highest glory a woman can aspire to is victimhood. Cheung's parents only want what's best for him and offer to make Mui a concubine, almost respectable in their day. And Cheung himself does genuinely love her, but is simply too weak to resist his parents and too cowardly to die. To be honest, de-spite Nina's outrage, I cannot think of Liu Ping as so evil after all. Who dies of love? Only Mui's character has the courage and the purity of heart. Her name in the movie is Fleur, and indeed that's how she falls, like a blossom overfilled with rain.

The film *Rouge* is made even more haunting by the real-life fates of its stars: On April 1, 2003, Leslie Cheung jumped from the twenty-fourth floor of the Mandarin Oriental hotel in Hong Kong. Reporters speculated that he saw his career peaking or that he had quarreled with his boyfriend, but the note he pinned to his body spoke of a long depression; thanked his friends, family, and his lover; and said, "In my life I've done nothing bad. Why does it have to be like this?"

The same year, Anita Mui died of cancer. She had struggled secretly for years, and when she retired from the stage, her series of farewell concerts went on for twenty-eight nights. She was working on the movie *House of Flying Daggers,* playing the rebel leader, when illness forced her to stop. Out of respect, the director, Zhang Yimou, removed her character from the story rather than replace Anita Mui. He dedicated the film to her. At the end of my DVD of *Rouge,* there is a message from the filmmaker, Stanley Kwan: "When Anita passed away, I finally learned the sadness in the saying 'the end of an era.'"

I've come up with a few possible explanations for this whole strange affair. If none are totally satisfying, at least they all share the virtue of being completely nonsupernatural. First, Nina simply saw the movie and then fabricated the entire thing. Maybe there never even was a channeler. Why she would go to such lengths, I can't say. To win me back? That seems unlikely.

Then again, the similarity to the film could well be coincidental. Chinese culture, high and low, is steeped in tragic love stories, which frequently end in suicides, double, multiple, whatever. The next, hardly shocking possibility is that the channeler was a con artist who squeezed Nina for more money than I knew and manipulated the details of her life. Perhaps she even knew of the real Liu Ping and his lost love. That may be pushing it, but I've certainly heard of other bogus psychics having a ready-made stock of glamorous spirits on hand. No one wants to know that in her last life she was a squirrel, or a bus driver who choked quietly at home on a cookie. Tragic courtesan who dies for love. This is very much the idealized image Nina carried of herself, and one talent psychics do have, like good shrinks and good lovers, is sensing what we long to hear.

As for Liu Ping and his matching tattoo, I now wonder what I saw, exactly. The man's chest was a quilt of scars, and the dragon is a common motif. Nor is he really the only Liu Ping. In Chinese they list the family name first. I forgot this and just looked under P. But if I look under the Americanized version of Ping Liu, there are more than two dozen in Manhattan alone. One thing is for sure: We did scare the hell out of him. I carried the copy of that scribble around in my wallet for months until I met someone who spoke Mandarin. What Liu Ping wrote on my hand, as if to warn me about the figure he saw standing beside me over his deathbed, as if he knew she had also been my lover, was "ghost." Then again, I read in a book somewhere that in the olden days, the Chinese called all white people ghosts.

I wrote Nina an email about the movie, simply suggesting that she see it. She didn't respond. But a few months later, she came into the Hungarian with that record producer. It was autumn, and she was still wearing my sweatshirt. I put a smile on my face and started to stand, but she didn't see me, or pretended not to, and they chose a table in front, far from my usual corner. She sat cross-legged and ate whipped cream and laughed at whatever he said. I understood. I didn't blow her play. I kept my face hidden in the paper till they left.

I haven't seen her since, but once in a while she visits me in my dreams, as do Su Li-Zhen and Liu Ping. They've joined that host of spirits who cloud the sparkling edge of my sight. You were right about that much, Nina: I see ghosts all the time.

I, Gentile

"Are you a Jew?"

A shudder ran through me. I'd been asked this question before, back in New York, by men like this: Ultra-Orthodox or Hasidic, bearded, confrontational, in dark suits and kippahs or fedoras, they accosted me like figures out of the past, returning from nineteenth-century Russia to nag me. I knew what they wanted. They wanted me to be like them, to pray with them, sometimes in the vans they called Mitzvah Mobiles and once, ominously, in the black box of a U-Haul truck. They wanted me to go to synagogue, to become kosher, to daven every morning, to refrain from tearing toilet paper on Friday night, because every wayward, secular Jew they rescued, every lost soul they pulled in, back into Biblical time, brought the Messiah's arrival closer.

My first reaction when I heard him was fear. Maybe it's genetic, five thousand years of conditioning, but when anyone, even an old rabbi, yells "Jewish man! Jewish man!" at me on the street, my instinct is to take off running. Instead, I just shook my head and scurried by. Or if it happened a lot, like when I had that temp job on Wall Street, I'd get annoyed and cocky and say things like, "Not today I'm not," or once, staring down a guy younger than me, dressed in a velvet hat and sidelocks: "Yeah, I'm Jewish. Why? You got a problem with Jews?"

But this was LA, and though I was living in the Fairfax District, a hot spot for old Jews, they were more familiar, modern old Jews, sun-worshipping Jews with leathery tans and bright warm-up suits, piloting huge old Caddies or standing on line with me at Canter's Deli, buying cheesecake. In this overbright, ahistorical world, it felt especially bizarre, almost dreamlike, walking in flip-flops to the Chevron gas station for a late lunch, to be waylaid by a tiny old *rebbe* and asked in a high, fairy-tale voice, "Are you Jewish?"

For one thing, nobody ever walked but me. Nothing moved on the street but cars and the occasional cat. And no one wore long black coats and hats. And no one sounded like this. Or if they did, I didn't know it, because unlike in New York, no random stranger ever, ever spoke to me here. So the sudden appearance of this little fellow, with his twinkly brown eyes, his crinkled brown rumple of a face, like a supermarket bag balled up and then allowed to half unfold on its own, his white Santa beard and black hat, his hand tugging at my sleeve, actually touching me, well, it was like meeting a leprechaun or an elf or one of those other happy but mischievous creatures that materialized before wanderers along the path. I decided to play it safe: "No, I'm not Jewish," I said. "Sorry."

"Don't be sorry," he trilled, in a lilting accent from beyond the Pale. "It's not so great, believe me."

I smiled and turned to go. But he didn't let go of my sleeve. I saw that his hand was actually very fine, soft and white as a girl's.

"I wonder, friend," he sang, "could you do me a little favor?"

"What is it?" I smiled warily. How did this go wrong?

"Do you know what means a Shabbos goy?"

I did, but I didn't think that as a Gentile I should. "Not really," I said, then added cleverly, "I think I know what a goy is."

"So. On Shabbos, which is the Sabbath, a Jew cannot do many things. He cannot drive or handle money or use machinery. Like for instance switch on the lights or the air-conditioning, or even the oven."

I was going to ask, why not, but just nodded. What answer could he give that would make it any clearer? God said so.

"So," he continued, "for these things we have a friend, a Gentile friend, who is kind enough to help us a little. But today my friend disappears. Unfortunately, he's a bit of a drinker."

"You want me to turn on your lights?"

"No, no. We cannot ask someone else to do what we would not. But maybe if you came to shul, just to visit, and you saw it was getting dark, you might turn them on for yourself. Of course, to such a friend we also like to be nice. If he stops to visit Friday night and again Saturday morning, then later in the week we make him a present. Say fifty dollars?"

"What time Saturday morning?"

"Eight."

"I don't know. The thing is I'm usually busy on Saturdays."

"Seventy-five. Plus you are doing a mitzvah." He fixed me a gentle smile. His soft eyes seemed ready to melt, but the pinch on my sleeve tightened, suggesting I had little choice. And I was broke.

"Sure," I said. "I'll help. This is cash, right? I have a tax thing happening."

"Of course." He pressed my hand happily between his cool, plump palms. "I knew when I saw you that you were a good boy."

I was actually a bit reluctant to go with him, despite the money. I'd been planning to stop by Olga's Beauty Saloon for a shampoo. That's how the sign was spelled, and I wasn't going to risk upsetting Olga by being pedantic. You see, my hair is a big mess, and I just trim it myself, since it's free and what's the difference, but for five bucks and a two-dollar tip, Olga or one of her girls would wash it, and I'd gotten into the habit of treating myself on Fridays. I told Olga it was because my place only had a tub. Actually, I only had a shower, but when I found myself feeling sad and a little vulnerable, it was nice to have a big, soft Russian lady soothe my aching head with warm water. Sometimes they'd hum a little tune while they worked in the suds. What can I say? This was my life then. I was between jobs, and trying to stay in between since I couldn't stand working anyplace anymore. Really. By the end, just looking in the mirror when I shaved for work in the morning made me want to cry. Mercifully, I got laid off from my phone-sales job. With my unemployment money, and the cash I made tutoring Armenian high schoolers and Korean college students, I got by and tried to do some thinking.

Sure, I ached. I was lonely. But I'd made my bed and I was going to lie in it, all day if necessary. Mostly I read. I had an old Norton anthology of English poetry and a warped stack of moldy philosophy books left by the previous tenant, an angry graduate student. I guess there'd been a flood. The wall where the books were piled was all stained. I read Nietzsche, Wittgenstein, Kant, the pages decorated with delicate flowerings of mildew and the margins scrawled with his thick pencil: "Bullshit," it said, or "Wrong," or just "No!" When my airless box got too hot, I went out on my front steps to smoke and talk to Merv, the manager, who lived next door. Our complex, or whatever you want to call it, was a village of miniature bungalows, studios like mine and one-bedrooms, camped around a cluster of dying palms and a dirt lawn where Merv would crunch and thrust and try to talk me into lifting weights.

"Don't worry, I'll spot you," he'd say. "You'll be ripped in no time."

I'd laugh it off. No kidding, ripped! Merv's crew cut and brush-stache were almost white, but his tattooed arms were the size of my legs, and what I pictured ripping if I lifted a weight was a testicle at least, or maybe a whole arm off at the socket. His nipples were pierced, and when I first moved in he scared me, but he let me slide on the rent, and if I didn't go over for Christmas and Thanksgiving, he'd come and pound on my door.

The shul turned out to be just a few blocks from my place. It wasn't what I expected. The building was plain stucco with arched doors and a few small Spanish windows. There was a tiny lawn and tinier parking lot divided into too-narrow spots. It lacked the haunted, chilly feeling I associated with holy places. In fact, I realized as I waited for the rabbi to unlock the door, I'd passed it before. It had been a Sikh yoga place then. I followed the rabbi around as he turned on the lights and air-conditioning so that when I did it later I could act like it was my idea. Apparently the deal they'd signed with God, all those centuries ago, was so harsh that the only way to get by was out-witting the boss.

I promised to be back at ten and then rushed to Olga's, but she was closed. That's what I got for doing a good deed. Still missing lunch, I swung by the Chevron for a snack. I'd poured my coffee and was waiting by the microwave for my breakfast burrito (they're good anytime) when she touched my elbow. The X.

"Larry, my God, it's really you."

"Hey, Claire. How are you?"

She opened her arms and we hugged, stiffly, in that awkward ex-fiancé way, me holding my coffee out to avoid splashing her white T-shirt and white jeans. Her sunglasses sparkled at me, and the fluorescent light purpled her dark hair.

"I'm good. What a coincidence. I just popped in to get some gas and some juice for the kids."

"Kids? Plural?"

"Yeah, Jonah and Jack, they're twins." She tapped a nail on the window. I saw a black Mercedes with a strong-jawed male at the wheel. I assumed the twins were in the back, like little celebrities behind the tinted glass. "What about you?"

"Me? Triplets."

"Ha-ha," she said. "I meant like, girlfriend, job?"

"I'm kind of doing this freelance work now. For a rabbi."

"A rabbi?" She brightened. "That's amazing. We're Buddhists, but I was thinking about taking a Kabbalah class."

The microwave dinged. I opened the door, and she considered the ham and cheese melting from my burrito. "He's Orthodox," I said. "But I'm Reformed."

"Anyway," she said, shifting nervously, "I've been wanting to call you. I want to say how bad I feel, you know. About the way things turned out with us."

"That's OK," I said. What else could I say? I took a bite of burrito to hide my sorrow. "Everything turned out for the best."

"That's so true," she said. "It really did. You know, I went into therapy. You should try it."

I remembered once suggesting therapy and getting a plate thrown at my head. But I let it go. "Well, you seem great," I said and pretended to look at my watch. It said 11:20. I kept forgetting to get the battery changed. "I should go. Gotta get to temple." I opened the door for her.

"Larry, I want you to know" — she squeezed my wrist and let go — "you're a great guy. And I'm so happy that you're getting in touch with your spirituality."

"Thanks." I followed her into the heat. She hustled over to the Mercedes and climbed in, talking to the rugged, sandy-haired driver. He waved and gave me a gracious winner's smile. I toasted him with my cup. I had to admit, he did look like husband material. Joyful participation in the sufferings of the world. That was what Buddhists like Claire and Sandy believed in. I looked at my reflection in the glass door and saw through my transparent skin to the brightly colored products inside. A strand of melted cheese clung to my lip. Had I known true suffering and true joy? Maybe not enough or not at the same time. I finished the burrito and flip-flopped back to my lotus pad. I took a shower and washed my hair, but it just wasn't the same.

When I got to the shul that night, yellow light was blurring the high windows and the blank building was hidden by two big trees that I hadn't seen before. I walked across the lawn and up the steps and pushed in the door. The place was packed. I had pictured a few old men like the rabbi, mumbling together, but there had to be a couple of hundred people in here. Where did they all come from? How come I had never noticed? They had to live within walking distance, I knew. It was as if these black-clad strangers had been hiding in the shadows of my neighborhood, like bats or dark butterflies, folded into leaves, motionless, invisible until, with the night, they swarmed. Except LA had no shadows. The sun laid this city bare.

An old man greeted me silently at the door, finger to his lips, and handed me a yarmulke and prayer book. I was early, the services weren't done, and I ducked into a pew in the back. The room was plain, just packed rows of wooden benches and a balcony running around three sides. The rabbi was in front, the Torah unscrolled on the lectern before him. He wore a white skullcap and a tallis. While the men around me rocked and muttered, the rabbi's prayer climbed higher, twisting as it rose up past the balcony to the roof. That voice that had seemed out of place on the street, too high, too singsong, too foreign, now unfolded its gorgeous feathers. Like a stick-legged bird that plays the fool on land, his voice was made for music. It sounded out of tune in mere speech. My gaze drifted up with the floating prayer and lit on a pair of eyes.

Now, the balcony was covered with a wooden lattice, and I knew that the women were hidden back there, where they wouldn't tempt the minds of men from God. So I really couldn't see much, and to be honest, I pictured a bunch of ancient, storybook women, with witchy noses and hairy warts, with head scarves and old-world woolens over their lumpy forms. I'd heard that they shaved their heads and wore wigs (or was that nuns?) and had sex through a hole in a sheet, like cartoon ghosts. Let's just say, I wasn't exactly scanning for hot prospects. But there, in the gap between two wooden slats, I thought I saw two eyes.

How? I don't know, maybe I was imagining things. I couldn't name their color or describe their shape, but my heart jumped and I gripped the prayer book like a believer. My vision narrowed to those twin points, and now it was I who was peeping through a crack in my cell, out on the world of light. The man beside me tapped my hand. I was on the wrong page. He pointed my finger to the correct line that I couldn't read anyway. I nodded thanks, pretended to scrutinize it for a second, and then turned my face back to heaven, searching the walls and ceiling, as if looking for a star in the clouded sky, but my eyes were gone.

After the service ended, I had to wait until the last of the worshippers left to turn everything off and lock up. I stood under a tree and searched the departing faces for that face, those eyes. No luck. Was it oval or round? Was the skin dark or fair and freckled? I somehow had the impression of dark curls, but maybe I was wrong. Now, dressed as shadows and walking through shadows, everyone looked the same. Finally, as the last stragglers moved off in groups of two or three and disappeared into the street, I gave up and went in to find the rabbi. He walked out of the sanctuary, arm in arm with a girl in her twenties. Of course, you've already guessed it was her, but I didn't notice at first. I was distracted by the limp.

She moved with a kind of up-and-down motion, her right

hip jutting sideways and her right foot turned out. She had those shoes where one is higher than the other, but not the big Frankenstein ones I'd seen before. These were subtler, like regular black leather ladies' boots, but with a good inch of extra sole added to the bottom of the right one. Maybe one of her legs was too short? It was hard to see what was what. She wore an ankle-length dark skirt and a white blouse that came to her wrists and buttoned high around her neck. But even those modest garments couldn't hide the fact that there was a live girl underneath: I sensed the spread of her hips, the tiny waist where the blouse tucked, the push of her breasts against the stiff fabric. A heart was beating in there. Her head was bowed demurely, with the hair piled on top, but I could see a graceful ear and part of a pale nape, like a slice of moon behind the cloud of lace.

"There you are," the rabbi said, then, "This is my daughter Leah."

"Nice to meet you." I held out my hand. Leah glanced at her father quickly and then briefly touched my hand. I realized that maybe I'd made a mistake: She wasn't supposed to touch a man but hadn't wanted to be rude. Blushing, she looked up at me.

Her eyes were brown but darker than her father's, less sad and with a gleam that, however shy the lashes, met and challenged my dim blues. There was a moment of awkward silence, and then the rabbi cleared his throat. He glanced around the foyer.

"Are you chilly?"

"What? Oh yeah," I said. "Mind if I turn off the air conditioner? And the lights?"

The rabbi groaned and Leah laughed, a small wild giggle,

like a bird fluttering out of my hands. Her eyes flickered twice, between two beats of their lids. As I ran downstairs to the switches, I heard the rabbi shout good night.

When I got back to my village, Merv was out front. "Hey, Larry," he yelled with a slightly drunken gaiety. "Have a beer." He rustled his paper bag. "Shit. None left. How about a Coke?"

"Sure." He went inside. His screen door banged, and the sky flapped above me like a dusty blanket. The stars shook out. Palm fronds scratched in the wind.

Later, Merv went out to a bar and I went home, but I couldn't sleep. I kept thinking about those eyes through the lattice, as if seen through a veil or the filigreed wall of a harem. About that high shoe and the body hidden under those clothes. I flipped through Nietzsche, Hegel, Kant, but it was no use. I went out on the steps and felt my sweat dry and watched my smoke go up. Then I lay back down and read the Norton till dawn, Wordsworth to Keats straight through. When the sun lit my window, I went to the Chevron for a large coffee and a donut. On the way back I noticed two feet sticking out of the bushes next to Merv's door. I parted the branches, and there he was, snoring away. He had his keys in his hand. Looked like he was coming home drunk and just missed by a few inches. I unlocked the door, and with a lot of prodding and pleading, he let me help him up. I got him onto the couch and covered him with a blanket. I noticed a pale band of skin around his wrist that used to be a watch. I wondered if they got his wallet too.

"Steve," he mumbled.

"It's Larry," I said.

"Larry."

"Yes?"

"Don't tell anyone."

"Of course not," I whispered, gently shutting the door. Who would I tell?

I left early for shul. Lawn sprinklers were throwing a glow on the grass, but no wind moved the leaves and I could see it was going to be another killer day. I unlocked the door and turned on all the lights. I got the A/C going. Then I took my book and sat on the steps to make sure I wouldn't miss Leah. But I couldn't read. My racing mind surged ahead of the lines. At last she came rocking up the path, holding her bent father by the elbow. It was unclear who was supporting whom. I quickly kicked the mashed cigarette butts I'd accumulated into the shrubbery and smiled.

"Good morning," I called.

"Shabbat shalom," the rabbi answered. Leah said nothing, a punch in the heart, but when the rabbi went in, she loitered out front, turning her closed eyes to the sun. I grabbed the chance to study her face, trying to store up every detail for later, when she'd disappear again behind the screen. Her skin was astonishing. There were no splotches or marks, only a blending, from milk to pink to deep rose. Her hair was a liquidy black, and each curl seemed to be alive, growing, twisting right then. I realized how long it had to be, coiled up like that. If she let it down, how low would it fall? To the small of her back? To her hips? She opened her eyes and caught me staring. I fled back down to my book.

"What are you reading?"

"A poetry anthology. Keats, actually. I'm up to Keats."

"Who's Keats?"

"Who's Keats?" I blurted loudly, then caught myself. In a rush, I told her everything I knew about Keats. How he was self-taught, really, working class, and died of TB at twenty-five, broke and bereft in Rome. How he wrote all his greatest works in only twelve months, and in that brief flash burned himself into the heart of English literature. He wrote some of the most beautiful love poems ever, yet some speculate that he may have died a virgin. Her throat bloomed red, and I realized that I'd said "virgin" to a rabbi's daughter. I blushed back and tried to extricate myself by getting high-minded but only dug deeper.

"You know what Oscar Wilde said?"

She shook her head no. Of course not!

"Never mind," I said. "Sorry."

"What did he say?"

"He said that Keats's grave was the holiest site in Rome."

"That's beautiful," she said and smiled. It was the first smile. "I'd love to read him some time."

"You can borrow this." I offered her the book. "I mean I've read it."

"No, I can't. It's so big."

"Well, there's just a few pages of Keats."

"No, I mean because of my father."

Just then the first worshippers appeared, coming up the block in their black, the young kids scampering ahead. One dropped his yarmulke and ran back. On an impulse, I opened the book to the page I'd turned down and ripped it out.

"Here." I crushed the poem and pressed it into her palm. For a second, her eyes widened like a startled animal's, min-gling fear and high spirits. Then she hurried in, pushing my paper rose under the sleeve of her blouse.

I sat through the whole service this time, eyes fixed on the higher realms. Again, I can't really say what I saw through that screen, but I believe I found her in the diamond of a lattice. I believe that the prayer book she held before her face hid the "Ode on Melancholy." I believe that when she looked up from the book and down into the congregation her eyes were searching for mine and that she found them, gazing up among the bowed heads, and that she looked right at me. And I believe she was crying.

The next few days felt like I had a fever. It was hotter than ever and my mind felt stuck, half melted and struggling to move. It would take me an hour to get through a page of *On the Genealogy of Morals*. Then I'd fall asleep, just for a moment, for a single breath, and have a long dream. Once I was in Turin with Nietzsche, when he was mad, walking in the town square. He put his arm around me. "*Cómo está?*" he asked, in Spanish I guess, but in my dream this was Italian. "I am God," he said, happily. "I made this farce."

I hadn't seen Leah after the service. I guess the women left earlier, while the men stayed all day, and my vision of her reading the poem faded and became as unbelievable as my Nietzsche dream. I spent a lot of time out on the step with Merv, but I didn't mention Leah, although my mind ceaselessly repeated her name. What would I say? The whole thing was better off forgotten. Still, when Wednesday came and I went to the rabbi's house to get my pay, all my nerves were shaking and a drop of sweat fell from my forehead as I knelt to tie my sneakers on his walk.

The rabbi lived just two streets west of me, on a block parallel to my own, but I had never been down it. The house was small, with a sloped shingle roof and a porch. The garden was rich but overgrown, a nest of wildflowers and vines and weeds, twining together without pattern. The rabbi answered the door himself. His arms were white as chicken in the short-sleeved white dress shirt, and I saw the knots of his tefillin hanging out. He sat me down in his book-choked back office and insisted, vehemently, that I drink hot tea with him, that it would cool me down. He served it in a glass with a lump of sugar on the side.

The floor was crooked, I saw sand and pennies glittering between the warped boards, and the stuffing in my chair was shot. I had to lurch forward to grab my tea, and a little splash burned my arm. I rested my eyes on the books. They were stacked everywhere, the desk, the floor, the couch, all Hebrew, and those rows of unknowable letters calmed me down. It was a relief to look at something beautiful without straining to comprehend it. There was a photo of a woman tucked between the volumes on a shelf. She was standing in the garden, which looked even more overgrown than it was now. It teemed with crazy flowers, blues and reds by her feet and the yellow heads of sunflowers nodding from necks taller than hers. She wore a head scarf and a printed apron over her dress. The sun blanched her face, made it indistinct, but the shape of the forehead and the dark smudges of the eyes were Leah's.

"Is that your wife?"

"Yes, that's my Miriam, *alav hashalom.*"

I must have smiled blankly because he leaned forward and patted my hand.

"In Hebrew this means she should rest in peace."

"Oh, I'm sorry."

"No, no. She's been dead now twenty-four years." Leah, he told me, had been a late last child, a surprise and they'd thought a blessing. But Miriam had died giving birth to Leah, who came with her twisted leg. Now the two lived alone in the house. His three other daughters, much older, were all long grown and married.

"You must miss her."

He shrugged. "I see Miriam every night in my dreams. And I hear her in the garden, singing. I haven't touched that garden since she died, but it just keeps blooming. Once, when I had a fever, she even made me one of her special teas. Better than this we're drinking."

"Sorry?"

"Yes," he said, smiling at his thoughts. His teeth were chipped and yellow. "I was lying in bed, and Leah brought me a pot of tea. When I tasted it, I was amazed. It was the tea my wife made, a special mixture only she knew. I drank it, and in the morning I was fine. I asked Leah, how did you know to make your mother's tea? She said, Daddy, you were dreaming. It was just Lipton's. But when I checked the pot, there it was, the herbs in the bottom. And in the garden those plants were cut."

"What did Leah say?"

"I didn't tell her. It would make her sad." He put his sugar in his mouth and crunched it, then raised the steaming glass to his lips.

There was no sign of Leah, and by the time the rabbi escorted me out, I was in despair. Pushing my way through the garden — it seemed to have grown denser since I came — I felt something, a leaf, a bug, brush my neck and I turned. There was Leah, in a window, watching me from the curtains. The sun was high, and the sky's reflection flashed on the glass. The truth was, all I saw clearly was blue air and clouds and a white gem of light with only the faintest silhouette of a girl behind it, a pale oval face framed by stirring lace. Still, I reached into my pocket and slipped out the page of Keats I had carefully cut out for her, "Ode to a Nightingale," and had folded again and again into a tiny bundle. I waved blindly and, hoping she was watching me and the rabbi wasn't, I dropped it in the tall grass.

"What are you waving for?" he asked.

"Oh, nothing. I just saw Leah."

He laughed again. "Go lie down. You're dreaming. Leah's at the market."

But I couldn't rest. I rolled around on my mattress until the damp sheets were strangling me. I went to the sink and splashed water on my head. I watched moths bounce against my screens. After two nights like this, I decided to stalk her. I knew I was acting crazy, but I didn't care. I had to get this thought out of my head. I crouched behind a parked car up the block, where I had a clear view of their house. After an hour, the car's owner appeared and I had to pretend that I was looking for a lost necklace.

"I'm sure it was here," I told the guy in the Lakers jacket and cap. My legs were asleep, and I stumbled around, head bowed low over the strip of grass by the curb. "You didn't see it?" I asked him. "It had a little charm shaped like a dog? It was my mother's."

"Sorry," he said. "Good luck." When he drove off, I saw Leah standing on the sidewalk by her house and staring at me. She turned abruptly and headed down the block.

"Wait," I called and went after her, but my legs were still numb and she moved surprisingly fast, considering her jerky, off-center sway. She was appalled, of course, to see me hobbling behind her, but I caught her by the corner, where she had to stop for the light.

"Leah, wait, please."

"What?" she demanded, catching her breath. "What are you following me for? It's Shabbos tonight. I've got to get to the bakery."

"It's Friday?" I'd completely forgotten. I could've waited to see her at the shul. I had to shower and get ready myself. "What time is it now? My watch stopped."

She sighed with exasperation and, checking both ways, undid a button on her blouse. She reached in and pulled out two folded pages, wrinkled and pressed flat like flowers in a book.

"Here," she said. "Take these." She pushed them into my hand — the Keats odes, still warm.

"You found this?" I asked. "How did you know I left it for you?"

She glared at me. "What do you mean? It was sitting on my front step when I got home. Thank God my father didn't find it first."

"But how did you know you'd see me today?"

"I didn't."

"Then how did you know to bring them now?"

She blushed. Her throat turned crimson, and the blood rose quickly to her cheeks. "I didn't. I was afraid to leave them anywhere, in case my father saw. Now just please leave me alone. My God, if he saw us."

"No, wait, you don't understand. If you knew the truth about me . . ."

"I know enough," she said and turned to go. I wanted to grab her hand, but restrained myself. I wanted to shout, "I'm a Jew. A Jew!" but now that seemed even worse: I'd denied my people and desecrated the Sabbath just to make a little cash. I watched her race away from me, her dark hair coming undone, her hips rising and falling.

Leah didn't come to shul that night. The rabbi arrived alone and said she was sick with the flu, a fever and a headache. "I guess it's going around," he said. "How are you feeling? Better?"

"Fine," I blurted guiltily, but I felt like I was dying. I hoped I was, anyway. I sat through the service and actually paid attention for the first time, keeping my eyes on the rabbi and off the balcony. It helped a little. The sound of those words I couldn't understand relaxed me, the prayers like songs, beautifully meaningless.

Leah wasn't there the next day either, and when I got out of synagogue, I went straight to the Saloon. There was a line of people waiting, but when she saw me, Olga squeezed me in.

"Darling, you look awful," she said, easing me into the chair and resting my head on the sink. "You need a nice shampoo." I sighed as the hot water washed over me. "You know what else you need?" Olga whispered as she lathered me up. "A manicure. Sonya over there gives a great manicure." I opened one eye. A buxom girl with long dark hair was polishing an old lady's nails. "She just moved from Russia," Olga went on. "She needs a nice Jewish husband."

"Maybe next week," I said, eyes closed.

Again that night I paced in my cage, thinking, thinking. I went by Merv's, but he was out. I sat on his step and was trying, with the help of a cigarette, to breathe, when I thought I heard a voice come from the bushes.

"Larry?" it whispered.

I looked closely. No feet were sticking out tonight. The shrub just looked at me like I was crazy, mad as Moses in his desert.

"Larry?" it called again, softly, and I answered, softly, "What?"

Leah stood up and pushed her way out, brushing the twigs from her hair.

"What are you doing here?" I asked her. She threw her arms around me and began kissing me randomly, blindly, kissing my cheeks, nose, chin.

"Leah," I said, guiding her back across the dirt yard to my place. "I can't believe you came."

"I had to. I couldn't stand it. I snuck out. But I didn't know which house was yours."

"Leah, I have to tell you, you don't understand about me."

"I know, I know everything, my love. I know you're not Jewish and you don't even believe in God. I know you don't care about my father. You don't care about anything. Good. I won't either. I'm glad you're a goy and an atheist who lives like an animal and doesn't care about what God or people think."

Animal! This was news to me. I looked at my dusty mattress, my cardboard carton of clothes, and the bigger carton I used as a table.

"Who said animal, your dad?"

"I know it because that's me too. I knew it all my life. I was just waiting for a reason to go. For you. I want to run away with you. I want to live and work and go to school and read books with you. And I want to have sex."

After that I said nothing because she took off her clothes, everything, she just peeled it all off and stood before me completely naked, looking me right in the eye and smiling, with her fists at her sides, like she was going to enjoy this fight. She looked so happy and brave. Afterward, we fell asleep, still clutching each other tightly, as if in fear, but my sleep was calm and without dreams. When I woke up, I felt as if I'd slept for a week.

Being careful not to wake Leah, I found my shirt and pants, stepped into my shoes, and went to see the rabbi. Halfway down the block, I realized that I hadn't brushed my teeth. Fuck it, I thought. There's no turning back now. The sun was out again and the morning smog was crystalline. The leaves and the grass blades were lit and blurred, the car windows like dusty mirrors. I found him in the study in the back of his house, head bent, beard in a book.

"Excuse me, Rabbi. Can I talk to you?"

He looked up from the book, his beard keeping the place. He smiled. "What are you doing here on Sunday? Today you should be resting and I should be coming to turn on the air."

I smiled back. "But I came to you for advice."

"Ah, you're not hot enough? You want my hot air too? OK, good, sit, sit." He waved impatiently at the worn chairs. "You make me nervous standing like a soldier."

I sat in my chair. A feather jumped out of the cushion with a little sigh. My hands were sweating. Those brown eyes, the same as Leah's, were beaming at me from the photo. Or did they look mad? I took a breath and said it: "Rabbi, I'm in love with a Jewish girl. She's from a very pious home, so I'm sure her family will be upset. I don't want to hurt them, but I love her. What do you think I should do?"

The rabbi's face showed nothing. "The girl, she feels the same?"

"Yes, Rabbi."

"How can you know it's love?"

"Because from the moment I saw her, I've felt sick all the time. No, that's not what I mean." I waved my hands, as if to erase that line, then slumped back in my chair. "I don't know how I know. It's a mystery."

He didn't speak, but his fingers and his lips moved a little, tapping the book, chewing his beard. His eyes focused on the space above my head, as if the truth were there in a cartoon bubble. Suddenly, he leapt up and came around the desk. I thought he was going to hit me. With that withered little body and those soft, white hands, it would've been like a child throwing a fistful of rose petals at me, but still, I would not have been able to bear it. Instead he sat on the other chair, which gasped and then exhaled deeply.

"Let's talk turkey," he said. "We're in Los Angeles here. It's not Minsk, thank God. If she goes with you, I can't stop her."

He shrugged. "This one I could never control anyway. She's wild. Like her mother was. But you, you think you can do better? How will you support her? How long do you think she'll be happy, living on air? She's a princess. Raised to be a queen. No offense, but she's stronger than you are, believe me. She'll crush you."

"It's true," I said. "She's a queen."

"Like her mother," he said again. I said nothing. We both looked down, and a moment passed there between us.

"Why don't you convert?" the rabbi said mildly, as if suggesting fish for lunch.

"What?" I looked up, to see if he was smiling, but he wasn't.

"Become a Jew," he told me, calmly. "Become a Jew and I'll give you my blessing. Then I'll help you with the money. I'll send you to study. To become a rebbe."

"Me?"

"Why not you? I knew it when I met you, that God had sent you to me for some reason. Maybe this is it. Who can understand God? We can only follow the path that he has written in our hearts. Now, I think I can see what he wrote in yours: 'Become a Jew. Marry Leah.'"

Madness, I thought, the most ridiculous thing in my whole ridiculous life. Leah didn't want a rabbi. She didn't even want a Jew. She wanted me. And how could I be a rabbi if I didn't believe? But if, by some chance, God did exist, then how could I refuse to play the hand he dealt me? With the stakes so high, how could I not bet my life? And if there was nothing? It was true: I did not believe in God, but I was beginning to believe in miracles, miracles and whatever is the opposite of miracles, terrible wonders. Yes, this life is a whirlwind, and what can guide us through it? Not our eyes, not our ears, not our brain. What difference does it make what we believe?

"OK," I said. "I'll do it."

He stood and grasped my hands, guiding me to my feet. His eyes were sad, wet, blazing. He squeezed my shoulders. "My son," he said. Then he kissed me, right on the mouth. I felt his beard on my lips. "Now go," he said. "Go to her. Run."

I ran. I didn't go back around the block. I ran out the door and across the street and cut through the neighbors' yards. I jumped over their bushes. I stopped for a second to yank a flower, a big orange flower, the best one, out of the ground, roots and all. A car honked and someone yelled and the dogs started barking and I ran past them, across the alley and over the wall, back to where my wild bride lay sleeping.

Vampires of Queens

My mother buzzes me in. I cross the dim lobby with its red tile
floor, its fake electric torches and threadbare, medieval furniture, and there it is, open, humming, as if waiting just for me.
I hesitate. I stalk ghosts through the hallways of this building, track assassins with my disc gun in the basement, fight off
hordes with spinning kung fu leaps on the stairways, three perfect scratches on my chest like Bruce Lee in the posters on my
walls, but I'm not allowed to ride the elevator alone. It tends to
get stuck between floors. Still, seeing it there, with no one looking, I walk toward it slowly, dawdling, planting a foot in the
center of each tile, almost hoping it will close and roll up past
the window in the door, but it doesn't, it waits and, as though
climbing aboard a ship in bad seas, I step on, one foot at a time.
The door slides shut behind me. It's only then that I see him
there, in the corner, the old blind man who lives on the top
floor. He's wrapped in the wings of his black overcoat, with the
high collar and the burn holes and the crusted egg yolk on the
sleeve. One white hand folds over the other on top of his white
cane, and in the pocket, I see the neck of a flat brown bottle
with a pink paper seal on the cap. His chalk head faces nothing,

the skin like old wallpaper peeling from his skull. A veined egg. I hold my breath and freeze as the cage begins to rise, turning the arrow above the door. He turns to me and shows his dog teeth and says, "I can't see you, but I know you're there."

As soon as he smiles, I know what he is.

That night it snows and, as if in celebration, my family goes out for Chinese food. Fat as petals, white as clouds, the silent flakes come parachuting in. You'd think heaven had finally invaded the earth. By tomorrow, all this will be gray slush and icy wind. But tonight it is a comforter spread by the sky, softening every sound, brightening every light, pillowing each mailbox and water tower and frosting every wire. Round, padded figures, barely recognizable as our neighbors, lumber about in mittens and hats, thumping and sliding, like furry, awkward creatures, newly made and just learning to walk on the slick ground, to catch rich flakes on their tongues. The lines between street and sidewalk, lamppost and tree, erase themselves like the line between horizon and sky. The stars flicker down like moths. They dance in the haloed lamps.

Later, at the restaurant, I toss a penny in the fake stone fountain of candy-colored lights and make a solemn wish that I am, even now, forbidden to utter. But fate answers, and before my soup is gone, my hands begin to itch. Tiny pink spots form like lichen, and the more I scratch them, the larger they grow. Burning pins jump across my arms, twitching and biting like wires.

By the time we get home, hives have risen on my face and my mother sends me to bed. The pink eruptions unfold in my skin like crushed flowers. Roses clog my throat. Electricity crackles over the surface of my body. I get lost in the living room and can't reach my door. A menacing brown couch blocks my way. The carpet sways like a field of wheat. When they find me, I'm burning up. All my features are blown up to twice their regular size. I'm a cartoon. I feel a black hand in my chest, squeezing my lungs. A skeleton hand, tight in a black leather glove. The air sings through my windpipe and fever eats holes in my mind, like salt burning through the ice. The doctor appears, pajamas under his gray pin-striped suit. White hair wings his pink skull. The needle stings going in, and I smell something burning, like birthday candles melting in cake. Outside my window, as frost grows on the glass and the world retreats into whiteness, a vast sky opens like a furnace above us, a black heart consuming stars and grinding them into embers.

I guess I'm allergic to the world or something. Invisible enemies inflame my eyes and skin. Microscopic mold spores in the air clog my chest. Bronchial asthma, some doctors claim. Others say asthmatic bronchitis. I can't have corn or cucumbers or eggs. And for the first time I realize how much I love these things that I've always been indifferent to.

"I want eggs, I want eggs," I moan over juice and toast. Milk is phlegm-producing, so I have to watch dairy too. Twice a week I go to the doctor's office for injections. He takes the steel needles from the sterilizing machine and pushes them through the rubber seal on the little bottles of clear fluid. It burns a little, but I don't care. It's a small price to pay for the miracle he has bestowed: a note permanently excusing me from gym. Finally, I am delivered from that hell they call phys ed. Awkward, weak, and timid, I can't shoot or dribble or hit. Balls thrown at me bounce off my hands, if I'm lucky. My eyes flame up in the light, and I can't see well enough to swing a bat. So my parents buy me mirrored sunglasses to shield my red, raw eyes, and during gym I sit on the sidelines with my book or chat with Bill, the epileptic kid.

On the weekends, I stay in and read. Then, as day ends, I am let out to play for an hour or two in the twilight. Sometimes, as I wheel my bike through the lobby, I see the blind man, sprawled and snoring in the tall, tattered armchair that commands a regal view of the mailboxes. My mother clucks and tells my father that she saw him passed out drunk again, but I know what he is really doing. I picked out my dark glasses to be like his. I go out when everyone else comes in. He is waiting for dark, when he is free and everyone else is blind.

Everyone feels sorry for me, but secretly I'm thrilled. Without the pressure of having to take part in something, do something, be something, I pass whole days without fear or boredom. Who could get tired of reading? I carry a book at all times, and at any moment, on the train, in a store, at Thanksgiving dinner surrounded by shouting relatives, I can open the cover like an escape hatch and drop through. I read to disappear and carry books like spies carry cyanide in their teeth. Real readers poison themselves with words. They close each book as though climbing, reborn, from a tomb.

After school Christine and I stop along Northern Boulevard and build a fort. The snow along the street is streaked with soot and shit, but pure flakes spiral in to shawl our shoulders. The plows have thrown up huge drifts, bristling with unearthed trash. Ducking low behind the wall, we pack the snow into dozens of hard bombs. It will be days before reinforcements arrive and we have to hold them off ourselves, sniping at the enemy supply line. Christine's straight blond hair has never been cut. Her eyes are a frozen blue. The wind whips gold strands around her hat and her tiny ears, and the tip of her small nose turns red.

"Fire!" We launch an attack on a truck going down the avenue. A snowball echoes loudly as it whacks the side of the truck. Direct hit. A bus comes along.

"Fire!" We stand and take careful aim at the windows. It's an express bus and not allowed to stop, so the driver can't get us even though he glances over just as I open up. The snowballs stick where they hit. A car comes next. This time we shoot too early, and a snowball thumps the hood. The car skids, lurching across the ice, and stops. The driver pops out, a big man with a beard.

"Hey, you little shits!"

"Retreat!" We run down the alley behind Woolworth's and jump on garbage cans to clamber over the wall. We come out on the other side of the block and slip into a basement window I know is never locked. We flatten ourselves to the pocked concrete wall, breathing hard, while my eyes adjust to the dark.

"Do you think he followed us?" Christine gasps, chest heaving.

"Shh . . ." I listen hard, trying to pick out our bearded pursuer from the landscape of crunching snow and hissing tires above. Now I can see the piled cartons and spiderwebs around us. In the corner where we're crouching, white cigarette butts and an empty bottle glow in the snowlight, covered in a lifetime's dust.

I see a plastic cap like the one from the needles the doctor sticks me with. I pick it up and put it my pocket for evidence.

Holding my breath, I stand on a box and peek over the windowsill. Suddenly, it's evening and the streetlights are on outside, burning white in the blue air, with a swarm of pinpoint snowflakes clouding each lamp like static. Legs go by. Cars bounce through potholes full of black water and shards of ice.

"I don't think he saw us," I report. "But we better hide here awhile. He might still be out there looking." We sit on the floor and pull off our wet gloves. My pants are soaked, and I've lost another scarf. I must have left it at the fort, but I can't go back there now. Christine takes a bag of M&M's from her coat pocket.

"Want some?"

"Thanks."

"Do you know what I do sometimes?" she asks, sorting the M&M's by color and giving me half the reds. "I hide candy under my pillow, and then in bed, after I've brushed my teeth and said my prayers and everything, I eat it." Prayers? I brushed my teeth but didn't say prayers.

"Why do you say prayers?"

"So that God doesn't kill you while you're sleeping. Otherwise you could die while you're sleeping and never even know you were dead." I suck an M&M until the chocolate bleeds through the shell. Christine finishes counting the yellows and looks up at me.

"Elliot?"

"Yeah?"

"What sign are you?"

I search my mind for a clue.

"We don't have signs. We're Jewish."

"Oh," she says, seemingly satisfied with that answer. Maybe, I think, that's why I don't pray either. God won't kill Jews. Although, according to my mother, almost everyone else will.

"Elliot?"

"Yeah?"

"Do you know how to kiss?"

I shrug. I don't.

"Me either." We sit in silence. I hear the blood booming in my ears, as if I were slipping over a waterfall. I want to say something but I can't.

"Should we try it?" Christine asks. I nod. We bring our faces close, and I feel her breath like a flower brushing my cheeks, like a warm snowflake feathering down. Carefully, we press our lips together. Her mouth is soft and tastes like chocolate. It's good so we try it again. She wraps her arms around my shoulders. I can't believe this is happening, so I kiss her cheeks. She seems to like it. I kiss her neck. It is even whiter and smoother than her cheek, the pale chill touched with rose, warm beneath the skin, like burning snow.

"Elliot, stop it. That hurt." I pull back. There are tears in her eyes. "Why did you bite me?"

"I don't know."

"It's late. I have to go."

Outside, the sky is a torn black cloak, wavering in the wind. Through the ripped stars a little light leaks in, from the world beyond. I bend my head beneath it and run home as fast as I can.

· · ·

That night at dinner I can't eat a thing. My lungs are full of ice crystals that ache and blaze when I breathe. Snow drifts block my chest. When my mother presses her lips to my forehead, she says I have a fever and puts me to bed, propped up with three pillows so I can breathe and sleep sitting up. On a snack table by my bed the humidifier steams, its mouth slathered with Vicks VapoRub. Straining at the shadows on the ceiling, my mind reels with bats, screaming in blind circles. I pray deliriously not to die while I sleep. I pray to the vampire upstairs.

Past midnight, a skull smiles. Its eyes sparkle like sugar. A hand crosses the windowsill, bloodless as the flat moon, each long finger bound in a different ring, the skull, the eye, the rose, the star. Fog hisses from the machine, reeking of menthol. The shadow of great wings spreads against the wall. He wraps his cloak about my shoulders. Everything that daylight hides, blinding us with false colors and the illusion of visibility, is dissolved and rendered clear now in the dark. He takes my hand, and we sail out over the city. He shows me what he sees.

What can I say about this night? That Queens rolls over like a snoring fat lady, in a shift of crumbling lace, and lays herself wide open, weeping in the arms of her dreams? Anyone could walk right in for a free show. The rooftops glow beneath us, pillows dusted in white. Roads curl up and draw their sheets over their heads. The white city is a bed brushed smooth by the sky, which rushes overhead in a river, moon and cloudy stars tossing on currents of wind. Every water tower, every ledge or sill or branch, every clothesline and antenna and each power wire is sugared with the same bright ice.

A man stands in a phone booth on a corner, pleading his case. He clutches the receiver in both hands, cupping it, afraid she'll let go of her end and cast him adrift in the waves. He is completely exposed in that glass box, like a lighthouse on the farthest point. Up the street, two men trade punches. Too drunk to duck or dodge, they just stand eye to eye, like dance partners, hitting each other in the face as hard as they can. They lean into the blows. Blood puddles between them. All that's holding them up is the support of a friend's fist. An ambulance cruises by, slowing while the driver considers the damage, then shrugs and speeds off. From the doorway of the neon-lit bar a woman watches in silence. Her face is bathed in glory, pink and blue.

I could tell you that the skinny trees have all gone python silver and black, that the buildings sway over their alleys, that the snow got dizzy and passed out in a vacant lot. But what then of the ice caves dripping under the bridges, and the crying train and the rats? The rats move through a city of their own, of dented steel garbage cans and dark mountains of plastic bags that tremble, as something we discarded but that isn't really dead at all, only sleeping, stirs. It's like muscles jumping and chirping under skin. Like eggs outgrowing their shells.

Tonight, we all dream the same dream under the same cold blanket, like we will one day in the grave. We lie stacked in buildings, like books on shelves, and behind each closed door we combine the same letters, talking to ourselves in our sleep. Even those dreamers who do wake up, and feel their way down the hall toward the bathroom, have to cross miles of drifting sleep, like blind men lost in libraries with blank books in their hands. The vampire watches. The vampire turns the page. He sighs, and his lips move in silence, sounding out the words in your head, the ones you've never heard spoken, like when you opened the big dictionary in the reference room, the one with the cracked black spine, and looked up "pudendum" or "viscera" or "groin."

He turns on Northern Boulevard, then left down Christine's block, and spots her walking home alone from gymnastics. She is scared, but he is not. He is the vampire. He has the strength of ten men. He takes the form of a wolf and follows, his paws in her footprints, her scent in the fog of his breath. Now the night is like a forest that she must cross to get home, where the only sound is her boots crunching snow, and the only moonlight that falls this far is on the flakes winding through the trees. When she finally reaches her building and climbs upstairs to her room, although she doesn't want to, she will leave the window open for him. She cannot resist. She will get into bed, say her prayers, and pull the covers up to her neck.

He drifts past the windows of her apartment. Her parents are grappling in bed together, the headboard clacking on the wall. Both their eyes are shut tight, each clenched in their darkness within the darkened room. The covers slide off, and I see Christine's father, a sweaty back and hairy thighs, climbing up her mother's doughy rump. Her nails pull the sheet off the corner of the mattress, and she wrings them in her hands, as though trying to twist out a stain.

Down the hall, Christine turns restlessly in her sleep. Her deer legs kick, straight and snappable as twigs, her thin arms folding and unfolding. In the wall behind her bed, a Virgin Mary night-light of luminous plastic is plugged into the socket, casting a holy glow. Her eyes open, and for a moment I panic, until I remember that I am invisible in his wings. She sits up, golden hair sifting, and reaches under her pillow, pulling out a

Nestlé's $100,000 bar, a Pixy Stix, and a pack of Bubble Yum. She tears into the candy, breathing hard as she bites into the chocolate and draws the strands of caramel through her teeth. She rips open a straw and pours the purple sugar into her mouth, dyeing her tongue and lips as it melts. Behind the wall, her father grunts as he shuts the bathroom door and Christine dives under the covers. She buries the candy in her blanket and lays her head on the pillow, baring her white throat. There's a smear of purple like spilled wine staining the skin around her mouth. Her tongue darts out to pluck the chocolate crumbs clinging to the creases of her greedy and shamelessly parted lips.

As soon as Mrs. Tannenbaum calls on me, I know I'm shit out of luck. When the papers are handed back, I am quick to hide my A, stuffing it into my loose-leaf, ashamed both of the high grade that marks me as a brainiac and also that it's not an A+. But when she announces that she will punish the authors of the best poems by forcing them to read aloud and calls me to the front of the class, I know there is no place left to hide. I take the long walk to the scaffold, past Ronald Scuznick, who mutters "dickbreath," and Terry O'Flynn, who hisses "wheezer" and flicks snot off his fingertips at me. I arrive at the blackboard and stare at the page in my shaking hands as though it had rewritten itself in Chinese. I manage to mumble:

> O Winter Wind
> Blowing so cold.
> Who knows if you
> Are young or old?

And so on. And as my classmates applaud, I glance up to catch the disgust in their eyes. I make it back to my seat without fainting or tripping over the feet that are sticking out and sit down, my heart beating on its coffin lid like a buried soul, to await the tolling of the recess bell, when I know my life will end.

In the school yard the boys slip off their jackets and backpacks in one shrug, dumping them still entwined in a pile near the fence, and run to play handball or stickball, the air filling with a constant roar. The snow has been plowed up into one dirty mountain over which they scramble and fight like goats in the bright winter sun. The girls gather in circles to jump rope or unpack Barbies and lipsticks and other mysterious artifacts. I slink along the building, hoping to go unnoticed, lingering near the huge, truck-sized dumpsters, with their sour tang of trash, their open wounds of rust bleeding into the snow. These are the worst times: play, lunch, gym, before and after school, whenever the lack of assigned places reveals that I have no place. I am never lonely alone. It is in the crowd, among all those who are supposedly like me, that my absolute strangeness is exposed. Somehow the shame of joining in is too much for me to bear. I can never get lost the way others can, in midflight with a ball in the air, in midsong with a fist in the air, or, God forbid, dancing, but am always myself, aware of myself, hearing the endless monologue in my head, unless that voice is stopped by another voice in a book.

And what is poetry, that thing in my chest, the heart's sudden, upward swim to the light and air at the top of the skull? Each set of lines is called a stanza. It doesn't have to rhyme. Poetry is anything you read out loud alone. At first, of course, I immerse myself in the classics: Horror, Sci-fi, Westerns, and

Kung Fu. Early efforts include "The Tell-Tale Fart," about a fat man who killed for a bowl of beans, "The Oriental Art of Death," in which a master demonstrates how to rip an enemy's limbs off, and the self-explanatory "Wolfman vs. Frankenstein," but already I am mysteriously susceptible to the temptation of certain phrases in old books I barely understand, the power of certain words in my ear, their look on the page, knowing more than they say. I recognize the scattered clues, a cooling of the forehead, a clearing in the eye. A sudden wind rushes up and lifts my chest like a leaf. I step into the world behind the world. Here, alone in my labyrinth with the garbage and the sun and the gorgeous rust, I know the secret name of things. I hold the thread.

Then Ronald Scuznick appears around the dumpster with Terry O'Flynn flanking to prevent flight. A cluster of boys follows, and behind them the girls gathering to watch. I see Christine among them. Terry intones with an Irish lilt:

> O Winter Wind
> You smell like shit.
> Why don't you suck
> Your mama's tit?

The response from the crowd is uproarious. Clearly this work is much better received than my own offering, and frankly, I'm inclined to agree. I even laugh along with the others, but this just seems to annoy Scuznick more.

"What're you laughing at, douchebag?"

"Nothing," I mumble, the smile drying on my lips.

"Damn right."

Ronald closes in, shoving my shoulders, and I stagger back. Ronald punches me, sounding my head like a gong, and I hear cheers through the hum. As he pummels me, I do my best to hit back, swinging wildly, but it's hard to aim with your eyes shut tight in terror. I can't bear to see what's happening to me. I pray only that unconsciousness will be swift and soft and that I am not permanently disfigured. I even entertain a brief image of Christine smoothing my brow in the hospital. My throat tightens, and I forget to breathe. It sounds like a leaf is caught in the spokes of my chest.

"You better watch out," Terry taunts from the sidelines as I sputter and heave. "The wheezer might cough on you!"

Everyone laughs again, but through the haze of fear an idea takes shape in my mind. "That's right," I manage to warble. "I'm contagious. You'll end up like me."

Scuznick closes in for the kill. Thinking fast, I plunge my mucus-clogged pipes, and just as he raises his fists, I lean my head back and spit.

Now maybe I can't fight, or catch, or hit a ball with a bat, but if there's one thing a bronchial asthmatic can do it's hock loogies. I bring up a beauty, gray slime flecked with yellow like a bad oyster, and rearing like Pegasus, I send it arcing perfectly through the air, splat onto Scuznick's ugly mug. It's everywhere, his hair, his shirt. He's like a villain caught in Spider-Man's web. Scuznick screams, "Oh Jesus, get it off me," and takes off running like he's on fire. The crowd of onlookers panics, trampling one another to get away as he wails among them, howling and rending his garments. I cough hard, loading up more ammo, and turn to O'Flynn, but he backs off. Scuznick runs over to Mr. Alpaca, who's on duty, reading the paper by the door.

"What's wrong?" he asks, looking up as Scuznick runs over, hysterical.

"It's phlegm."

"Well, don't get it on me," Mr. Alpaca says, batting him away with his newspaper. "It's disgusting. Go see the nurse. Or ask the janitor to hose you off."

This gets a huge laugh from the kids, and as Ronald rushes inside, they trail along, laughing and skipping and jeering happily. I can't believe it: I've won a fight, sort of. Or at least I haven't lost it. It's the crowning moment of my life. But surprisingly no one seems to be flocking around to cheer and clap my back or lift me on their shoulders as they do with other victors. Instead they cluster in little groups, staring at me and whispering. Christine is among them, wide-eyed and pale. When I take a step toward her, she turns away, then changes her mind and, glancing over her shoulder, runs over. Is she racing to me, hair streaming, cheeks flushed, to finally confess her love, now that I am a schoolyard hero? This thought makes it all seem worth it. Maybe we can run away together, take a raft down the river or live in a cave in the woods.

"How could you?" she asks.

"Hi," I say.

"How could you kiss me when you're infected? What if I have your disease now?"

"No," I stammer. "It's not really like that."

"I hate you," she says, eyes tearing. "Don't ever talk to me again. And don't you dare tell anyone we kissed."

I can't sleep, but still dreams come to haunt me. I throw the covers off. I'm slick with sweat. I can't stand it any longer.

Whatever the cost, I have to speak to him. I creep down the hall and listen at the door of my parents' room. They are asleep. I go to my window and silently lift it. I put a bare foot on the cold slats of the fire escape. Below me the street is empty. The wind makes my eyes water, and as I climb the ladder, the skin on the bottom of my feet sticks to the rusty iron. On the fourth floor I look in the window. There is the Spanish lady sleeping with her face in the pillow, black hair fanning out. I keep on climbing, hoping the vampire isn't there.

The light in his room is off, but the TV is playing. I can see if I creep up to the window. It is a large room, the same as my parents'. All the walls are covered with books except for one space, where a painting of a nude woman hangs. The floor is bare. On a night table crowded with jars and pill bottles, a cigarette is burning in an ashtray. On a narrow bed like mine, not a grown-up bed at all, the vampire lies, eyes closed. An old hand goes out and picks the cigarette from the tray. He brings it to his lips, then stubs it out, exhaling a fog of smoke that spreads to fill the room.

I tell myself to knock. I tell myself to go back. So I hold still, shivering. My breath clouds the window. My teeth chatter. There is a cramp in my legs. I have to move. I unbend my limbs, shifting the weight, and something falls, a pebble maybe or a paint chip. It clanks from floor to floor. I freeze. The vampire sits up. His eyes are wide open, revealing two floating, clouded blue marbles. I want to scream. I know there is no point in taking off; he'll only find me. He reaches out and turns on a light.

"Come on in, boy. You'll catch your death out there."

I hold my breath.

"I said come in. It's not locked."

I slide the window open and climb inside where it's warm.

"Close that window. My blood's thinner than yours."

My eyes widen at this, but I turn and shut the window.

"Now then." The vampire reaches for his cigarette pack. "What's your name, boy?"

"Elliot."

The vampire rummages through the litter on his night table, cigarette hanging from his lip. He turns to me, dead eyes rolling like Gobstoppers. "No, you wouldn't have any." He lifts the lamp, and his hand finds some matches. The shadows on the wall grow and change. "Ah, here we are. Now we can get down to business."

I wish I were in my bed asleep. But I'm not. This is real.

"Tell me, Elliot," he asks. "Why are you here?" The bony hands strike a match and lift it to the cigarette. I don't know what to say.

"I, I have to ask you something."

The vampire runs a hand over the ridges on his scalp.

"I'm waiting." He grins. The points of his teeth gleam yellow.

"Are you" — I swallow — "a vampire?"

The old man starts laughing like an engine trying to catch. I blush while he laughs and wipes the tears from his eyes. I didn't know blind eyes could cry. Then he starts coughing. He sits up, pounding on his chest, and leans over to spit on the floor. I stare at the gray lump. I notice some dry splotches in the same area. The vampire leans back against the pillows.

"Yes," he says, "I am."

My hand goes up to the collar of my pajamas. The blush fades from my face. I'm right, but I wish I were wrong.

"Really?"

"Yes, I have been for years. For longer than you've been alive. Since before your grandparents were born. And I've been all over the world. Europe, Asia, Africa. You name it, I been there."

My fingers wrap around my throat. "And you really drink blood?"

He draws on his cigarette.

"Sure. I have to. But not just any blood. It's got to be pure."

"But you can fly? And change into a bat or a wolf?"

"Yeah, all that. But it's not an easy life. Wherever I go, I'm hounded. Sooner or later they find me."

"Who?"

"The vampire hunters. They come while I'm sleeping and try to hammer stakes into my heart. The last time, just as they were about to kill me, the sun set and I woke up. There were five of them."

"What happened?"

He shrugs. "I broke their necks. And then I came here. I thought I could rest easy. Who ever heard of vampire hunters in Jackson Heights? But now I guess you'll tell everyone."

"No, no, I won't." I rush to the side of his bed. "I came because I want to be like you." For the first time I look up at him, meeting the blank eyes that I'm sure can see me somehow. Now there's no turning back. The vampire is still for a moment. Then he bursts out laughing again.

"So you want to be a vampire, huh? Can't blame you. Tell me something, though. What tipped you off?"

Now I smile. "Your teeth." I can picture myself with fangs like those. The vampire puts out his cigarette and reaches into his mouth. He pulls out his teeth. I gasp and jump back. He laughs.

"Don't worry. They're not going to bite you." He slips them back into place. "Come here, there's something else I want you to see."

I lean forward, ready to run. The vampire pulls back his robe. There is a thick, lumpy scar running all across his frail chest.

"A doctor did this to me."

I can't take my eyes off it. It's red against the milky skin, and I can see where the stitches had been.

"What's more, I paid him to do it," he says. "I had this thing in me, see. A tumor. It was eating me up. They took it out. The damn thing had hair on it. And a couple of teeth too. Now that's what I call a vampire."

He laughs again, quietly. "Now you go back to where you came from. And don't tell no one you were here."

I open the window. Then I turn back.

"Go on, I said. Scram."

I climb out the window and back down the fire escape. I get into bed and pull the covers over my head. I curl into a ball and shut my eyes tight.

My mother and I watch the arrow above the elevator move from number to number. We've been shopping, and she holds a bag of groceries in each arm. The elevator door slides back.

"Step aside please," a large man in coveralls says, backing out. He's holding one end of a gurney. A black cloth covers the shape of a body.

"Oh, that poor old blind man from 6C," my mother says as the wheels squeak by. "He's finally passed on."

"Maybe he's just sleeping," I say. The sun isn't down yet.

"Yes, dear, it's like he's sleeping. Only he won't wake up anymore."

I think about the time I woke up and found a long blond hair that wasn't mine in my mouth and about the soreness in my chest sometimes that burns like a tooth when I breathe. I say the word to myself: "Tumor."

Matinee

Philip's family's apartment is bigger than ours and better. His parents must be rich. There is a fireplace and a bar. My father has a dusty, unopened fifth of Scotch someone gave him last Christmas. Philip's parents have rows of gleaming bottles filled with liquids the color of gold and autumn leaves and ice. There is a crystal decanter, an ice bucket, seltzer in a blue glass bottle with a siphon. There are three bedrooms. I've never seen an apartment with three bedrooms before. My sister and I share a room, but Philip has his own and shares the adjoining bathroom with his sister while his parents have one to themselves. A bathroom of one's own! Somehow the idea entrances me more than even having my own room.

But the most amazing thing is the state of Philip's room. It is like a bomb crater or the inside of a dumpster, the most incredible room I've ever seen. There is a giant heap of dirty laundry sloping against one wall. The bed is a tangle of covers and stained sheets. A bird flies around, shits on the chair, and returns to its open cage, where a melted Spock doll sits beside an armless G.I. Joe. There is a scorched black spot on the floor where an experiment went wrong and a bare bulb dangling from the broken fixture. He has his own black-and-white TV, with paint spattered on the screen. A carving knife is stuck in the wall, a memento of an attempt on his life by his older sister. But he got vengeance, he confides, by secretly peeing on her bath towel and hanging it back up to dry, and also by sticking her toothbrush up his butt.

This is an impossible life, utterly beyond my imagination. My dirty clothes must go directly into two separate hampers, a wicker one for shirts and pants and a plastic one with a lid for underclothes. My bed is always made. It is unthinkable that I could say, "Fuck you," to my mom like Philip says he did to his. And though I fear my father worse than death, I can't even imagine him striking me. Philip tells me how his father, when he heard Philip cursing his mom out, came flying from the bedroom in his boxers with a doubled belt and chased him, barefoot and half naked, down the stairs and out into the street, where he finally cornered him between two parked cars and whipped him in front of the neighbors. To me the Plotkins live like movie stars, like beasts, like mad kings and queens. They sleep and eat whenever they want. They have TVs in their bedrooms and hairballs under the beds. Dust rises in clouds when you sit down on their couch, and when you stand, pet hair coats your jeans.

Philip's mother is like no mother I've ever seen: She has a perm and smokes Eve cigarettes and never cooks us lunch, but Philip and I fix our Cheerios in lumpy bowls that he claims she made herself out of clay. His father wears a double-breasted suit with a bright tie and pocket hankie and works as an advertising executive in a skyscraper in the city. It is a mysterious and exotic profession, and even Philip can't really explain what he

does. My father works in the subway, selling tokens in a booth.
He has been down there a long time and has seniority, but still
works all kinds of shifts, holidays, weekends, graveyards. He
needs the overtime, he says, and what's the difference, it's always night underground. Sometimes he goes down at dawn
like a miner, when only a few working people and the bums
are drifting through the station. Those who slept in the subway
come creeping out, poking in the garbage, taking up their begging posts before the rush. Strangest of all the creatures my father describes are the Tokensuckers, a subspecies of drug addict
who feed by stuffing bits of paper down the turnstiles' token
slots and lying in wait until a normal traveler's token gets stuck.
Depending on his mood, the passenger will either jump it or
complain to my father, who buzzes him in the service gate. The
Tokensucker then presses his lips to the metal slot like a wood-
pecker tapping for an insect and sucks the token up into his
mouth. He'll try to cash it in with my father, who, of course, re-
fuses. The Tokensucker will sometimes become enraged and
pound on the bulletproof glass. Then, as rush hour begins and a
line forms at the booth, he'll sell the tokens to other passengers
at a cut rate.

Every day, during the rush hour, my father sees humanity
pass by. They line up and push through the turnstile like cat-
tle and cram onto the train cars as if packing themselves off
to the slaughterhouse. The trains scream and moan. The overhead speakers bark. It's like a mass deportation. Quiet returns
at nine, and it's back to housewives and students and bums till
evening. He sees the same people each time, coming and going,
tired in the morning and tired at night, when they stagger up

exhausted and angry, as if from hell, but none of them recognizes him. He's invisible. After the evening rush come the night people, dressed up, going out, then later the drunks puking on the tracks. No one even knows he's there. He's seen people mugged and beaten right in front of him. He calls the transit police, who show up an hour later, after even the victims have gotten bored and left. One night, he spent a whole graveyard watching a Spanish kid spray-paint BOOTY BURGLER in giant letters over the wall.

I keep asking my father why he doesn't become a conductor, my own dream job, but he says he's not interested. Finally, to stop me from pestering him, my mother tells me that he tried but was rejected because of his accent when pronouncing the street names. Of course, she says, that's ridiculous since you can't understand anything over those speakers anyway. It's true; they sound like dying walruses or Mayday calls from foreign wars. The real reason, she says, is because he's Jewish and the Irish have those cushy jobs locked up.

Philip gets a box of Fudge Town cookies (a whole box, mind you, not a numbered handful negotiated with promises not to spoil dinner) and shows me where to squat and spy through the keyhole at his sister in the bathroom. She is sitting slope-shouldered on the toilet with a look of distraction on her face. At first the only skin visible is her knees and thighs where the jeans are pushed down and of course her bare arms in the T-shirt. As she slumps forward and stares blankly into space she might as well be sitting on a bus, except for the thrilling sense of violation I feel and the faint trickle of water in the bowl, like the tingling of a tiny golden bell. My heart pounds. I squat in a runner's crouch, ready to flee even as my legs cramp into stone. I hear Philip crunching cookies over me. Fine crumbs skitter down the back of my neck. Then Philip's sister reaches for the toilet paper and tears a few sheets off the roll. Just two or three weightless squares, a crumpled flower, nothing like the massive wads of paper I use to bandage up my mitts. Instead, holding her dainty pink corsage, she dips into the shadow between her legs, arching her back to reveal a soft belly, white as the porcelain, smooth as the tile. Carelessly, she drops her damp tissue beneath her, like the princess in a story, leaving her perfumed hankie in a forest for her favorite courtier to retrieve. I'm no Galahad, but still I am kneeling, like any knight should before the Grail. Then she stands, jeans falling around her ankles, T-shirt riding up her ribs, and not three feet from my sweating eyeball, I behold, at last, the mystery that lies at the center of the world.

Philip whispers wetly in my ear. "What's she doing?"

I shrug.

"She's got a nice little cunt, right?"

I'm outraged, but I nod, thinking it the easiest response.

"She's fingering herself, isn't she?" he asks.

I hesitate, then nod again. He chuckles, and I can smell the chocolate on his breath.

Anyone who lives in a high place knows the happiness of dropping things. You feel sorry for deprived city children who've never seen a cow or picked an apple? Big deal. I pity those who've never lived more than two stories off the ground.

Philip and I have it down to a science. We know just how long it takes for a wad of wet toilet paper or a tomato to fall six floors. We know where, allowing for variable wind conditions, an egg will land if you hold your arm straight out from the sill and let it go. As a target comes down the block, we gauge its speed, and just as it is two or three paces from the kill zone, we let a payload fly. A mailman saunters along unawares as an egg spirals toward his head and explodes down his shoulders. A fat lady shrieks as wet toilet paper splatters over her housedress from out of nowhere.

Then Philip has a stroke of genius. He rushes into his parents' bedroom and returns with a blue box of tampons. Cackling to himself, he disappears into the kitchen. I follow curiously and find him in front of the open fridge. He has unwrapped several tampons and, holding them by the string, is stuffing each one down the throat of a ketchup bottle. The effect is strikingly realistic. Gleefully, he dashes to the window and leans far out while I watch from an adjacent sill.

At first there is nothing promising in sight. A few kids squat in the dying sun, trying to set a newspaper on fire with a magnifying lens, but they are out of our range. Cars go by, but this is too good to waste on a car. Then a big blue Cadillac pulls into a space directly below our post. A balding man in a suit gets out with a briefcase and an overcoat over his arm and locks his car. As the man steps onto the sidewalk, Philip lifts a tampon by the string and flings it straight at him. There is a queasy moment as I hold my breath, watching, and then she lands true, sticking to the man's right shoulder. Startled, he stops and picks off the object, a look of pure horror overtaking him as he realizes what it is. Moaning like a shot animal, he drops the foul thing, and tossing his coat and case aside, he tears off his suit coat, throwing it to the ground. He scans the heavens in anger, and we duck out of sight behind the sill, shaking with fear and excitement. Cautiously, like a trench fighter, I peek over to see the man shaking out his coat. Philip drops another bomb. It streaks through the air and slides like a snail down our enemy's back, leaving a red trail on his white shirt. He jumps and starts running, leaving his belongings behind. As he sprints down the block, he pulls off his shirt and throws it away, fleeing for his life.

How can I describe the laughter? It's like being tickled by an angel's wings. It's like farting on a cloud in heaven. It's like having your heart go mad with delight and take off running for the hills. We laugh till our guts hurt and we cry. We bend over double like God-stricken men. We crawl howling on the floor and roll in the dust like drunks, and the dog licks the tears from our faces. We laugh till we're miserable, until there's no happiness left in us at all but an empty, delirious ache. Those who say that throwing dog crap at a bus isn't funny are mere Philistines and will never know true joy.

At breakfast my mother asks if I want to invite a friend to go to the movies and dinner for my birthday. I ask to bring Philip. My father snorts over his cereal.

"He's a loser, that kid."

"Well, Philip is a bit wild," my mother says.

"He's soft," my father says. "He couldn't make it two days without his refrigerator and TV."

"Don't you have any nicer friends?" my mother asks.

I blurt out the awful truth. "I don't have any friends."

My mother waves it away. "Of course you do. You're just shy. And you can't play sports because of your health. And they're jealous because you're smarter. "

"I had a friend once," my father breaks in. "They shot him and left him lying in a ditch. No one could go to him because the guards were looking out. So late at night, I crawled out to him. I tried to help him, but he was dying and he knew it. All he wanted was for me to knock him out so that he wouldn't feel so bad the pain. So I hit him as hard as I could. But he was tough and I was weak from cold and no sleep and to eat only one rotten potato a day. I tried and tried, beating him until my hand ached, but it was no good. Then I took up a rock and hit him on the head, but he was still too tough. He bled, but he stayed awake. So finally I smothered him, with my hand like so."

My father pinches off my nostrils with his left hand and covers my mouth with his right. "It wasn't hard because he didn't struggle. Just squeezed my wrist until it was bruised." With that he turns back to his bran.

My mother waves him off. "Don't listen to your father," she tells me. "You'll make plenty of friends next year. Why don't you try joining the math club?"

I brighten as an idea comes to me. "Can I take karate lessons? Or join the scouts with Philip? They go camping in the country."

"Come on now, honey," my mother says. "You know you're allergic. The woods are full of airborne mold and pollen."

"Please?"

"Ask your father."

To my father, "Please? I promise I won't touch any plants."

My father points his spoon at me. Milk runs down his wrist. "Forget plants. There's a lot worse things than pollen out in the woods."

"You mean bears?" I ask.

"He means rednecks," my mother explains. "And hicks."

My father shrugs noncommittally and opens the newspaper. "So go if you're so smart. You'll find out."

"Over my dead body," my mother says. I finish eating as fast as I can and race out to meet Philip.

We decide to cut school, but it is raining out, so we go to the Earl with Philip's sister, who threatens to tell on us if we don't let her come and buy her ticket. The ticket booth at the Earl Theater is freestanding, like a subway token booth, with bullet-proof glass, a steel grille to talk through, and a curved wooden threshold worn smooth with hands pushing money, but it also has carved columns and a scalloped roof, and it stands beneath a huge marquee, with stone floors under the grime, and ornate moldings under the paint, and burned-out tulip bulbs around the empty glass boxes where the movie posters used to go. The fat lady in the booth never questions your age. She doesn't even speak English, except to say "three dollar." Sometimes she falls asleep in the booth, her breath fogging the glass, and you have to tap on the glass and show her your three dollars. You give your ticket to the old man in the threadbare jacket with epaulets, and he grants you entrance to an unearthed tomb. With each step, dust rises from the pattern of the ancient carpet, and in the dim light you can still make out a water-stained, speckled mural depicting Greek ruins on a hill above an olive grove.

Silver ashtrays the size of funeral urns stand guard outside the gentlemen's lounge.

Entering the great cave of the theater, with its balding plush seats and the shifting curtain marked with the masks of joy and pain, the gaze lifts to the limitless roof, rising away on buttresses and columns, thick with soot but still painted, here and there, with stars. Glimpsed through the cracks and plastered fissures, mottled with mold, this night sky no longer matches the one outside. It has deteriorated, regressing to an older, unfinished sky, mapped with different constellations: the Key, the Snake, the Handgun, the Pizza Man, the Three-legged Dog. Drops of rainwater seep along the cracks and fall, one at a time, across the huge vault, to clang in the buckets placed in the aisles. No one ever sweeps up in the Earl. When the lights go down, you want to keep your feet up on the seat in front of you. Rats scratch in the candy boxes, stale popcorn in their mouths. Bottles roll. Don't go to the bathroom either. The toilets are always backed up, and there's usually blood or vomit in the sinks. Often the floor is flooded, with toilet paper sailing around. There are no doors on the scribbled marble stalls, and one time I saw a man stripped to his waist and soaping his armpits at the sink. Another time there were two men in a stall together, one on his knees before the other.

Still, the Earl is the best place in the world to see a movie. It draws a great crowd. The dozen or so patrons spread out and relax. Some sleep, although the usher with the baseball bat will poke you if you snore or wave your hand in front of the projector. Otherwise, he doesn't mind; you can smoke or drink from a bottle in a bag. You can throw candy and yell at the screen.

In fact, the old dark-skinned men at the Earl appreciate every-thing that your parents would yell at you for doing in a theater or even in front of the TV. If you burp or make a fart noise, they laugh. They will discuss with interest the birth of Godzilla or debate who would win in a fight between Clint Eastwood or Charles Bronson. If you shout, "It's ass-kicking time," when Bruce Lee takes off his shirt, they cheer, and yelling "Yo' mama" at the bad guy is always appreciated as a classic riposte.

It's warm inside the theater today, as the three of us find our favorite seats in the middle of the middle row. Raindrops ping in the buckets. The lights ease down. There is a double fea-ture, *Blood of Vengeance*, starring Bruce Klee (Bruce Lee's cousin, someone explains), and a picture about knights, *The Curse of Doom*.

The movie starts with Bruce Klee as a simple fisherman rowing his boat in from the sea. He pulls it up on the beach and jumps off, barefoot in white pajamas. Then he sees smoke ris-ing from a hut and starts running. It's too late. They've mas-sacred his family. His sister has been raped and killed, and his dad's hanging from a hook. He spots a few hoodlums at the local waterfront tavern, drinking rice wine and hassling the old innkeeper with the long white whiskers. One of the trouble-makers is wearing his sister's jade necklace! With his bare feet, Bruce pushes his toes against the edge of a brick lying on the beach and pops it up like a soccer ball. He catches it and rams it right into one guy's chest. Blood shoots out of his mouth. Then Bruce gouges the other guy's eyes out and snaps his neck side-ways. Covered in blood, he puts on his sister's necklace and, falling to his knees, lets out a warrior scream of vengeance.

Next he has a whole long journey. He learns from clues that

the killers are from the Dragon Temple, so he shaves his head and joins, throwing his ponytail on the ceremonial fire. He has to hang out with the Dragon Monks, swallowing his hate like poison, letting it seep into his heart. The contest starts. Guys get their arms ripped out. They shatter ice blocks with their heads. Monks who have rubbed iron dust into their hands for many seasons split logs with one chop and break bricks. Bruce beats everybody in the tournament, even the Dragon Champion. The Champion, who can't stand it, dishonors everyone by throwing a razor star at Bruce when he's not looking. But Bruce catches it and throws it right back into the Champ's forehead. They reward him with the Dragon Robe, but we see his smile is bitter.

Now he's alone with the Master at last. Bruce tells him who he is, and they fight, first monkey style, then praying mantis, then crane, where they jump up twenty feet in the air and hang like hummingbirds, arms and legs whirling. Finally, Bruce gets the Master down, and we know, from the twisted look of horror on Bruce's face, horror at himself, at what he is about to do, that this is the deathblow. He plunges his fist into the Master's chest and rips out his heart. While the Master, still alive, watches in terror, Bruce wraps his sister's necklace around the beating heart and throws it on the fire, where it explodes. Everyone in the Earl roars in approval. A man leaps to his feet and turns to face the audience, fists raised in glory. Somewhere a bottle breaks.

"That's true," the black man in army fatigues sitting in front of us says. "I seen it in Nam. They'd split you belly and take out you whole intestines, like twelve feet of it right in front of you. But the brain is still alive and watching it all."

The fat white guy a row back agrees. He's so fat he never has to wear a coat, just parachute pants and a *Blizzard of Ozz* T-shirt. We can hear him breathing there behind us, wedged into his seat, sipping from a bucket of diet soda.

"Over thousands of centuries," he explains, "your Chinese has mastered the Art of Death."

The Earl is a ruined temple, open to the sky, and in its endless night, dreams arise from the void and fall again. The same wise men, in beards and long coats, gather here each time, to see the great forgotten tales retold. Stored on metal reels, a million tiny pictures, bright as stamps, come spilling out into the dark, floating down in a row, dancing like merry soldiers or angels along the dusty beam of light that crosses the vast, empty heaven of that cave. It is like the unscrolling of a lost parchment, unearthed and read aloud for the first time since history began. And as the magic words are uttered, these dead images begin to move. Skeletons gather their bones and march. Monsters awake and crawl out of the sea. A terrible force is unleashed on the earth. Good and Evil fight to the death on the screen. The dead rise up to feed on the living. An army of heroes invades hell, and mutinous angels turn to make war on heaven. The courtesan of Babylon, full of strong drink, does a belly dance for the nobles. The king swears he'll slaughter a nation to have her. Blood runs in rivers. Heads weep on sticks. There are crucified soldiers on hilltops and fires in the pits of the night. Kings perish and the kingdoms fall at the breaking of the sword. During a storm, the queen gives birth in secret and dies. The orphan prince, born under the curse of Doom, and raised by wolves and peasants, does not know his own name.

Philip's sister takes my hand and puts it under her skirt. It's like putting my hand in an oven. Her legs are smooth and coated in soft hair. She moves my hand up her thighs to where the flesh splits and it's warm. I close my eyes, and another movie forms in my head, as the blood bursts behind my eyes, breaking into roses and flaming hearts against my lids. I am afraid to move or take my hand back. Philip is right there, next to her in the dark. She presses my hand harder against her with her two hands, and grinds her hips until something gives and she gasps. Then she grabs my jacket off the back of the seat and drapes it over my lap. She unzips my fly and touches me down there. She knows just how to work it, better than I do, light and then hard until it shoots. It's never done that around other people before. She laughs, a mean laugh, and I blush with shame in the dark. Somehow I have been tricked, made a fool of in a way I can't even understand. Then the film jams and starts to burn. The frame bubbles, and a white hole opens like God's eye peering in on us. The old men howl in pain. A treasure is being lost, like a Torah thrown on the flames. The lights come on, and everyone looks around, blinking, wondering where they are and how they got there. I sit absolutely still. My pants are still open under my jacket, and my legs are sticky. The audience begins to hoot and clap, yelling curses and throwing empty soda cups at the screen. Philip's sister wipes her hands on my jacket and reaches for the popcorn. She has a defiant look on her face. Her eyes glitter wildly and her smile curls into a sneer. She is proud.

Finally the lights go down and the movie starts up again. But it's a different reel, some other part of the story with no connection to what happened before. I can't even tell if it is from earlier or later. The king is dead, but the wizard he killed before is back. The prince is grown and on a quest to find the sword. He dismounts in the mist and gets on the barge that will take him across the River of Forgetting to Snow Mountain, where everyone who died in part one is alive, where everything lost is regained, where flowers fold their petals back into seeds and scattered leaves leap back in the wind and dance into the arms of the trees. But before you may enter, you must answer questions three.

One. Where do you come from?

Two. What have you forgotten?

Three . . .

It is always night when you come out of the Earl, as if, distracted by the movie, lulled off guard by the darkness and warmth, you fell asleep without realizing it and now you are exiting into a dream. I walk carefully down Roosevelt Avenue, under the steel girders and openwork roof of the El. Headlights rear up, exposing the rain's invisible connections, the strings of a puppet theater tying the sky to the street. Then the car goes by in a rush. Ghostly faces glance from behind the windows and, splashing through a pothole, it's gone. Philip and his sister turn off to go their own way. Only Philip says good-bye. His sister holds Philip's hand and gives me a sly look. Now I'm alone, and whatever has been pursuing closes in. The rain parts and the buildings lean in, closing out the sky. The clouds descend to earth. The streets have rearranged themselves, shuffled like a pack of cards, and I am no longer in my own neighborhood. I have gotten turned around somehow and wandered into the city behind my back, like when you lay your head on the pillow and sink through to the other side of sleep. I pass rows of closed shops with bars drawn across their doors and here and there a lit store window. The door is locked, but a bright box still displays peculiarly chosen objects. It is impossible to say what they mean. One storefront is heaped with foreign candy, pink circles and pyramids tipped in green. Another offers only a broken clock, a fork, an old-fashioned lady's hat, and two black leather gloves. They are like the clues left behind at a crime scene. A headless mannequin signals from behind her glass. The only place still alive on the street is a bar, a neon beer sign glowing through a steamed-over window, but I'm not allowed in bars. A man stumbles out, arms gripping a fat woman like a buoy in a squall, and they vanish down an alley.

Trying to find my way back to a main street, I end up in a park I don't recognize, or perhaps it just seems different in the dark. Fog seeps through the picture, gathering on the swings. With each step, I grow more apprehensive, as if something is there, watching me, holding its breath when I stop to listen. I hear the crush of feet on leaves and duck down behind a bench. I strain my ears. The park has become an orchestra. Each leaf leans out, a tuned instrument raised in anticipation, awaiting the breath that will move them all. Rain comes, a sheet of water, from a single cloud passing over me. It descends like a flock of sparrows landing everywhere at once, with tiny, light steps, picking at the grass, checking under each blade. Drops line up on the branches and wires. They gather together to draw resolve before falling to the ground. Then it's gone, leaving only the scent of water and its splotched tracks on the ground, a delicate, unreadable scrawl.

It was then that the world first revealed itself to me in all its awful beauty, rising up suddenly, like a lion in the path, like a monstrous swan beating its wings to say: Everything you know and dream of is nothing, not even a speck of what is. The life of even the tiniest ant is as infinitely complex as a man's and the life of a man is like a god's. And even this vast whole is enclosed in my endlessness like the faintest glimmer of the first thought on the dawn of the first day of creation. Everything is still possible. You have not yet begun to live.

I Think of Demons

THINGS TO DO THIS SUMMER
Natural History Museum/Planetarium
Central Park
Subway
3-D movie
Camping

This list is taped to Philip's wall, written in multicolored pastels and markers on thick paper torn from a sketch pad. In case his parents wander in, he has left off the end of the title: ON ACID. As it is, when we cross off an item, Philip's dad grunts in approval and gives him more dough. There is a list of records too:

The Piper at the Gates of Dawn — Pink Floyd
    (with Syd Barrett of course)
Larks' Tongues in Aspic & *Red* — King Crimson
Bitches Brew — Miles Davis
Metal Machine Music — Lou Reed
There Comes a Time — Gil Evans

The idea is to put on the record, or better yet pop in the tape so you don't have to change it, then drop the acid. Lie back with your eyes closed, headphones on, and try your best not to move or stir or blink until the album ends . . . no matter what happens next. It's harder than it sounds. Some records are interminable, the pressure builds, and your eyes burst open. You sit up, gasping, as if you were drowning in your own mind. Others bury you so deep in dreams you can't get up at all. The record spins and clicks and ends, and you keep your eyes shut, afraid to open them, or forget they are even closed, as you wander, lost, trying to remember where you are, your name.

Then on July Fourth, the hottest weekend of the year, Philip's parents drive us up to Harriman State Park to go camping. I let my parents think Philip's family will be with us, but really they just drop us off with our sleeping bags and a cooler full of food. He brings paints, paper, charcoal, and pastels. I have a leather-bound notebook and a pen. I hope to be a poet, he an artist.

"No," says Philip. "We already are. If I paint a stroke" — he blobs Kremnitz white on a tree — "then I am a painter. Just like when you write a word, you become a writer." He taps my new book, leaving behind a white ghost of his fingerprint.

I nod but don't tell him that all I've written inside is the date, now a couple of weeks old. We start setting the tent up, and two hours later, as it leans crookedly against a tree, we eat the acid, two hits of blotter each, and step out for a nice stroll in the forest before lunch.

We wander along, wading through the tide of old mulch, brushing back the branches that hide the inner, leaf-lit chambers, chatting and chuckling, until we hear the silence and it shuts us up. I listen to it, that ocean of silence that is always back there, into which each birdcall and dying leaf falls. It is a presence, this quiet, a medium. I am struck by the fact that everything around me is alive. In the city everything is dead but us. It is a graveyard of ten-story tombs, and we are the ghosts who haunt it. In the suburbs the people are dead but don't know it, and in the empty, groomed streets and blank windows, only cars and TVs move. Here the trees, the weeds, the hills are all breathing, and the air hums with insects. Even the dead matter, the torn leaves and rotten trees, the earth itself, is alive and seething with bugs, worms, microbes. Of course, I knew this before — but did I really *know* it? Did I sense it the way I do now, embracing the flanks of a roaring oak and feeling the power surge through me?

"Everything around us is alive," I whisper to Philip, who is up ahead of me on the path.

"I know," he answers flatly without turning around.

"But do you really *know* it?" I ask.

"Oh, I fucking know it all right," he says, his voice choked with feelings. I realize he's crying, clean streaks through the dust on his cheeks.

"What's wrong?"

He wipes away the tears.

"Nothing. What's wrong with you?"

"I'm thirsty," I say, and it occurs to me, we have no water, no sunblock, no food. I look around: trees. The cicadas cough like throats choked with sand, dropping their discarded bodies. I see a skull full of pebbles.

"Do you know which is the way back to our camp?" I ask.

Philip stops and peers around, turning in a circle. The back of his neck is bright red. His T-shirt is soaked through with sweat.

"No," he says. "Which?"

"I don't fucking know. That's why I asked you."

"Asked me what?"

"Oh fuck," I say, panic starting. "We're lost." I institute emergency survival procedures: preserve moisture by collecting saliva in my mouth and smear damp earth on my face to shield it from the damaging rays of the sun.

But Philip stays cool. He pats his pockets thoughtfully, looking for the cigarettes that aren't there. "No problem," he decides. "We merely ascend this hill and look around. The whole topology will be laid out before us."

Comforted, I follow as he proceeds upward, beating his way through the brush. A cloud of gnats swirls around him, whining like static; I picture little helmets, goggles, parachutes. They buzz me and I try to wave them aside, but nothing happens. Are they only motes in my eyes? As the incline grows steeper, I begin to slip and slide in the loose earth. Crooked trees lurch at us like dying old men in the locker room at the Y, trunks covered in black goiters, moss hanging from their armpits.

Now I see: It is only language that separates, say, the tree from the earth that feeds it, or from the sky that it longs to embrace and lose itself in, if it could only tear free. The cicadas might as well be the leaves themselves, brushing together under the blanket of heat. Everything pushes toward the surface. You can smell the sun cooking on the skin of things, bubbling and cracking, melting over the branches, sticking to the soles of your feet. It fills my lungs and eyes with gold. I hear the blood beating in my veins, shaking my hands like rattles. I hear the energy crackling in the twigs as I break their connections. I see the fire frozen in the wood.

"What fire?" Philip asks, turning to me with a wild look. Is he hearing my thoughts? I try another one, beaming him an image of a saint. Philip slaps the back of his neck.

"These fucking bugs are drilling right into me."

Everything is alive, that is the horror of it. The grass screams when you tread on it, and the trees bleed when you snap their twigs, and the stream rolls over and rocks itself, crying in its sleep. The stones are watching your every move; it takes a thousand years for them to blink once. And the mountain? The mountain is the mind itself, the true and hidden mind. Everything is alive and dying.

We summit on our hands and knees. At the peak sits a boulder the size of a two-car garage — coarse, black, porous — thrown from a volcano on the moon. I read the alien inscriptions through my fingertips: A star is about to be born. The black rock breaks, like a giant egg, and blows light into my hair. My mind splits like a rotten peach spitting out its pit.

Philip screams. As I watch, a halo of white fire explodes around his skull, burning his hair like nerve endings. His voice is dust. His face is wind. The hill is heaving, throwing trees sideways and cleaving rocks. He sticks his finger down his throat, trying to puke up the poison.

Just then, lightning shoots from my hands, blasting trees

into flame. Struggling for control, I wrestle them into my pockets. Clouds rush into the sun and are burned away. I realize that my brain is now linked, as if by wired roots, to the world. I can't tell the difference between thought and action, between the voices outside or inside my head. Anything I think will happen, so I must not think the wrong thing, the evil thing. I must hold still. I freeze my face, trying not to breathe, and follow Philip with my eyes as he crawls over.

"Evil," he hisses, crouching like an elf in the shadow of the rock. His ears and nose grow points. "This place is fucking evil," he whispers in my ear. "Let's get the fuck out of here."

He takes off, stumbling back down the mountain we just climbed. I rush after him. Shadows swoop and dive around me. Trees grab at my legs. We plunge into a swamp, and I stop short as Philip howls. He has sunk into the mud up to his knees. He thrashes around, grunting and baying, like a brontosaurus stuck in tar.

"Wait, don't fight it," I say. "The quicksand will pull you under."

But he ignores my advice and plows through, leaving one sneaker in the sucking wounds. In their depths, eyes open for just a moment and then forever close.

Trying to circle the sinkhole, I quickly lose my bearings and tumble into a campsite. I crash blindly through a bush, yowling as switches lash my face, and there they are, squatting over a fire, a bald dad and his young son, limp wieners on the tips of their sticks. They stare at me, aghast, as if I were a Sasquatch: long hair full of leaves and twigs, body covered in cuts. The mud I've layered on my face for sun protection is flaking off.

But then again, who are they to judge? Look at their fucking faces — swelling horribly with pustules and throbbing rainbow colors. The little boy is actually aging, wrinkling right in front of me, while the dad morphs backward into a pudgy hairless baby. Somebody screams. It's me. I turn tail and flee back into the forest, trying to outrun the screaming, which follows me like an echo. I'm dodging right and left, ducking the trees that keep throwing themselves in my path, when I collide with a deer. A fucking deer! At first I just see a brown blur, knocking me back as it darts by, startled no doubt by my idiotic thrashing. He brushes past, high chest blazed with white, antlers, neck, back, tail. So fast and so strong that I am left vibrating, like I've plunged my arms into the quick of a freezing river. Stunned, I sit in some mud. The deer stops and, as if taking pity on me, looks back to calm me with a noble gaze.

"Follow the drums," he says. Or thinks. He seems to be licking a leaf, but his thoughts sound too deep and profound to be coming from me.

"Thanks, friend," I say, rising slowly. But now there is a disturbance in the force field, angry crashings in the woods, like a giant hunting for meat. The deer starts.

"Don't listen to the cat," he whispers quickly and springs away. I cringe. The leaves tremble. Philip comes toppling out, dragging his shoeless foot.

"Hear that?" he asks. We listen. Far off. Drums.

The drumming is faint, and we can't see where it's coming from, but the sound is steady, like a beacon, and wherever there are drums, there must be people.

"It's some kind of ritual," Philip suggests as we hobble along. "A tribal gathering. We'll be cured."

That sounds good. There is definitely something wrong with me now. I don't know how long we've been tripping, but I feel years older: half blind from sweat, swollen with insect bites, and limping painfully. The drugs and heat have cooked my brains down to where I can't tell what's real anymore. Trees mumble and sigh as I pass. Rocks squint in the sun. Nymphs flash and giggle nudely among the pines. Day and night rise and fall randomly, every few minutes, or is that just wind in the leaves? Maybe I'm laughing at the birds instead of them laughing at me. At first I think I see the deer again, following me, but it's a satyr, grunting and thrusting with a girl down under his hooves. His horns tangle her long hair into a crown of fine-spun gold. He sinks his teeth into her neck. She moans and her eyes open, fixing me. I know her, but I don't recall from where. She smiles, showing her fangs. The blood seeps out between them, purpling her mouth like wine. I wipe sweat from my eyes and walk faster and don't mention it to Philip. I don't want him to worry.

By following the drums through mud and brush and swarm, Philip and I reach paradise at last. Paradise, it turns out, is a man-made lake surrounded by a sand beach on which a hundred Puerto Rican families are picnicking. The ritual drumming is the sound of all their radios and boom boxes playing and echoing at once. Hitting the sand, we break into a run. We are alive. Philip peels off his shirt as he sprints toward the concession stand, and I do likewise. But I slow to a jog when I see him pulling down his shorts. I stop in horror as he makes a beeline for the water fountain, a fat, sunburned, sweaty white boy, covered in filth, wearing briefs and one sneaker, pushing and shoving little kids aside as he forces his way to the front.

"Cutter!" they yell.

"Water, water," he moans, knocking a scared child to the ground. He guzzles from the tap, and then, as the passersby watch in disgust, he splashes the water under his arms and crotch. Now several burly guys in Yankees shirts and razored haircuts are being dragged over by their kids.

"Hey, man, what's your fucking problem?" they want to know.

Philip bolts, and the angry dads chase him across the sand. The barking pack quickly outflanks him, but they pause when he charges into the lake, hesitant to follow a half-naked madman into water. A crowd gathers as he howls and splashes around. He blows waterspouts, snorting like a whale, and waves his sodden underwear over his head. Old women cross themselves. Mothers cover their children's eyes. Philip begins to urinate, laughing tearfully at his own little stream, while swimmers panic, scrambling up the shore.

A park ranger's truck and a cop car arrive, and the crowd parts. The officers sigh and shake their heads. They get the bullhorn.

"You in the water. Stop what you're doing and come out."

But they know there's only one way this is going to end, and finally, resigned, they go in. It is a brief, disturbing struggle. They wade out and take him down, flailing and screaming. It takes four guys to drag him like a seal onto land and get him to the car, tears and snot streaming. He screams numbers between sobs.

"Seven seven nine point three two one. Nine seven six seven two. One oh one oh one oh one. Nine. Nine. Nine. Nine. Nine. Nine."

The police call our parents. Philip's folks meet the ambulance at the emergency room. Mine drive me home in silence. But in a miraculous twist, we get off scot-free when Philip's freak-out is blamed on sunstroke and dehydration. We're lucky to be alive, the doctors say, which confuses my parents and takes the fun out of punishing me. In the end I am simply forbidden from camping, which is fine by me. I never want to see another tree.

Summer returns to normal: bong hits, air-conditioned double features, and nights playing Frisbee in the Dunkin' Donuts parking lot, but looking back, I realize now Philip is never quite the same. Maybe he never really manages to rehydrate. He complains that one eye sees in a rectangle and the other a triangle, or that he can only perceive two dimensions, though he actually finds this helps his painting. There is a grumbling under his bed that he can never make out, that starts just as he is falling asleep, but when he checks, there is nothing but dust balls or the cat. I mock him, laugh it off.

Then, one weekend that August, Philip's parents go away and we do angel dust at his house. We lie on the floor and listen to Miles's double album *Agharta* with our eyes shut. When it's finally over and I sit up, it's too late — it doesn't make any difference. I keep seeing the same thing, planets forming and imploding, the history of the universe speeding up. We go to the kitchen and try eating fun things. Ice and grapes are best since they change state in your mouth: the exquisite torment of the melting ice, the sunny burst of a grape against the tongue. Philip goes into the bathroom to pee, and I hear him laughing hysterically.

"It's like I have this sort of hose sticking out of my body," he announces. He laughs so hard he pisses all over the floor. "You've got to try it."

"Later," I say. I'm not sure I am ready for that. Then we sit facing each other on the couch and do "impressions."

"OK, I'm Humphrey Bogart," I say and Philip immediately hallucinates that I am Bogart, complete with the cigarette and raincoat.

"I'm Eleanor Roosevelt," he says, and I howl as I see it: the big lips, the dress, the hair.

"I'm Jimi Hendrix."

"I'm Hitler."

"I'm Cher."

Soon of course, we raise the stakes and get into the scary ones.

"I'm your dead grandmother," I tell him, and his eyes widen crazily.

"Stop it. Stop it." He is jumping around and punching my arm. So I turn back into myself. Then he gets up close in my face and grins, looking me in the eye.

"I'm you."

Philip decides to go to sleep, so I go lie down in his sister's old room. I am worried. I know I won't sleep, and the cat is giving me the creeps. It keeps growling and clawing on my chest, muttering like a soft engine that I can feel digging toward my heart. When it leans over me, eyes aglow in the dark, I know right away: It is a demon. I remember the words of the deer and lie there, paralyzed with fear. Finally, I work up my nerve and, with a superhuman effort, I jump up, toss the beast into the hall, and lock the door. All night, I huddle under the blanket, staring into the dark, while the cat scratches and meows in the hall. Around dawn I hear crashes and screams, but I don't dare peek. Who knows what that creature is doing? Quiet returns, but that scares me even more. Now I really do have to piss, but there is no way I am stepping out there. I get up and look around for an old bottle or a plant. There is an air conditioner in the window, so that's out. When I press my head to the glass, the lawn and shrubs look like a black mass closing in on the house. The trees seem to float an inch off the ground. I hear the muttering that Philip complained of, from behind the door, and I understand: It's the demon speaking numbers. Finally I just piss in the corner behind a dresser. I'll blame it on that fucking satanic cat.

I crash out, and when I wake up, it is midafternoon. I feel a lot better about everything. I want to head to the diner for pancakes, ham, and eggs. I want coffee. I venture out to Philip's room, hoping he will be in the mood for breakfast. Everything in there is smashed and torn to bits: the furniture, the stereo, every single record and book. The windows and mirrors are shattered. Philip is lying naked and unconscious in the middle of the floor with a hammer in his hand and blood smeared on his feet from the broken glass. I split immediately and go home to have lunch with my parents. Later I hear that Philip's parents have packed him off to some kind of rehab or nuthouse and after that to a special school. A year later, I will start college and move away.

Decades pass. I enter my own dark period and finally emerge, a reasonably sane sort-of-grown-up living a seminormal life. At least I learn to fake it, more or less. I move back to New York, where I find work as a teacher. Not long after I arrive, I bump into an old classmate, Christine, browsing the stacks at Strand Books. Despite loving her madly through grade school, I don't recognize her at first. She's a mother now, with her hair in a long yellow braid and red knuckles above the wedding ring, but up close, in the smile and the eyes, she's the same. It's Christine who brings up Philip. I admit I haven't thought of him in years. She says he's back in a mental facility in New Jersey yet again, diagnosed as a paranoid schizophrenic. Feeling guilty, I write him a letter, raising the possibility that maybe, if he stays off drugs, he can find another, freer life, like me. I offer to visit. "After all," I write, "you are my oldest friend." The reply is succinct, printed on a plain lined sheet: "Glad to hear you are well. Please do not contact me again."

I never see Christine again, but from then on, Philip, you are in my thoughts. I hear that you've been seen panhandling in our old neighborhood or gotten arrested for sleeping in Central Park, and although I know it's ridiculous, I begin looking, randomly, peering close when I pass a dirty scarecrow begging on a corner, or spot a wastrel snoozing on the train. Then one night,

I am on the subway, heading home late from a party, a fund-raiser for a magazine that has just published a story of mine for the first time. It was a fancy dinner, and I am dressed in a suit and feeling pretty good for once, with a free copy of the magazine on my lap. My story is right up front, and I am rereading it one more time when I notice a bum who matches your description passed out at the end of the car. He is slumped forward under a droopy old hat, but his hair is the right brown, down past his shoulders, and his face is all beard. Leaves and twigs stick out, as if he's only just returned from that bad trip in the woods, a time-warped refugee from the wilderness of the mind. His gathered shopping bags are all filled with paper, and I can see there are drawings in marker and crayon and pastel. Other pages are covered in numbers. As I draw closer, I see too that there are numbers scrawled on his arms and legs, covering all visible skin.

And there it is: 999, the number you cried in your agony, written on the backs of your hands, facing me now upside down, right and left, 666 666. Did only one of us escape from the evil we met on the mountain that sunny day? Or did you carry it back down with you, like a mark?

"Philip," I say, soft at first, then louder. "Philip! Is that you?"

Then your eyes open. They are blue. Not even madness can change your eye color, I don't think. It isn't you. So I apologize, handing over a dollar with a shaky hand, as we pull into a station. The bum takes the bill with a grave bow, removing his hat in dignified thanks, and that's when I see them: two red horns protruding from the storm of his hair, bone hard with sharp black tips. The demon smiles, and a black tongue slides between his sharp white teeth. Terrified, I edge away as the door opens behind me, but a grimy claw grabs my hand.

"Hey, David," he says, in a voice I know. "Let's do impressions." Then he gets up close in my face and grins, looking me in the eye.

"I'm you."

Hawk

The hawk wheels east toward Riverside Drive, low above the playground's shrieking kids, soft and slow but too big to eat, seeking fat rats that breed in warm co-op pipes, feeding on white garbage, brie rinds and organic fruit, writhing like muscles under black, plastic skin when you walk your little doggy at night. The river is stuck like a sleeping shark, mouth frozen open, eyes clouded. The river rolls over and shows a spotted gray belly to the sun. Bare trees pass by with abandoned nests in their throats. Old smoke drifts back down to earth, and a veil of soot spreads on the snow, like a shawl covering cold shoulders. Surging swaying riding on the trembling point of a branch,
the hawk
stands
still.

"I saw the hawk today, over by the river," Jack said, breathing a last lungful of ice-sharpened air into the dim and stuffy room. It was an old building, and the radiator sang and sighed like an old man's guts. "He was cruising the promenade by the dog park with some kind of dead body. It was crazy, just sailing along in a big V, not even moving its wings, holding like a mouse or sparrow in its claws. It gave me an idea for something." He pulled off his hat and gloves, squeezed out of his sneakers and thermal top, and searched the messy desk for a pencil, trying to remember the lines already crumbling in his mind. "Hey, what's wrong, why are you crying?"

She sat on the edge of his bed, facing the window, weeping with her hands in her lap. Was someone dead? His mother? The thought appeared from nowhere, a dumb and wild fear. Why would they call Janet and not him? Her family then? Her dad's heart at last? He felt his damp hair drying, cooling his scalp as he knelt, hands on her knees.

"Janet, what is it?"

She turned her wet and shining face to him, as if in pity.

"I've been thinking about breaking up."

"Us?" he whispered. The small word clawed his throat.

She nodded.

"About wanting to break up with me?" he confirmed.

She nodded again, and tears dropped from her cheeks. In a cracked voice, she screeched, as if in horror: "I've been thinking about sex with other people." Her eyes were wide with shock at herself. "I can't help it."

"Have you slept with someone else?" Dread made his own voice sound distant, as if he were hiding under the bed.

She shook her head. "But I'm afraid that I'm going to." With this she began to sob so hysterically that he leapt up and held her, crushing her small head softly against his chest and stroking the knotted curve of her spine. He loved her very much at that moment. He admired her bravery.

"It's OK. These are normal feelings. Everyone has them. You're just more honest than everyone else." He sighed. "Much more."

"Do you?" Her gleaming eyes searched his eyes.

"Sure." He answered her question carefully, as if testifying before a congressional inquiry, a tiny lawyer buzzing in his ear. "Sometimes. Everybody does."

"What does everybody do about it?"

He shrugged. "They live with it. They just stuff the feelings and don't talk about it. Or they act on it and then they lose their relationships and are single till they find someone else, but eventually it all happens again. Until you're too old to care, maybe."

"I don't want to lose you."

"You will," Jack said, self-pity washing over him. He was older and he'd been through more, which gave him a tragic, fatalistic angle on life, but not much practical wisdom to go with it. Once a relationship began to turn like this, to decline, there was no way back. Or if there was, he didn't know about it.

"Have you ever thought about an open relationship?" she asked.

"You mean dating other people?"

"No. Well. Having sex with other people. Do you think that could work?"

"No. I've never heard of it working. Have you?"

"No. Well. There's that couple Rita has been dating. They have threesomes with other women and men. Or couples. Or there's swingers clubs."

"I don't want to see you with another man. That sounds horrible."

"I think it would be hot to see you with another woman."

"It would be. I'd like to see you with another girl too. But not some dude's hairy ballsack."

"That's not fair. I have to see your hairy ballsack with girls."

"But you don't have to. Anyway what does fair have to do with it? We're talking about what turns us on. Thinking about you with other guys makes me nauseous. Sorry."

"It would be so much easier if you thought it was hot."

"Easier for you. It would be easier for me if you wanted to stay home and bake cookies while I date other girls."

They laughed finally. A small dry laugh but some relief at least.

"I guess maybe . . ." He spoke in a measured, wary tone. "Maybe if I just didn't know. Like if you were going on a trip and had a little fling or took a weekend off from me to fulfill some fantasy. Like wanting to fuck a guy with a strap-on. I suppose I could live with that."

"Gee, thanks."

"And I'd do the same. Like, if I wanted to have sex with, I don't know . . ."

"Who? Someone I know? Who is it?"

"What? No. Nothing like that. I just mean, I don't know, a different kind of girl."

"Bigger boobs?"

"No. I love yours. I told you."

"Then what?"

"Just whatever, some sort of physical variation. Something out of the ordinary."

"Like a midget or a blind girl or something?"

"No! I don't know, Jesus, I haven't given it much thought. A black girl maybe."

"Oh, I see. Or Asian. I know you like Asian girls. They're your favorite."

"Actually they're your favorite. You watch those videos of Asian girls kissing."

"Whatever. You get to bang hot Asian and black girls, and I get to stick a dildo up a guy's butt? That's your idea of fair?"

He laughed. "No, that's my idea of hot. But don't worry because it's not going to happen. The truth is you would have a thousand guys lined up around the block in five seconds, standing at attention, and I'd be home alone watching Netflix. So stop saying 'fair.' Sex and desire is the one realm of life where justice is not only impossible, it's inconceivable. What would fair even look like? Everyone you want also wants you, and no one desires anything that would upset you? That's not fair, it's total despotism. The fact is you are free. Do anything you want, fuck anyone you want. I'm not trying to change your mind. You'll just hold it against me, and we'll break up anyway. So there is nothing to lose really."

He took a breath. He wasn't sure if he believed even half of what he'd said, but he was desperate and felt he had to make a play with whatever cards were left.

"I just don't want to do nothing now and then do something worse later," she said.

"I understand. I think you're right."

"You make it sound like we're breaking up."

"Aren't we?"

"No."

"OK then," he said. "Good."

That night, after extensive debate, Jack and Janet will agree to begin talking to other people without telling each other about it, but also not to proceed to sleeping with anyone without further talks. And just as Jack predicted, over the following weeks she'll receive a staggering amount of eager male attention while he awkwardly attempts to chat up a few women. However, she will also prove the more jealous, jealous even of his (entirely feigned) lack of jealousy, and though he specifically asks her not to, she will tell him all about the men pursuing her and insist on knowing everything about the one poor girl who actually seems interested in a fling with Jack, cyberstalking her and carrying on about what a skank she is until finally Jack will have to tell the girl he can't talk anymore. They will decide to go back to normal, but normal will be gone, they can't unknow what they now know about each other, or themselves, and finally Janet will say she needs some time apart, to think, and they'll separate, though they will still talk on the phone about maybe having kids one day, and meanwhile Jack will try to reconnect with that skanky girl, who will refuse to answer his texts, till at last he somehow ends up as the jealous stalker, tracking her and Janet both, living in dread of the day when she will, inevitably, tell him she has found someone new.

But all of that was yet to come. By the time Jack and Janet finished talking that night, it was very late and they were exhausted. They crawled under the covers, his arms around her waist, and Jack fell into a deep but dream-troubled sleep. In the dream, he was going to see Janet at her place in Brooklyn. He got out of bed, dressed, walked to the subway, and got on. Looking back, the only suspicious thing was that it was dark and there were no people and no traffic, not a soul in sight, yet the train came right away. He entered an empty car. He rode a long time, rattling through the tunnels, the glaring lights stinging his tired eyes. Then somewhere under the river, the conductor came through and asked for his ticket. He handed over his MetroCard, and the conductor swiped it between the fingertips of his gloved hand. Sorry, he said, you are dreaming. You won't be allowed to exit. Jack was confused. He was only a few stops from Janet's. But you're sleeping, the conductor explained. Go home and try again.

So he got off at the next stop and crossed the platform, where another train was waiting, and rode the empty car back uptown. He walked through the empty streets, passed his snoring doorman, and took the elevator upstairs. He took his clothes off and climbed into bed with Janet, who lay naked and curled on her side, and he cuddled up to her, nose behind her ear, breathing in her scent, which he knew so well but could never describe or even imagine until he held her again and closed his eyes.

Then the phone buzzed and woke him. It was Janet, texting again, asking him to come to her place, and again he got dressed and left. Again the train was there and, rushing through the turnstile, he jumped on just as the doors slid shut. But somehow he must have drifted off, because the next thing he knew, the conductor was shaking him and demanding his ticket. Confused, he fumbled in his wallet and his MetroCard fell out, fluttering like a leaf in midair until the conductor caught it in a gloved hand. Sorry, he said. You're sleeping. No one can exit on the other side until they are awake.

This went on, repeating a hundred times, a thousand, one of those dreams that last lifetimes and leave you more exhausted than when you went to sleep, until finally I woke up and was shocked to see that it wasn't even day yet. Why was I up? Then I realized my girlfriend was awake and sitting at my computer, her face lit in a window of blue.

"What's going on?" I asked in utter confusion.

She looked at me. She was crying. "What is this?" she asked. "What are you writing?"

Had I left some email open? Some old note to a girl? My mind searched the darkness above me, wheeling over the walls. "What's wrong? Why are you crying?"

"Who are Jack and Janet?" she asked. "What is happening to us? Is this the end?"

"I don't know," I said, but as I rushed across to hold her, I knew it was not. This was the beginning.

Retrospective

I

On October 21, 2004, I saved my friend J's life. Well, maybe not saved, "saved" is a bit strong, but I reacted favorably in a clutch moment and removed her from harm's path, although as it happens there was no real chance of harm. (Her name is Jenny, by the way, but so is my sister's, and my dear old friend's and my recent ex-lover's, so best to call this semifictional character based on the real person J.) In any case I was happy, happier than I'd been in a long time. I was back in New York after years in Los Angeles; I was just emerging from a painful and exhausting divorce; I was in graduate school, a student again, finishing a long-paused doctorate in comparative literature (at times this felt ridiculous since I was in my thirties and had spent the last decade imitating various sober professionals, sometimes even in a tie, but that day it felt great to be in a place where everyone at least pretended to take books and culture seriously). It was a crystalline autumn day, with superfine white sunshine dissolving in a pure sky and firing the edges of the leaves, and I was accompanied by a beautiful woman, my friend J. We were pals only, I will make that clear, but it was a pleasure to walk through that air speaking to her, she was brilliant as well as lovely, and we'd just had lunch (a pretty good lunch special at a so-so Japanese restaurant) and were heading back to class, and she had just been teasing me about my terrible math skills and general frivolousness with money (there'd been four of us at lunch, and I'd pronounced a total of thirty-six dollars to be indivisible by four, suggesting we round up to forty for convenience). Anyway we were laughing together about me, which was fair enough, but it was the lightness of it that delighted me, the fact that we were laughing lightly about me, when all I had done for months and months was feel grim and serious about me (I had still laughed then, but grimly). I felt that, against all odds, my life might turn out all right after all. It still wasn't too late.

The spiritually advanced are always pointing out to the rest of us how only the present moment exists. This is true of course — the past is gone, and so not worth feeling resentful or regretful over, and the future is, famously, unknown, thus not worth fearing or worrying about (unless what you fear happens to be the unknown) — but what I want to point out is a less comforting corollary of this assertion: If only this moment, here, now, exists, then everything, everyone, everywhere else does not. Your childhood, your old friends, the sex you had last night, your husband or wife, your own children, the person you just hung up with when you called into work to say you were running late: all gone. And since you yourself are constantly becoming, reemerging as it were from darkness into the light of each moment, so too the person you were back in grade school, the person you were yesterday, or even a moment ago, is also vanished, lost to who you are now. You are trapped in the present. Your connection to others, to the past, even your own continuation as a human being (the "being" part, I suppose), it is all a matter of memory really. Slip for a second on the ice of the mind, as when you space on a name or forget where you parked the car, and you might be lost forever.

Thus is each moment a risk, each breath and thought a gamble, a play in the game of fate, and even as one steps off a curb on the Upper West Side, a little late for class at 2:01 on a beautiful fall afternoon, the dice are tumbling, sparkling like diamonds in fortune's crooked eyes.

That's when the accident occurred. Right at that moment, when J and I were about to cross the street, laughing at how bad I am at math, two cars collided in front of us, one that had been in the middle of Broadway, trying to turn onto 116th, and one that was proceeding downtown. I didn't actually see it. I heard it, the scream of tearing steel. I felt it, a shudder in the air, a blurry rush, the blow, and I jumped, my left hand instinctively shooting out to grab J's right arm and pull her with me back onto the curb. And from inside that tiny split second, due perhaps to some affinity, some analogy or alignment, or else due to the violence, the rift and rupture, I was transported back in time.

2

I did not get very far. I traveled approximately three thousand miles and seventeen months, five days, two hours to Los Angeles, May 2002. I was driving my car, the Volvo sedan that now, as far as I know, belongs to my ex-wife, and she, still my wife for a little while longer, was beside me. We were in downtown LA. The light was warm, yellow, dense LA light, not at all like the pale fall light of New York. This was thick sunshine, layered like butter across the dusty windshield, dazzling and dancing in my eyes like a constellation of motes. (Of course I immediately forgot where, and when, I'd come from, forgot the future, though I felt a pang, the pull of losing time.) We were smiling, laughing, chatting, but unlike in the New York moment with J, I was not content or at ease. I was nervous and edgy and a little ill. Why? I was on a date. Sort of.

I don't know if anyone is ever really comfortable on a date, I'm certainly not, but this date was extra awkward, extra weird and disorienting, because it was with my wife. We had been living apart for some months, attending couple's counseling and trying to see, sometimes desperately, sometimes despairingly, if our marriage was still salvageable. One of the counselor's suggestions, along with the lists and books and positive mental exercises, was to go on dates, to rekindle the romance by going out to have fun together and relax and, for once, meet without discussing what was wrong with our lives and whose fault (mine) it might be.

For our date, I had chosen a trip to MOCA, LA's museum of contemporary art, then I believe still referred to as the Temporary Contemporary since its new headquarters was being built. We were seeing the Lucian Freud retrospective. I didn't really know much about his work at the time. I was aware of him mainly because of his grandfather (Sigmund), his close friendship with Francis Bacon (I admired both Sigmund and Francis very much), and his use of Leigh Bowery (the enormous and thrilling performance artist) as a model. Still I was intrigued by what I'd heard and it was the sort of thing that my wife had once liked to do with me, so I proposed and she accepted. It was a Saturday afternoon. I drove to our house, where she was staying (alone, I thought, but in fact she was already dating her yoga instructor, a disturbingly muscular blond woman), and we took her car (this being the new car, the Volvo sedan, which had somehow ended up as hers despite the fact that we'd bought it to replace my old Audi), but I drove. I always drove, by her choice and to my relief. I was a much better driver.

The paintings were hung more or less chronologically and, not being an especially knowledgeable or subtle observer of art, I didn't really get them at first. They looked like pretty standard realistic likenesses, slightly stiff perhaps and with none of the conceptual flash or stylistic personality I usually admired. Also, in my defense, I will remind you that I was distracted to say the least. There she was, my little wife, the source of all my joy and grief, my comedy and drama, for the last seven or so years, a person I'd woken up next to thousands of times, and now I had no idea what to say to her, or even whether I should take her hand. So much for the "date" idea. What the shrink forgot to figure into her scheme was that everyone hates going on dates. The incredible awkwardness, as though you were suddenly dropped from outer space into your own body and didn't know where your hands went (pockets? crossed? twisting the museum brochure to bits?) or how to stand or what your own laugh was supposed to sound like. (Mine was much too loud now, bursting through the museum like a barking dog.) Maybe the shrink's real plan was to scare us straight. Just settle for each other, she was saying. It's still way better than trying again with someone else.

But in some ways the woman I found beside me was already someone else, as ungraspable as the painted women on the wall, *Girl with Roses,* or *Girl with Hand Around a Kitten's Throat,* with their oversized liquid green eyes and side-parted hair, their looks of alarm and allure, of hungry curiosity mingled with terror and tears.

Had she always been this small? How could such a little person cause me such big trouble? She wore a light skirt, thin socks, cute shoes, a necklace I'd never seen before, a long chain dangling before her low-buttoned blouse. Her shoulders seemed like a sparrow's, her head tiny and perfect as a newborn's. She was very tan, like fresh-roasted coffee beans, from a girls-only bonding retreat to the desert she'd just been on, to help her get in touch with her feelings about me, accompanied by the woman I didn't know then was already her new lover. I read the names of the pictures from the strangled brochure. She nodded and pretended to look. We talked about the weather and a sick friend. (The friend died a few weeks later after a long, drawn-out battle with lung cancer. I remember our last visit to her hospital room, again as a kind of official or ceremonial couple who no longer slept in one bed. The friend's ex-lover arrived, yelled at the staff, and then told us, tearfully, "I begged her to get a Jewish doctor. Begged!" No one else present seemed surprised by this medical assessment. I was the only Jew there. Did people in Beverly Hills think we were magic?) In the bright light of the white-walled museum, my wife noticed fresh veins of gray in my hair. (Now it is the black that runs in streaks through the gray.)

Then we wandered across a threshold and reality struck. Reality in this case was a huge naked man seen from behind, squatting on a red plush stool, a meat mountain fissured at the base by a hairless, chapped ass crack and topped by a smooth round head. (The model was Leigh Bowery, who shaved his whole body for showbiz reasons.) Yet this raw reality, encountered in the flesh, is (in reality) not flesh at all but paint, and that fact is made plain as well: Every stroke, every brush, every line is visible. There is no illusion. Just paint pushing itself as it strains to realize, to understand reality, to register the actuality of flesh, of meat and skin and plenty of blubber, sagging, stretching, peeling, pulsing, beating and bursting, alive and also dying, cracking, flaking, sinking and subsiding into decayed matter. (As it happens, this death was already inside and growing. Unknown to the painter, the model had contracted the HIV that would slay him.) Those organic and biological truths are not the whole, though they are the first and the last, aren't they? They are primary, and that is why only a very shallow mind indeed considers these matters, these merely fleshly matters, shallow. Why would he need to transcend this? What is more profound than the painter's mother's lined and noble brow, her closed mouth set in the thousand sittings he did with her as she traveled toward death, his grown daughters' vaginas and thatchy pits, his dog asleep on the bare floor, his own naked ghost in unlaced boots, like a tattered veil of splotchy paint that appears in a mirror, holding a palette and knife? But not just those animal facts are attended to (an ass that surely farts and possibly accepts cocks, shoulders that could bear a world); you can see that bald head thinking. The eyes, in the painting where he is cast back naked on the floor, leg up, thick dick draped on fat thigh, sad shriveled sack dangling like soft walnuts — those blue eyes have another world behind them. What is it? How can the artist know? He can't and won't lie, won't surmise or presume. But he can see it's there, like a shadow behind a screen if he peers hard enough. He does. He looks hard enough. Many, many times, and for each glance a stroke and for each stroke he mixes his colors fresh. (Every time, he does this. He thinks and plans and tries once more, with each touch of brush to canvas, to get it right.) Ten thousand strokes are ten thousand shots at trying to see what is right there before us right now.

Sometimes you hit the target; sometimes you miss. So what? Reality is back again, a moment later, a day later, different body, different light. Another roll of the dice. Each moment leaves its mark, if you are looking, if you are present for it. (It takes a lifetime, it is so hard to do.) Until all our moments are gone.

That day, the naked woman I discovered in the next room — with her eyes shut, stretching like a big cat, breasts high on the rib cage, pussy wet in paint, or the one with eyes open, alert yet somehow more shy, glancing off the side of the canvas, pinkish-yellow thighs closer over her furred groin — was somehow more real, more present to me, than the hidden, clothed body of my wife, which I had not held in forever. Which was nevertheless right there, an inch from my fingertips, as we stood side by side, and yet already fading, becoming unreal, disappearing as I hurtled through time. (And now? Today? Has her body aged like mine? Have her beautiful breasts sagged? Are the veins too risen to the surface of the skin, blue against the brown? Would we know each other again in darkness by touch? Could I paint her from memory, if only my hands knew how to paint?)

3

It was on the way home from the museum that the accident occurred. Still awkward, but quiet now, elated or stunned by what we'd seen, we stopped at a light. It turned green. I lifted my foot from the brake, rolling us forward, then pressed the accelerator as we eased into the intersection. Another driver ran the light and hit us, full speed from the left, striking the front of the car, fortunately, or I would have been wounded, at the very least. As it was, we spun around completely and ended up parked in the middle of the intersection, more or less where we'd begun. (God bless Volvo.) I was dazed, my mind still turning a moment behind my body and the car, but I was fine.

"Are you OK?" I asked her.

"Yes," she said, checking herself. "I'm fine."

A white lady with short dark bangs appeared at my window. "I saw it all he hit you out of nowhere he ran the light," she said. I looked where she pointed. A blue LTD was sitting a couple yards away at an angle from my crumpled front quarter panel. I saw a curly brown head regarding us in the rearview. Then the LTD puttered off, leaving a gray cloud of stink behind.

"Motherfucker. He's leaving the scene of the crime." Instinctively, I restarted my engine, lurching into gear, and incredibly my bent car came to life. We began in a creaky sort of way to pursue the blue LTD. (It was an old '80s model. My grandfather had a red one.)

"What's happening?" my wife asked, her mind clearing.

"He's getting away," I said. "Call the cops. Tell them we are in pursuit."

The curly head glanced at me again in the rearview, a tan man with sunglasses. He sped up. So did I. He turned right at a stop sign without stopping, and I did too. My wife sat bolt upright, grabbing the dashboard, as if she were the time traveler.

"What are you doing? You're chasing him?"

"You said you were OK, right?" I said.

"I am OK. You're not. You lost your mind."

On a long empty street that ran between parking lots, he hit the gas and shot forward. I stayed close behind.

"What if he has a gun?" she pointed out.

"Why would he? An armed red light runner? Anyway" — I gestured at his vehicle, reassuringly — "he can't shoot at us if we're behind him."

Luckily it was a weekend afternoon and downtown was vacant. As we sped through empty, peaceful streets and wide-open intersections, pausing through lights and winding between corrugated warehouses, it seemed to me less like a death-defying, body-smashing, car-flipping movie chase, and more like a mild, cheaply made TV show, an episode of *The Rockford Files*. Still, the blood was pounding in my ears and in my hands as I gripped the wheel. My wife was on the phone with the cops.

"Give them the license plate number," I shouted, trying to keep his plate in clear view as we bounced and twisted along. I could hear our tire scraping in the bent wheel well. A high-speed blowout would not be fun. "What do the cops say?"

"They say stop chasing him. He might have a gun."

"Tell them to cut him off before he gets on the freeway," I

suggested. "Give them our location." I went faster, leaning into the race. We squealed around a corner and came to a major thoroughfare. Traffic rushed by in both directions, and a line of cars waited at the light. He hit his brakes, screeching to a halt, and I slammed mine, almost banging into him this time. We lurched forward and bounced to a stop. I chanted his plate number under my breath, trying to memorize it. Then his door opened. He stepped out, hands extended, not so much in surrender as a kind of hey-you-got-me shrug. He was a thin older man in a polo shirt and cheap slacks. He smiled and waved, kind of shyly. I started to open my door — "No, no, please don't," my wife begged — but as soon as I put a foot on the ground he hopped back into his car and fled, cutting off the other mergers on the right and drawing a chorus of honks. I stayed put. (We had his plates and make. The cops did indeed find him, but it didn't do much good. He was driving without insurance, on a license already suspended for drunk driving.) Sitting there, at rest, my heart pounding like a fist inside me, adrenaline leaking through my stomach and rage running in my veins, I felt victorious and alive. I turned and grinned at my wife. She was trembling and her face was crossed with tears, and I could see in her eyes that at that moment I was no one she knew. We had no further dates.

4

"Wow, that was close . . ."

I was back. J and I stood on the corner of 116th and Broadway, staring at the two crimped cars before us. We realized we

were holding hands and let go. The two drivers got out, unin-
jured, and chatted calmly. Traffic adjusted and began to flow.
Time resumed, closing back up like the skin of a river closing around a drowned rock. We realized we were late for our
hermeneutics seminar and quickly crossed the street. By the
time class ended, two hours later, it was dark out, and this entire incident was forgotten.

J now lives in Brooklyn somewhere. I never see her, but from
what I hear she's doing very well. My ex-wife lives in LA in our
old house and, as far as I know, drives the Volvo (the insurance
paid out since we were found 100 percent not at fault), with
her new husband beside her, or maybe now she prefers him
to drive. She is also doing fine. In the years since, I have had
a number of adventures and relationships and jobs that have
taken me to Paris and Taiwan and the Lower East Side, but I
have somehow ended up alone at last and living back uptown,
just a few blocks from where that accident took place, when J
and I were walking. I pass that corner all the time, but even
standing in that exact spot, waiting for a red light to turn, now
transports me nowhere but across the street. That autumn day
has vanished, joining the spring day in Los Angeles, out there
in the past, that afterlife of lost space and time, which I cannot touch or even completely believe in any longer. Everything
seems equally far away. Leigh Bowery is dead. Lucian Freud is
recently dead, though I still go to see his work every chance I
get and hope there will be another retrospective soon. I am reminded of something he said in an interview long ago: "I visit
museums as I visit the doctor, for help, and with some urgency."

White Tiger on Snow Mountain

Last fall I became impotent. Well, not literally. For one thing I wasn't having sex with anyone and so couldn't verify any specific incidents of impotence. But I began to suspect that if I did, I would. More precisely, I became afflicted with the fear of impending impotence. I developed various alarming symptoms, including numbness and tingling in my fingertips (though this may have been caused by texting outside in the cold), insomnia, the slackening of my normally oppressive sex drive, and a general feeling of unsettled weirdness below (and often above) the waist. It was a vague malaise, an attitude problem, really, as if my own body were shrugging me off and refusing to participate further in the ridiculous antics of my personal life: Call it impudence.

I had recently ended a relationship with a girl who managed to combine a fascinating and compelling kinkiness with a sluggish libido. At least it was new: She wanted to be tied up, spanked, and talked dirty to. She liked to perform stripteases. She loved to watch me masturbate and, believing it good for her skin, even offered her dainty face up to receive my offering, which she then spread over her pores and let dry like a flaky beauty mask. Nevertheless, she had almost no interest in actual intercourse, and insisted that it was unbearably painful for her, despite assurances from several doctors (and one dedicated amateur) that she was, at least anatomically, normal.

She was forthright if nothing else, and told me after our first kiss that "basically" no one had ever given her an orgasm, including herself. But the problem intrigued me, from the scientific point of view, and besides she was extra cute, so I volunteered to mentor her. At first, it was thrilling if exhausting: a tremendous amount of naughty talk and sexual busywork, of role play and foreplay, all building up to what was often, for both of us, rather an anticlimax. If for a while it seemed like my coaching was bringing her around, in the end the influence worked the other way. My own libido began to falter. I started losing interest halfway through the routine and even found myself reconsidering whether orgasms — my own included — were actually worth all the effort. Defeated, I flopped beside her on the bed.

"Fuck it. I'm exhausted." I felt like I had carpal tunnel syndrome.

"Well, it's soft now," she said, poking my deflating hard-on like an undercooked sausage she was sending back to the kitchen.

"It's depressed."

"Never mind," she said, hopping to her feet. "I'll put on my cheerleader outfit."

I was trapped in a pornographic nightmare: I could talk about my cock with her, wave it at her with impunity, threaten her with it, even slap her in the face with it, but I couldn't put it inside her without her cringing and urging me to get it over with while she lay rigid as a corpse. I even found myself reminiscing about the latter nights of my marriage, those doldrums before the final storm when, still more fed up with life than with each other, my wife and I would just roll into position on our sides and take care of the sex chore that way, with the Food Network whispering seductively in the background, or else we'd multitask with morning sex in the shower before work: Sex as soporific or stress reducer. Sex as cleanser and detox. Sex not as a drug — dangerous, glamorous, addictive — but as medicine, to be administered in sensible doses.

Finally, even those dubious pleasures I was sort of enjoying with my oddball girlfriend came to a shuddering halt one night when, just as I was about to spank her, she burst into tears. I panicked, as I always do when women cry.

"What's wrong? What's wrong?" I hadn't laid a finger on her, yet.

"I don't want to play any games," she gasped. "I just want to be you and me."

I grinned and kissed her. "That's fine, sweetheart. That's the best." We went to bed, and it really was the best, but only for a night. It turned out that being you and me didn't work at all. There was no you and me. So we broke up, out of exhaustion really, but instead of being driven by horniness back out into the cold world, I found myself retreating, reclusing, recoiling at last, even from my own touch.

The solution, I decided, was to quit smoking. I'd read, somewhere on the Internet, that impotence could be brought on by smoking. I smoked! I'd been trying to quit unsuccessfully for the last fifteen years but was so hopelessly addicted that once, after a week of Nicorette, a shrink actually advised me to smoke again: He was afraid that my outrages and crying jags, my bank line tantrums and post office panic attacks, were building up to a real breakdown, perhaps even an arrest. So I went back to my trusty Camels, comforted by the knowledge that they had been medically prescribed. But now the same obsessive, compulsive mind that used to make me climb into dumpsters at 3 a.m. to retrieve the pack of cigarettes I'd ceremoniously thrown away at noon flipped on me and, in a stunning reversal, my own neuroses came to my assistance: I became convinced that I could actually feel the cigarettes killing me, one by one. I could sense my nerves dying, my capillaries withering as I inhaled, and began constantly testing the numbness in my fingers by snapping them as I walked around town. Any second, I expected my penis to shrivel away like a dead vine and blow off down the street. Finally, in a fit of hypochondria, late on a cold November night, I spit my last butt into the street.

I should have been grateful to be impotent, really. I should have welcomed it as a saving grace. My relationship history, long and arduous, comprising brief episodes of ecstatic agony relieved by epic stretches of dull despair, had often driven me to "pray" (in the atheistic, communistic, profane sense of the word) for relief from that most intolerable of all itches, the one you can't scratch yourself. I had been married and divorced, both against my will. I'd been moved in and out of various shared dwellings. I'd been hopelessly in love with tragic, troubling beauties ever since Cindy Blumberg stabbed me with a pencil in kindergarten. And never once, in all that time, had I made a sane or rational decision. Always I had thrown myself in harm's way, obeying the loon call of love. And each time, when I found myself shattered still further, into still tinier bits, I had thought, If only desire would leave me, if only that hunger would cease and desist, I could find some peace. Now, at last, the prayer had been answered: I walked the streets, and though my eyes still reflexively tracked this smooth curve or that flash of shining hair, there was, in the heart, in the groin, no real response. I chatted politely with waitresses and shopgirls, but nothing in me grasped for anything in them. I'd lost that desperation, that howling in the soul, that made the dog in me chase the scent of a passing cat. Woman delighted not me. No, nor men neither. Nor porn. I was, I realized, completely without desire. There was no one I loved or hated, needed or missed. I was free. I immediately rushed to the doctor.

Of course I didn't walk into the doctor, a female doctor no less, and complain of Theoretical Impotence or Penile Impudence. I asked for help quitting smoking. I had gotten Dr. Chang's number from a friend who claimed she cured her psoriasis with acupuncture and herbs. Her office was on Canal Street above a bank, on a floor with two dentists. The waiting room was packed with elders and a few matronly women who had brought along snacks, cut carrots, or goldfish crackers in baggies. One had a small boy in tow. I was the sole non-Asian.

The doctor herself was in her early fifties. She had some gray in her black bob and wore glasses and a white lab coat. She said that she could help me with the smoking, but only if I was truly ready to quit. I assured her that I was. I was afraid now for my health. I had symptoms. Such as?

"In bed," I managed to stammer. "You know."

She didn't. "Problems sleeping?" she asked me in fluent but accented English.

"No. Well. Yes. Sure, I always have that. But I meant you know, down there." I nodded discreetly at my own lower half as if it might overhear us.

"Problems with erections? With your girlfriend?"

"Well, I don't have a girlfriend."

"So then no problem, right?" She smiled.

"Ha, yes, but . . ." I lamely explained my "symptoms," the compulsive finger snapping, the impudence. She gave me a look that said, "Who let this idiot in here?" and proceeded with a thorough exam. She took blood and urine. She checked my heart and blood pressure. She got a pointy needle thing and poked my numb fingers, checking my nerves and reflexes. She boinged my knees with a mallet. A week later I came back to hear the troubling news: There was nothing wrong with me.

"So then I just have to live like this? Forever?"

She frowned, dubiously, but took pity on me. She peered into my eyes, first one, then the other. She considered my tongue. Then she took my pulse, checking each wrist separately.

"Are you sensitive to cold?" she asked.

"Yes. That's right." Her office was tropical and I had a sweater on, but I felt a sudden chill.

"Frequent urination? Getting up often at night?"

"Yes!" I was thrilled. This was true. I had been urinating often, getting up several times a night, even planning my daily errands so that I'd be sure to pass a bathroom. One might say, technically, that I pretty much always had to urinate. I actually had to go right then and there in her office; I just chose not to.

"I urinate constantly," I told her. I hadn't thought to mention it, naively blaming it on the gallons of coffee I guzzled, because it hadn't occurred to me that it could be a symptom of anything, that "peeing a lot, being chilly, and snapping your fingers while being less lascivious than usual" could add up to something real — but apparently it did, in China.

"Kidneys," she decided.

"Kidneys?" Frightened, I clutched my stomach, then remembered my kidneys were in back. "That's serious. Something's wrong with my kidneys?" I saw myself on dialysis, shuffling through life in paper slippers.

"No." she smiled. "Don't worry. Only Chinese kidney."

"Chinese kidney," I repeated, relieved. "That's different. I don't need my Chinese kidney. Just cut it out."

We both had a good laugh at this. "In Chinese medicine," she told me, "we have something called chi, which is like an energy in the body."

"It's like a spiritual life force," I suggested.

She looked at me doubtfully, then continued. "This chi has two aspects, yin and yang, which we are always trying to bring into balance. Your chi is very out of balance. Maybe from smoking a long time and stress. And other factors maybe?"

I nodded. Other factors. Maybe.

"And now I think quitting smoking also makes you out of balance even more. Takes a long time to make this balance!"

I shrugged sadly. A long time.

She showed me a poster, which looked like a chart of the night sky blanketing the outline of a sleeping man. It traced the meridians of power that crossed the human body, clustered galaxies and orbiting spheres, terminating in points where the acupuncture needles would hit like stars of pain. These lines, she said, were associated with different organs. My particular constellation of symptoms placed me under the sign of the kidney.

It was both comforting and disturbing to learn that this odd jumble of "symptoms" actually made sense, became legible as it were, when read through another language, the map that a different culture laid over the flesh to explain our experience to ourselves. To me, and to Western civilization as a whole, my story was meaningless gibberish, neurotic noise. But my body whispered in Chinese to Dr. Chang.

She wrote me a prescription for herbs and then had a talk with her assistant, Amy, a stout, middle-aged lady with thick forearms, thick glasses, and a part in her short hair. She led me into another room with massage tables sectored off by sheets hanging from shower rods. Amy spoke almost no English, but using signs and brief exhortations ("All off!"), she had me strip to my underwear and lie on my back. The table was edged into a corner, and I had to turn on a slight angle to fit. "You too tall"—she laughed—although for a Caucasian man I'm average. "Too tall!" She lightly slapped my feet. I giggled. Then she spread a little towel over me and patted my head.

"You so weak," she clucked. "I have to help you stronger."

Her first step was to stick needles in my face. One in the forehead, one in each cheek, and one into the cup of each ear. It didn't hurt exactly. There was a small prick as she worked, quickly and expertly, first poking lightly to find the spot, then flicking the head of the needle with a finger to drive it in. The hardest part was just lying there and thinking: She's sticking needles in my face. I shut my eyes and did what I vaguely remembered as yoga breathing, which seemed to help, though of course I knew that yoga wasn't Chinese. She put more needles in my hands, right in the meat between the thumb and forefinger, in my forearms, my shins, and especially my feet, a fistful sprouting among my toes. You couldn't really predict what would hurt. The left hand stung more than the face, but the right hand I didn't even notice. Then, when she stuck my thigh, I felt a wild surge of pain, but not where the needle had entered. I felt it on the bottom of my foot, in the curve of the sole. Lightning shot up my leg, like someone had jerked an invisible wire running through my body. I twitched uncontrollably and hissed like a severed snake. Amy laughed good-naturedly and patted my head again.

"Sensitive," she chanted in a teasing lilt.

"What is that point for?" I asked through gritted teeth.

She smiled. "That kidaney."

I was now pinned to the table like a butterfly, with a dozen needles standing in my skin, but we weren't done yet, not by a long shot. Amy got out some alligator clips attached to electrical wires and started clamping them to the needles. I felt like a prisoner about to be tortured. I was desperate to confess, but to what? She turned a knob and began ticking up the current.

"Too strong?" she asked. "Is too much?"

How much electricity in the face is too much, really? I'd never pondered the question. It came in pulses, a bristling tingle like heat rash breaking out. When it hit blister stage, I said, "Too strong!" With another chuckle — "you so sensitive" — she dialed it back to bearable, then aimed a heat lamp at me, tucked in my towel, and left me there, little needles jumping in my skin, flesh flexing of its own accord. If I opened an eye, I could see a silver pin trembling in my cheek. "Relax," she ordered, and drew the curtain.

Weirdly enough, I did relax. One of those spikes must have fired off some endorphins because I drifted right to sleep. It was a sleep that spread over me like a light blanket, very dark but very thin, stirred by the pulse of the needles and by the staticky Chinese news radio playing in the next room. The current came in waves, building and then receding. It was immensely pleasurable in that way a nap can sometimes be, when the constant little wakings, instead of disturbing, return us to the joy of sinking back to sleep. For a few minutes I forgot where I was. Then one of my face needles popped out.

It must have been in too lightly because it just jumped loose with its wire attached. I could see it from the corner of my eye, hopping around my chin. But I was afraid to move or even lift a hand since my other needles were still buzzing away.

"Hello?" I called softly. "Help?"

All I could see was the curtain, stirring with the heat vent above. I could hear the other patients in their tents, moaning and snoring. Beyond that, the radio and a burble of voices in the waiting room. I searched my mind for its tiny bits of Mandarin.

"*Ní hao ma!*" I called. And louder, "*Ní hao ma!*"

Although it's used as a greeting, like "bonjour" or "shalom," the phrase actually means "how are you," and I was well aware of the absurdity of a white guy lying there and yelling, in a panicked voice: "How are you! How! Are! You!"

I heard some giggles from my neighbors, who added their own calls in rapid Chinese, and a minute later Amy came in.

"The needle came out," I told her. She laughed and put it back, giving it a little twist that stung.

"You talk Chinese!" she said.

"Just a little." I recalled the couple of other words I'd learned. "*Bing-lang!*" This was the weird betel nut stuff old Asian guys chewed and spit in purple wads on the ground. I'd tried it once, as a tobacco substitute. She laughed, delighted.

"*Xia xia,*" I said, trying to pronounce the lovely word right, swallowing the soft *shhh,* as she adjusted my current: "Thank you."

I started going twice a week. Amy gave me acupuncture front and back and usually a great massage. Dr. Chang attached little seeds to my inner ears, like discreet piercings I was supposed to press when I wanted to smoke. I also went to the herb store and showed them what she wrote. Perhaps it said, "Let's screw with this fool's head," because what they gave me looked like a sack of garden trimmings: sticks, fungus, berries, and dried brown leaves that I had to boil into a foul tea. But sure enough, when I showed the note to the old guy behind the counter, he took the cigarette from his lip and said the magic word, "Kidneys." Smiling wide, he pronounced the bag of scraps he sold me as "Good for man." He made a virile fist around his burning cigarette and waved it in my face. "Very good for man!"

Phase Two in my stop-smoking program was running. For years, I'd been urged to take up some exercise, but the thought of a gym triggered traumatic wet-towel-snapping locker-room flashbacks and visions of myself crushed in some mythological torture machine: The Tantalus Maximus. The Sisyphus 5000. The Abdominator. I was too poor and angry for yoga in Manhattan. Running seemed, if not easy, at least simple: If you could walk at all quickly, I figured, you could run. Also it was free. When I'd tried before, however, I had been smoking. Not while I actually ran, perhaps, but I smoked on the way there and back, and ran only in short bursts, as if chasing a bus, passing everyone, then stopping to wheeze and choke a block later. The real joggers eyed me curiously as I tore by, then fell behind, gasping. All of which led me, when I finally quit, to make an amazing discovery: Smoking is actually really fucking bad for your lungs. Or at least for mine, because in a few weeks I had doubled the distance I could run.

I ran two miles, then four, then six, up and down the waterfront. I didn't go very fast, and at my rate it would be ten years before I could attempt a marathon, but I had caught the habit and I kept going, even as the winter days grew cold and dark. My outfit was a bit odd compared to the high-tech warriors I saw darting along the paths: thrift store polyester pants, a hooded sweatshirt, black socks. When it snowed, I layered on thermals, a hat, and gloves. When my ancient long underwear sagged, I had the brilliant idea to safety pin them to the tops. I even got sciatica from running too much. Amy cured it with one vicious stab in the hip, and I was back, across Houston Street to the West Side Highway and out to the river alone. Just like I wanted.

My other new obsession was Internet sex (Intersext? ISX?), specifically the ads on Craigslist. I was freelancing then and spent all of my working and most of my nonworking hours immobilized before a screen in my basement apartment, making it rather hard to tell the difference really. And how far that once noble term has fallen: a free lance! Once it was a knight, unbound, ready to fight for fortune or honor, to ride out and meet victory or death. Now a freelance(r) was a pale, impudent nonsmoker hunched in his bathrobe, grinding out captions for an organic Brooklyn roof farm's veggie pics, ad copy for a revolutionary line of wrinkle-free chinos that came in a tube, and rhapsodic bloggings about a new hotel for dogs.

But if not smoking was great for breathing, running, and living in general, it turned out to be terribly unhealthy for writing. It was just as I'd suspected: Writing was antithetical to life as a whole, and my smoking cure had apparently relieved me of both compulsions at once. So I waited, staring into the blankness, and added work to the list of things I was busy not doing.

Then, when a rumor in the building made me fear, erroneously, that I'd have to move, I searched for places on Craigslist. The housing scare passed, but I found myself checking the personals. The ones that seemed sincere, actual people seeking actual happiness, were far too depressing, and at first I mostly enjoyed the silly misworded ones. "I'm the girl next store," a lady declared. A wise woman insisted on "condemns," while another's "testy pussy" had to be licked "just now." Then there was the plaintive cry: "So moisten, can't wait!"

Finally, perhaps inevitably, I answered. I estimated of course that at least 60 percent of the ads were spam, drawing traffic to commercial sites. Another 35 percent or so I figured were hookers, pranksters, or men. Of the remaining "real women," I assumed most were housebound invalids who had been scarred in terrible acid attacks, since, as far as I knew, pretty much any woman who wanted casual sex with a stranger could find it walking around the block. This left one in a hundred, maybe, who was normal enough, attractive enough, biologically alive and female enough, but harboring some dark secret (she was married, she was kinky, she was a nun lusting for rabbis) and so venturing online to engage in a bit of fantasy, with no intention of actually meeting up.

That was fine with me. I had no intention of meeting up either. I never intended to meet anyone ever again, unless she sat beside me in my doctor's waiting room, or to chat "off-line" with another human, except across the counter of a deli.

So I targeted this perverse minority. In fact I took it up as a (blocked) writing challenge: I knew each girl would get hundreds of responses from desperate dudes drooling over their keyboards. Could I, purely through the magic of language, rise to the top of the pile? To make it really sporting, I answered only the dirtiest, nastiest, and most twisted of the posts, the masochists and the submissives, the self-named whores and sluts, the daddy's girls, the slaves, the bitches in heat, the toys. Henceforth, it would be among my fellows, the fallen, wounded, and lame, that I would find my only friends.

HELLO DADDY . . .
I just read your response and it turned me on so much!! I do have a pic, but I am on campus right now and cant send it . . . But i wanted to let you know that you got me thinking such filthy filthy thoughts. There was a few things that TOTALLY peeked my interest . . i have interested in a while to do pee control . . when you make me hold it till

you say so . . or me holding your dick when you pee . . I have 3 little
girl outfits that i think you may like . . and i hope i get to wear them for
you! I deo have to tell you . . i am not that experienced . . but I love to
rollplay and pleasure my daddy . . i tend to be naughty a lot . . nothing
a punishment cant handle . . hope to here back form you . . Lyla

Hi Baby,
It's Daddy. I'm glad you liked what I wrote. And I'm
very happy to know that it turned you on. Did you get
all wet reading my letter? Don't worry about being
experienced. After all, that's what Daddy's for . . . to
teach his lttile darling to obey and please him. I will
certainly train you to hold your pee till I say so and to
have you show me how you learn to go like a good girl.
Yes, sweetheart, you will get to hold Daddy's cock while
he pees, but that is a reward for when you are good:
If you're naughty you will be punished: Daddy knows
what to do with naughty girls too.

Hey Daddy . . . I want to play with you soon . . . i read your first
2 emails . . and they were soo hot . . lol . . . Your little girl had a
confession to tell you . . i am not sure if you are going to be pleased or
upset . . I have recently found out that I like playing with girls too. . . . i
am not sure if you are into playing with 2 little girls . . maybe having 2
daughters . . but it could be fun . . once in a while . . she is into older
men too and we played together one night and it was great since
then me and her play a lot . . i jsut wanted to let you know . . . we are
both 20 . . but we look like we are 15 . . lol . . . I just turned myself up
totally . . lol . . .

If you have a special best friend, of course you can bring her to play with Daddy. There's lots of fun we can have. Although she has to be a good girl too, or she'll get spanked and punished also.

Well we both are sometimes bad . . we would both need to be punished from time to time . . . sometimes we argue over our toys and clothes . . . we usually share nicely . . but sometimes we get snotty . . we are little girls . . lol . . we love to experiment on eachother . . but for our daddy we would do anything he told us . . . I forgot to tell you i did mention to her this situation and she got excited . . i told her about pee control and holding your cock when you pee and she said she has doen some dirty stuff like that before . . i never have . . she said her last daddy liked to pee on her . . do you like to do that? i am not sure if i would . . but you can do it to her . . . i mean if you really wanted i guess i would have no choice . . bc i know what you say goes . . love Lyla

I complained to Dr. Chang about my back, so she added a new item to the menu: cupping. Amy had me lie on my belly with my head to the side. I could see a fellow patient's white-socked feet, tiny as cat paws, poking from her curtain, and a cheap calendar hanging on the wall, printed in English and Chinese. It was January. There was an ink drawing of a tiny village, thatched huts cuddled in chimney smoke at the bottom of a hill. Brushy trees climbed the heights, and a ram posed at the peak, his horns curling like shells. A line of check-mark birds flew off the edge. "Morning in Cold Village," the caption read. I meditated on this image for a month.

Meanwhile Amy placed a small clear bowl on my right lower back. Attaching what looked like a giant turkey baster or small bicycle pump, she began to suck the air out, until I felt it bite my skin like a leech. It sealed and stuck when she let go. It didn't hurt precisely; it was more like being molested by some futuristic parasite. She put another one on the left, repeating the process until my entire back was covered with these globes, like giant blisters bubbling from my skin. When removed, they left big circular welts, super-hickeys from an octopus. In the men's room mirror, I looked like I had some terrible disease that made you break out in polka dots. I covered up when some guy in a suit walked in and gasped.

What could I say? I'd been horribly beaten by a mugger with great design sense? It was impossible to explain, even to myself. But as I bent to tie my sneakers later, I noticed my back pain, my neck pain, my shoulder pain: all gone.

That day, while I was running, New Jersey disappeared. The river froze white into fog and rose like a ghost from its grave, becoming first a curtain, then a mountain that covered the far shore. As if I were witnessing the geological past, or peering into the drowned future, the river now went on forever, blending into the horizon, with only the clock atop a mall's tower still awake. Farther uptown, the black stubs of a fallen dock appeared, rows of broken teeth in the river's mouth, a folded white gull asleep on each, like an envelope or a handful of snow. I ran along the edge, against the wind, with a scarf over my mouth to warm my breath, and snowdrops stung my face like sparks.

IM with sweetsally

hi Master

Hey slut where are you?

in my apt

Are you wet for me? Did yr pussy start to drip?

its always wet for you

thats right. Your horny little pussy should melt as soon as you see me online . . . you should drool at the thought of my cock like a starving bitch in heat

i neeeed ur cock i am drooling for it

you'd love to crawl and beg for it . . . worship it . . .

yes Master

you'd come crawling as soon as I come over . . . with your leash in your mouth

yes Master

I want you nake on all fours with your collar on . . . what is your body like?

Althletic, curvy

what size are your tits?

34DD sometimes 34D depends on the bra

Real or fake?

real i work out a lot i lost like 40 lbs a couple years ago and now im a workout junkie

good . . . Shave? Wax?

wax

good . . . I'm strict when I inspect you . . . if I find a stray hair . . .
legs, armpits, pussy . . . you get whipped

yes Master

if you asshole isnt pink and clean when I stick my finger up it
you get slapped

yes Master

maybe I should weigh you too.

**oh god that makes me so wet and if we go out to get coffee
or anything and i try to order a cookie or put cream in my
coffee u stop me right there and humiliate me in front of
everyone by slappin gme accross the face and saying you
think you can have a cookie?!?! i dont want a fat fuck for
a slave and then i have to apologize and thank you for
stoppin gme**

Then I'll eat a big brownie and drink a cappucino while you
watch, haha . . .

**mmm god im soaking wet tell me more about how u would
humiliate me please and make sure i dont get fat and the
names you would call me like slapping me if i ordered a
cookie and making me apologize and thank you and show
everyone that i cant get fat**

ok . . .

I'd take you shopping and pick out the tightest sluttiest little
clothes and make you try them on and come out of the
dressing room and parade around . . . and if they dont fit I'd
call you a fat pig in front of the other customers and laugh

at you with the cute salesgirls and talk about how hot they
looked and how you should lose weight and maybe bring
one home to fuck in front of you and eat cake and hot fudge
and let you lick us clean after

oh god i am soaking wet

oh my god that is so hot

**the more u make me feel like i am the MOST worthless girl
in the universe**

the more i want to please you

the more you humiliate me

the wetter i get

please tell me more

im begging you

the more you treat me like shit the more i want to serve you

you have power over me

I know, you are my slave. I have to go . . .

just stay two more min

please

please

please

im beggin you

two min

PLEASE

PLEEEASE

can you talk on the phone? tired of typing

i cant talk on the phone my bf is here

but im so wet please if we talk for 2 min i know i'll cum

please

im begginng you

please stay and let me cum

or at least tease me some more

please i need you so bad

I know what you need

you need to craw lover here and take my cock out and put it in your mouth

mmm yes while you call me a fat fuck

and kick me in the ass

telling me its jiggling too much

I better be able to bounce a quarter off that ass

u inspect me regularly

and put me on a diet

tell me more about it please

and even if im in perfect shape what would you do if i wanted to eat a real dinner

like a full meal

If you are perfect and have served me well . . .

I will let you cook me a steak and then kneel beside me

for scraps that I feed you from my hand

mmmmmmmm yess tell me moreee

maybe you can lick the plate

that is amazing

for desert . . . I stick one grape up my ass and let you nibble it out

mmmm yes

shit i gtg bye

I passed through to the acupuncture room, where the hands and feet, shoes and hats of my fellow sufferers poked out from the shifting edges of the curtains. I drew my shade and disrobed before lying on the table. It was February now, and the calendar showed a new picture, which I had been eagerly awaiting, sick to death of that wee winter village. This one was a puzzler, though: a slope, several vertical slashes representing bamboo stalks, and a cluster of curvy strokes that meant nothing to me, until I saw the small slit eyes, the tiny teeth, the claws. Then, like one of those 3-D puzzles, the image snapped into shape: The black waves were tiger stripes. Though lacking an outline, the form was there of a feline hunter leaping in the air, like a ghost rippling through space. The title read: "White Tiger on Snow Mountain."

Just then a cell phone blasted a jangling pop tune, and the old lady lying beneath the calendar sat up and answered, yelling in Chinese with a nest of needles poking from her face and hands. I looked away.

Amy entered and greeted me with a slight chuckle that seemed to both express her general joy in life and hint that there was some joke I was missing. Maybe that very joke was in fact the key to her joy in life. Or maybe the joke was me, a goofy, pasty white guy lying in his undies, paying her to poke him with pins.

I turned facedown in the donut hole, and Amy pummeled my back, sore from typing, and worked my legs, stiff from running, and dug her fingers into my neck, hard as cardboard from the stress of supporting my mind. I fought to hold still while she battered me, gripping the edge of the table, flexing my toes, and grimacing horribly at the floor, in part so she wouldn't snort and call me sensitive, but also because each wrench or rip of pain was followed by a surge of pleasure, the one seeming to unlock the other, until the line between them blurred. Just as one imagines, or in my case recalled, ecstasy as a rising pleasure whose intensity approaches the unbearable, beauty as the door to terror, so too I now felt pain build into its own relief, blossoming, just when it seemed most fatal, into happiness.

I sighed as she pierced me and attached the electrodes.

"Too strong? Pain?"

"Good, good," I said. Lightning sparkled up and down my arms, twitching my nerves like prickly heat. My skull vibrated like a gong. I ground my teeth. But I had learned that the power came in waves, waves that swelled and towered, and just when you thought they were going to take you under, they broke. So I hung on.

"Good," I said, as the needle in my third eye danced, puckering my forehead skin. And oddly, while my left eye gazed calmly at the calendar and then went to sleep, my right eye, aimed at the blank wall, began to weep for nothing. I wasn't even sad.

. . .

I started chatting with a new girl, who went by blkrose. She was, her ad claimed, a "submissive masochist seeking dominant man." Sort of. It was all very complicated and vague: She had been a good kid and a virgin until a slightly older girl became her mistress at fifteen. However, a lot of what that mistress had her do was "service" men. At twenty-one her contract expired and she was "free." She was sometimes dominant with other women but never with men unless ordered to do so by a dominant woman or man. As of right now, she was her own mistress, dominating herself, which seemed not only less than satisfying to both parties but also extremely awkward and frankly exhausting.

So what do you do to yourself?

lots of stuff

tell me some details

lots . . . of . . . stuff

You dont want to say? I know you cant really humiliate yourself alone in your room . . . haha

i humiliate myself plenty, thanks, most of it not alone in my room

like how?

like lots of ways. why do you wanna know so bad?

no big reason . . . just bored. Nevermind.

what do you wanna know? i'll be an open book.

ok well, the last time you played alone . . . what did you do?

bondage, clamps, wax, plug, ball gag, collar, corset, ballet boots.

slapped myself, spent the night in my cage

what are ballet boots? Toe shoes?

they are fetish shoes. feet on point with a heel

how do you bind and gag yourself? your hands are still free . . .
I cant picture it.

i do really complex ties i couldn't begin to describe

but there wasn't alot of free movement sans immense pain
going on

and how does the humiliation and degradation come in if
there's no one to see?

among other things i moonlight as a stripper

you find that degrading?

Yes! dude go into a skeezy strip joint some time and watch how
girls get treated.

We get slimeballs. it's a rundown place in the middle of nowhere
new jersey like a 20 min drive in either direction to civilization.
i found it when i got lost in Newark trying to find the turnpike
way the fuck out past the airport.

fully nude or g-string?

nude

you make a lot or not cause its out in bumfuck?

I make alot more at my real job

What kind of work? Office you said, right?

I said I work in an office. non secretarial.

Still thats a lot of dough for filing or word processing no?

I don't file or word process unless you count memos or emails.
I'm not in a support position. that's why I specified non
secretarial.

then I guess everything is "office." Lawyer, real estate tycoon,
dentist . . . hey a masochist dentist! I bet there are a lot

lol I work for a private investment firm. I oversee the buying/
selling/leasing of real estate. I'm like all kinds of underqualified
for the job. I only got it because my father's very good friends
with one of the directors.

you sound smart to me . . . all that math and stuff . . . I can
barely add and subtract

not much math, really. that's for my pa

So you dress all conservative at work? Skirt suits?

in the office? casual. if I'm meeting a client it depends on what
they're like

do you wear a butt plug or clamps ever to work?

yes

nice . . . you feel like a whore talking to clients and your dad's
friend?

he just got me hired i don't interact with the directors

do you give lap dances at your strip club? hustle drinks?

yes

you give handjobs?

over the pants . . . yes, many. out, less.

you find that degrading huh . . . having to touch the
sleazeballs

i find the whole thing degrading.

the chumps come in their pants?

i take it you HAVE never been to a really skeezy club. this place is great for someone who really enjoys suffering

anyway i think its just a front for drug money anyway

a laundry

yes. everything about this place is weird. i feel like i'm on drugs when i'm there. a totally different universe from the one everyone else operates in. Even how i found it.

How?

dude. alright, i was out meeting a client at a site but i got lost, there's NOTHING on this road, just warehouses and like a closed gross clam restaurant. it's dark, i've been driving around in circles and finally i see the sign for this place in the distance, like revolving, so i pull up and there's this guy standing outside smoking so i get out of my car and ask the guy where the highway is he tells me where the highway is and i start to walk back to my car and just on impulse i ask if they're hiring

keep in mind i'm driving a 50k car and i'm wearing, like, very nice conservative clothes, expensive jewelry

haha

the look he gave me was priceless

so what happened they made you try out?

i had to give the 'management' a private show

you showed your pussy?

i took everything off except my shoes and my jewelry

they put a song on?

yes

what?

Cam'ron

?

Oh Boy a Cam'ron song it was popular a couple years ago

I dont even know what the fuck that is. Ha

lol

what do you dance to now? you pick yr songs?

i have my own cds, actually

whats on there?

black eyed peas a couple britney spears songs. Fergie

At least I know those names

Shakira. the ying yang twins

Shakira I heard of . . . but I dont know her song . . . ying yang I dont know, ha.

download dangerous by ying yang not shakira that's my current favorite

that and I got that boom boom which is britney and ying yang

it's an r*b song although it's got a "rock edge"

I like r&b but to me thats like james brown

Where's your straight job, in NY?

they're both in NJ but different planets

hey

you want in on my big secret?

sure

i'm planning my destruction.

?

of my life

how?

everything. that's what the strip club's for. a place to land.

so you dont mean suicide.

no i don't mean suicide i mean permanent suffering

I suffer every day baby

lol

so tell me about your plan for total suffering?

i'm going to be a 24/7 slave without an owner

whats that mean? like a wandering samurai? a free lance warrior?

???

Nevermind. Explain.

i'm gonna turn myself into a bad joke at work until i'm fired. im going to stop making payments on the car and the house. burn through my savings and then after that i'll be my own mistress. torturing myself and ordering myself around 24/7, cruel and vicious as i can be. i'm gonna live out every single fantasy i've ever had such as?

dude the shit i'll do to myself i don't even know where to start.

for a masochist i'm the most twisted sadistic person you'll ever meet

nice combo

what do yo imagine most?

sorry sailor bed time

On the way home from my run I swung north through the NYU campus, impulsively, randomly, perhaps stupidly seeking Lyla, the daddy's girl, who had told me she was prelaw. I scoped out the law school, sloshing through a lake of gray slush under the brick arches, wandering in and out of doors, smiling and nodding, impersonating a busy grad student on the move. Crisscrossing Washington Square, I saw a dozen Lylas: in their Uggs and sweats with "NYU" stamped across their rumps, in their Wellies and fur-trimmed parkas, their jeans and boots and clown-sized wool hats. For an instant, across the street or around the corner, each one became my nymph at play in the city. Each turned into a different human girl when I approached. Snow fell. I could feel the sweat chilling along my scalp and spine. An older black lady, in a heavy coat, said, "My, don't you look lovely!" And when I glanced in a shop glass I saw my hair was beaded with frozen crystals. I hurried home.

Still, searching for Lyla became another of my strange compulsions, my secret habitual rituals. Every time I cut through

Washington Square, I looked. Every time I saw a blond girl, I wondered. I worked the law school and library onto my routes to and from the river. Once, when she claimed to be surreptitiously typing to me and even touching herself under the table while studying in the student union, I entered "BRB," putting her on hold as it were, and dashed over, wandering the hall, scanning the faces. None seemed like hers. Was she lying? Had she moved? Was she even in New York, even a girl? Once we spoke on the phone and the voice matched, female, young, Long Island accent, but beyond that she could have been anyone. I didn't know her last name and doubted of course that Lyla was her first, but while the odds of finding her in this downtown jungle of young blond women seemed ridiculous, it seemed equally bizarre that this person I was in intimate communication with was hidden a few blocks away. But "looking" for her only made this paradox more palpable: Searching snowy lamplit streets for the tracks of a girl I'd never seen felt like walking into a fairy tale, while shut in my room, seeing her words appear and form lines across the white box, she felt, if not exactly real then present, and if not present then at least closer, as close as anyone else, right there, almost, breathing behind the bright glass.

IM with blkrose 1:32 AM

> hey
>
> **hey, whats up?**
>
> not much, down in georgia on business trip
>
> **hows it going? been slutting it up lately?**

lol do you know what i did last night? i almost didn't get out of it. you know those stupid hangers they have in hotel rooms?

the kind you can't steal?

Yeah i hung myself on one by my nipples, standing on my toes

nipple clamped or pierced?

clamped but i also bound myself i thought i'd be able to like lift myself up a little higher with my toes but it turned out i couldn't get high enough

see this is where you need pics to send me!

lol seriously though i was stuck for like 6 hours

hahaha . . . the real humiliation wouldve been if the maid came in and found you!

i was pretty close to yelling for help but i don't know if anyone would've heard me

haha . . . shit I have to crash . . . I have a busy day tomorrow

psh

psh?

mmhmm

pish pish? psshaw? is that some kind of georgia saying?

you should hang around for a few and help me use myself. i'm in a mood

where are you? What have you got?

my hotel room

clamps, cuffs, rope, plug, dildo, our respective imaginations, duct tape its a hotel or like a motel with seperate units and cars parked outside?

it's an actual fairly nice hotel but they're seperate units with cars outside

hmm . . . ok . . .

you should strip to only high heels, tie your knees together, stick the plug up your ass, write FUCK ME on your stomach, clamp your pussy lips open, stick the dildo in your mouth, tape the room key to your forehead, cuff your hands and then walk around the parking lot and back.

Hahaha that's awesome

haha . . . thought you might get a kick out of that

hmmm . . . ok i'll tell you how it goes next time we talk

I should get to see this!

hopefully i'l be lucky and no one will

see you, space cowboy

gnight

IM with blkrose 2:26 AM

so i licked every license plate in the parking lot last night.

hey . . . did you do what I said?

yeah. and licked every license plate in the parking lot to make sure i didn't rush it took me like an hour and a half to get back to my room

did anyone see?

not that I'm aware of although some cars def went by as i

walked by the road and the guy at the desk was giving me weird
looks this morning

**maybe they got some complaints about a weird whore
wandering around scaring folks**

lol i was a sight i'm sure.you don't wander with your legs bound in
heels.you teeter

**like being hobbled . . . i like that . . . too bad you didn't get
busted. Headlights. Cameras. Little kids jeering.**

lol that happened to me before, sort of. at the beach. i was
wearing a bikini that ties

and someone untied it both peices, not just my top

wow who did it?

i have no idea

where?

the. beach. i was in the water.

they took it with them?

or they got caught in a current or something. i definitely didn't
have them and i was trying to like

you had to walk out naked

signal my mom

yr mom

and she didn't see me

haha when was this? How old?

so yeah, i had to walk up the beach to the blanket

how old were you?

15

classic everyone was looking?

i was mortified. no, who'd look at a naked 15 year old?

::smirk::

but you like being mortified . . . you thought about it later
when you fingered yourself

yeah i did think about it later but at the time i was just
mortified.

i couldn't run bc i couldn't cover myself and we were waaaay the
fuck up the beach and i couldn't cover everything bc i only have
two arms

cover tits with one arm and yr pussy with the other . . . just
show yr asscrack running by

no i tried my tits kept coming out and then i wouldn't be thinking
so i'd like stop and throw my other hand up over my tit and then
i'd realize i was standing there naked also i fell

were people yelling or chasing you down the beach kids and
dogs barking

i got alot of catcalls. a couple old ladies asked me if i was ok. i
didn't stop to chat

they wouldve given you a towel

i wasn't really thinking about much but getting to MY towel

and then!

i had to help carry shit to the car and the towel kept falling
because i couldn't hold it and the other shit and my mom kept
yelling at me like i was doing it on purpose

haha . . . you probably were you little slut

no i really wasn't i had the towel tied at first and then i had
a cooler in one hand and chairs in the other hand and it came
untied and then i was just trying to juggle everything and keep
the towel up so i could get to my clothes in the car

shit its late . . . i'm going to run 8 miles tomorrow . . .

psh

it's 2

?

oh 2 o clock

you called it late.

yeah well I'm an old man

blah blah i can do about 5 before i collapse

I used to but when I quit smoking I doubled my running in like
2weeks

whatevs I met a slave out here.

oh yeah . . . slave for you? since when are you dom?

you remember when I was like "i'd make a cruel domme"?

I decided to find someone

a girl or a guy?

fem i don't like male slaves

well me neither, haha so who's your little slut?

she just graduated hs. she's never done anything before. at all.

i told her she'd be sorry she started with me lol

whats she look like?

she's alright looking. she could lose some weight. and will be.

so howd you meet?

personal ad. we emailed for a few and then she met me at the
hotels restaurant

you used her yet?

yes.

how?

right now she's bound to the table being my ashtray shaking
like a leaf. im about 90% sure she got kicked out of her house. i
wouldn't untie her when it was time to leave.

you smoke?

yup

and you're tipping ashes in her mouth?

and on her stomach

hows she bound?

on her back, arms and legs to the tables arms and legs

can you send me a picture?

i don't have digital camera with me although she was kind enough
to pick up a disposable camera to blackmail her with. it's going in
her mailbox tomorrow

she already wrote a letter

whats it say?

basically that she's a whore who exists only to serve her
mistress

the funny part is she only came her for a session

so she's going home with you?

Maybe. I might just leave her tied up here or drop her off naked downtown i'm undecided

what else did you do to her?

cut all her hair off

haha

haha it's not shaved it's just all kinds of fucked up some spots are a few inches some spots are less than an inch

anyway time for one of us to sleep and the other one to shake all night

I'm not shaking.

I mean her.

Oh right.

IM with blkrose 11:14 PM

Haha

hey . . .long time no chat . . . whats so funny

i left her there

who?oh the girl tied to the table back in georgia?

hung up in the closet

why?

just cause. i told her was if she could find me she could stay with me.

did she want to . . . or she just wanted a date that went tragically wrong? haha . . . for her i mean she wanted to.

jeeze clingy

well. we kind of got her kicked out of her house.

yeah well maybe she was looking for a way out of noweresville georgia too I guess

lol maybe. i wanna see if she can find me.

does she know your name or anything?

she knows my first name. the kind of car i drive. the state i'm from or at least the state i register my car in and she knows my cell #

still a big effort tho

if she's clever she knows the name of my company but i don't know if she's clever

haha

if this girl comes up here i'm gonna buy a new house

wow must be love. You're settling down.

Lol if i ever dont want her i can kick her out. i just want to build a special little hell

and did i tell you i'm limiting myself to slutty clothes? gave everything else to goodwill

what about work?

they can deal. i wanted to make myself a joke anyway, remember?

then you wont get that big new dungeon

why not?

I thought you said you'd get fired and lose yr house

hard to lose it if i'm selling it

?

i couldn't lose the house without blowing through my savings first

i'm a trust fund baby, remember?

no I didnt know . . . but it figures . . .

well. i kept a pair of sneakers, sweats and a hoodie for working out. besides that, everything's 5" heel or greater.skirts are all 12" or shorter. tshirts are all very thin. a couple little button up things. at home i'm in ballet boots, a corset, a posture collar, a ball gag and a butt plug.

so you said . . . but I havent seen the proof

lol when i decide i'm almost done there, like completely done i'm going to buy a pair of jeans to piss myself in at work. maybe at a meeting. maybe with a client.

go to bed now though

bc i am

right adios

In March I got sick. I thought I had a sinus infection, strep throat, bees building a hive in my nose. But Dr. Chang said it was allergies.

"Allergic to what?" I asked.

She shrugged existentially. "Some plant. A pollen. A mold. A dust." Post-smoking and with recharged chi, my body was changing. As Amy would say, I was sensitive. "You want to find out or just fix it?"

My eyes ran. My nostrils were sealed with cement. I could feel the pressure in my teeth and cheekbones. "Just fix it. Please." She smiled and spoke to Amy. Maybe she told her that I hadn't paid my bill because Amy spread me on my back, rolled up her sleeves, and got right to work pummeling my face. No needles yet. Just strong fingers molding my flesh like dough, digging in around the temples, jawbone, lips, as though sculpting me into some finer form. It hurt a lot. I lay still and tried not to whimper. I focused on the calendar, which depicted cranes descending on a wetland, perhaps in promise of spring, but shut my eyes when Amy lowered her trembling needle above them. She popped a couple in my cheeks, and a moment later, as if by magic, my sinuses cleared.

"Nose good?" she asked.

"Yes!" I demonstrated by drawing a huge gulp of sweet air through both nostrils, something I rarely did even on a good day. "You're a genius," I murmured like a battered spouse in love.

She chuckled — "OK, bye" — and bustled to the next prone body, its head murmuring in a hole.

IM with blkrose 6:09 PM

so she found me

who?

that sub girl

Aw, true love

lol

what sort of games have you two been up to?

I broke her. like, completely

how?

i kept her caged, no contact with anyone. sleep dep. i'd wake her
up pouring water on her or with a stun gun. i'd drag her out of
the cage and hold her head under water. not say anything to her.
then throw her back into the cage. just random and vicious.

we've done a bunch of shit

for real i don't know where to start. i told you i lost my job?

Nope how come?

i was dismissed for lewd conduct

specifically?

giving someone a blow job in the copier room

haha you got caught?

yeah someone walked in

who was the guy? Random or you'd been fucking him?

not quite either but sort of both he still works there. ironic, eh?

maybe he got a raise

lol

did yr dad find out?

my family's not talking to me

so.

probably.

so what have you been doing since then?

i get by.

stripping?

some. savings. sold my house, traded down my car.

where are you living?

jersey

apt? house?

i don't know if i'd call it a house really but yes

tent?

lol no it's just a peice of shit

why dont you put yr slave to work?

fuck that

why not? Get her stripping

the basis of her life is that she is worthless

did you ever take her and get her used?

yeah, we both have

oh yeah? What happened?

lol like it was once

i ache.

ache? what happened?

i slept on a concrete floor for 4 days among other things

where?

we volunteered to be frat sluts.

so how was that?

it's ongoing. i like it.

whats the deal? What happened? How many dudes?

the deal is when we're in the house or accompanying frat members outside the house we do as we're told. fuck. suck. clean. lick shit off the floor. anything they could think of. the nastiest food

how many guys?

about 16 in the house

so how many used you total?

so far . . . 16

how did you meet them?

i put out an ad. met a couple diff guys, talked about what we were both looking for, found the one that meshed

so they just line up and fuck you or what?

they use us when they want for whatever they want to use us for

what is the nastiest shit that happened

the food.

Haha how many times fucked in four days? how many blowjobs?

i got fucked at least twice by everybody in at least 2 holes

and if you're curious, my pussy and ass are both killing me, as is my throat and jaw and also my back and legs and feet and arms and everything else

so you got fucked like like 65 times, ha

raw in every hole

raw, like bareback?

no raw like i got rubbed raw

haha frat boys . . . thats a new low.

yo they're fucking mean i wish i had known

how so?

theyre just vicious

it doesnt sound like they did much but fuck you and feed you nasty food

yeah that and letting me get 4 hours sleep on cold concrete

making me lick their piss of the floor and get splinters in my tongue

taking us out and showing us to the other frats

they made you perform or what?

a bit yeah. saturday night i got to drink stale beer with piss and cigarette butts

haha how much?

more than i ever thought i would

did you chug it, frat style?

i had to it wouldnt've gone down otherwise. it would've been fine without the cigs

that's what gives it the kick

lol i can't speak unless spoken to i'm not supposed to meet their eyes. i'm on call.

what do you have to wear? are you leshed when your there? Tied up?

depends on what they feel like i've been leashed, i've been tied up, i've been chained to the floor, locked in a closet

and your slave too?

mhm

How will you top this? I can take you around to a home for retards and let them loose on you

Lol there's always something next. God i've turned myself into such a slut.

a life of this? can't wait for whatever turns out to be next

how old are you again?

25 i think i was 24 when we met.

ha . . . well you might be pretty worn out if you go 20 guys a week by the time yr my age

we all pay a price

also I met a sadist

oh yeah? As opposed to what? your usual gentle sweet hearts?

you're always so funny

its part of my charm. tell me about the sadist

what about?

Dunno who? What? where? how? the usual basics of good reporting . . . I wont bother asking why!

lol lots of pain

like what? tell me the harshest thing this new sadist did to you

making me kneel over lit candles

like bend so the flames touch your tits or belly?

i had to lower myself slowly to put them out

Wow that is harsh, ha ha, you were all blistered or what?

minor burns

hmmm . . . not that slowly then! what else did he do to you?

he has a metal whip

metal tips you mean? or like chain links?

it's like 4 lengths of stamped tin twined together

that must sting. howd you meet him? Whats he like?

through a friend. he's alright but that whip fucking hurts

no doubt

i had to count off 500 strikes restart when i lost count

thats a lot! across the back?

back, ass, thighs, stomach i was howling

im seeing him again actually

cant wait to see what he does next

as soon as I heal

lol

The birds returned to the park first. I saw their little prints, a fossil record on the old packed snow. I spotted them from afar, black marks on the flat sky above the river. Then, on a grassy bank under the arms of the West Side Highway, I saw a fat, sleek goose bobbing across the path, with a troop of goslings toddling after, piping puffs of fur on tiny sticks. A sign warned dog owners to keep their pets on-leash and away from the birds. But no one warned parents to leash their mutts, and the little screechers chased the goose family, some getting squawked at, some sliding down the bank and ending up green with goose shit as the flock escaped by water.

I saw sparrows pick and twitter at grass seed in the dirt. I saw a robin throbbing like a heart with a worm in its mouth. I heard crows bitching and saw them lined on the wires above me, flapping and falling and cawing in their ragged cloaks. Far off, I saw a hawk circle, sweeping in beautiful arcs, swimming on the wind currents, watching for food to make a move below.

In April, Lyla announced that after graduation her dad was sending her on a trip to Europe. Then she was starting law school out of town. She was full of pep, bubbling about Italy and Greece and the car she would get for school, but I couldn't help feeling disappointed since this meant we'd probably never meet. Then I remembered: That was the whole point. I had wanted fantasy, with no threat of real life, and I got it. Still, realizing that I was as imaginary to her as she had been to me hurt my feelings somehow: the sensitive, touchy pervert. The Melancholy Master, sad because she didn't really want me to abuse her after all. She was just toying with my rotten evil heart.

I knew this was ridiculous. I was a fool, even worse than I had imagined. Utter impudence! Wasn't there some potion the doc could brew that would break this fever? A needle Amy could drive into my heart to shock it sensible, or insensible, whichever?

I resolved to withdraw still further into my shell and for a few rainy days I didn't even run, staying inside to watch old movies, do my laundry, and even get some work done. In fact, I was meeting a twice-extended midnight deadline, sending the chino folks their copy, when I saw blkrose's name appear online, blinking and winking pinkly, like a pesky digital itch on my screen. I ignored it and emailed my work. Then I swallowed my Chinese herbs, which I usually forgot. I brushed and flossed thoroughly. When I came back, she was still there, dangling. I clicked.

Hey sup slut?

Who is this?

It's me. Your old pal. How's frat life?

blkrose is not available at the moment . . . she is indisposed ;)

Who is this?

I am the One controling her accounts now

She can't talk anyways, her hands are tied up, her tungue is clamped, she can only cry

That's all I want from her, her tears and sorrow

I AM REAPPER

You will reappear?

REAPER! FUCK OFF JEW SHE IS NOT PRETTY NO MORE

I signed off in a panic, as if he could reach right out and choke me with a black glove. Then, scowling at myself for being such a sissy, I signed back on, but by the time my computer reloaded the program, her little icon was gone. I watched part of a movie and fell asleep for a few hours, until I woke up to pee, of course. Passing the computer in the silent apartment, I found myself drawn to its dark face, empty as a mirror, or the polished black stones into which magicians once peered, breathing pipe smoke, believing they could see through time and space. Smoke. I realized it had been a whole day since I'd craved a cigarette. It was working. I brought my computer to life.

IM blkrose signed on 5:10 AM

> hello?
>
> hello?
>
> ru there?
>
> My Owner the Reaper gave me permission to write you since i told him you were my friend and the only person i will miss . . . i know u understand i found what i needed
>
> but please free my slave who is in the closet at my house! 42 Pinest
>
> 5:12 AM blkrose has gone offline
>
> 5:14 AM blkrose signed on
>
> I AM THE REAPER I GATHER PRECXIOUS TEARS
>
> HRVEST OF SORROW
>
> 5:15 AM blkrose has gone offline

I went back to bed but could not sleep. I rolled around and thought about cigarettes and sex and all the other things it hurt to want until I felt strangled in the sheets. I kicked free and got up to make coffee. Then I went back online, glancing quickly at the email from my client, requesting more rewrites and a conference call. (Did I think they should say "khakis" or "chinos"? Was khaki a color or a whole lifestyle? Did the word "chinos" sound more Hispanic or Chinese?) I answered quickly, then switched to Google Maps, but there were a great many Pine Streets in New Jersey, and restricting my search to those with houses numbered 42 didn't help much. Then I remembered her story about stumbling across the strip club: Way the fuck out on the turnpike, she'd said. Past the airport. It stunk.

I was pretty sure I knew where that was, having smelled it myself, the fumes from chemical plants mingled with rotting wetlands. I guessed that when she found the place, she'd been living in one of the richer suburban towns, heading out to some slum or crap strip mall her dad's friend built. So the club had to be along the roads that crossed the stink zone from the rich neighborhoods into Newark. Also, I guessed that if the club was "a place to land," then the cheap house she'd rented after getting fired would be nearby. I started searching for bars and strip joints, pinning them on the map, and found one, J R's Cafe Fantasy, that had a Pine Street 7.2 miles away.

Then I rented a car and, for the first time in a long while, I left the island. The rain lifted, at least to the rooftops, where it clung like a sequined shroud, and with the GPS calmly urging me on in a seductive female voice ("Go straight, go straight, two miles . . ."), I felt my way through the spiraling infrastructure of on-ramps and off-ramps, junctions and waste fields, with planes plowing the low clouds and poison leaching from the smokestacks, here a black scribble across woolen gray sky, there a sudden belch of fire, like a bubble rising from a petrochemical plant's silver tower. I followed the signs and signals, ignored the quietly insistent voice telling me to turn left into oncoming traffic, and found the right exit at last.

Weeds, corrugated warehouses rusting purple in the damp light, an auto body shop with a guy in a ball cap out front smoking in a swivel chair, a giant sleeping Costco, a mass graveyard of smashed cars stacked stories high, a cat squeezing under the fence. There were no addresses on the buildings or signs on the streets — this was nowhere, and the people who came already knew where they were headed — but I arrived eventually at an intersection where something called New Palermo Clam House and JR's Cafe Fantasy faced each other, lit by shafts of sun that had found a way through the murk. At first glance it was the thought of those clams that gave me chills. The strip club seemed merely sad, its garish sign rotating for no one atop a pole. There were no windows on the black building, only one shut door with a sign forbidding entrance to those under twenty-one. The potholes in the parking lot shone with silver rain.

I parked and went in. It was impossible to see anything in the dim, carpeted foyer except a vague figure behind a counter.

"Welcome to Junior's," said a kindly voice. An old man in a mustache and pink golf shirt materialized. "ID please."

I showed him my license, paid ten bucks, and went inside. It was a low-ceilinged, windowless space, like a basement with no upstairs. The walls were mostly mirrored, the ceiling was sparkled black stucco set with spotlights, and there was a long stage where a couple of girls listlessly turned on poles and a bar in the back where a muscley dude in a cutoff T-shirt lounged, absently fingering his phone. There were three other customers: Two were IT types in short sleeves and tan slacks (badly wrinkled, they should switch to my employer's chakhinos), one with an ID still on a lanyard around his neck, the other with his Bluetooth in. They sat stiffly at a table, ogling the girls. Huddled at the end of the bar was a lone gunman type, frazzled fringe of hair and army jacket, staring in fury through thick glasses. The girls looked tragic. One was crackhead thin with limp boobs and lanky red hair. The other was brown-skinned and composed of soft rolls, with deep creases between her thighs and ass, ass and belly, belly and upper belly, upper belly and breasts. Her purple nipples stood out like valves on overinflated tires. Neither of these women, moving like zombies at aerobics class, could possibly be blkrose.

I approached the bartender. "Excuse me," I shouted into his face. The music was very loud. Some kind of dance pop number.

"What do you need?" he screamed back.

"Actually I'm looking for a friend. I think she dances here sometimes. White girl. Dark hair. Big boobs." I felt like an idiot, realizing how little I really knew about my pal. Her background, education, religion, everything was a blank. We were inside out: We knew only the things other people hid from one another. We shared our shameful secret identities and turned around our masks. Then I had an idea: "She goes by Rose. She dances to Cameron Diaz and the Ying Yang Kids?"

"Rose Black?" he said.

"That's her. She around?"

"Nah, not in a while."

"Know how I can reach her? It's kind of important."

"Nah, sorry."

"You don't have her contact information on file?"

"Maybe if you ask the manager. What's her real name?"

"Sorry?"

"Her parents didn't call her Rose Black, dude. That's her stripper name. What's her real name?"

"Oh, right. I'm not sure."

"Some friend. You must be close."

"No, ha-ha, it's true, we're not. But there's been an emergency."

"Sorry, dude. No can do. So unless you want a drink, relax and enjoy the show."

"Listen, how about this?" I went on. "You call her. Don't give me the number. Just please call and see if she's OK."

He leaned in and poked my chest, as though pressing a mute button. "Dude, I told you. No. Can. Fucking. Do."

"But . . ." I felt a shooting pain in my shoulder. It was a set of large fingers in a Spock grip, pressing some nerve in my neck, almost as hard as Amy did. The fingers belonged to an even larger man in a black T-shirt, parachute pants, and ponytail. He smiled down at me.

"Problem here, sir?" he yelled into my ear.

"No," I gasped. "Everything's fine, thanks."

The bartender came around, grabbed my other, nonparalyzed arm, and began twisting it up around my spine. "You were just leaving, right?"

"Yes," I said. "But can I just see the manager on my way out?" I was now bent double, as though I were trying to touch my toes with my face. My limbs were numb.

"I'm the manager," Ponytail said. "Step into my office."

Holding both my arms, they ran me out the door and into a mud-filled pothole. The sunlight was dazzling. The clouds had cleared. A rainbow appeared over Newark.

"You know, sir," the manager said, looking down as I struggled to my knees, "what creeps like you don't get? These girls are just entertainers trying to make a living. They're not fantasy objects or property or something. They're real people with lives, thoughts, feelings of their own, just like you. Except, of course, way hotter."

I nodded. It was true.

"Cashmere in there has three kids to support," the bartender put in. "Dude, her husband lost a leg in Iraq. And Sparkle, the redhead? She's working her way through social work school. She's going to focus on homelessness."

"Go home," the manager suggested as they walked away. "Forget about the girl. And get a life."

42 Pine Street was being renovated. There was a dumpster in the driveway full of old furniture and a stack of paint cans and tarps on the porch. No one seemed to be around. I approached cautiously and peeked through the unshaded window. A ladder stood in the middle of the empty room. There seemed no point in knocking, but also no point in giving up. I pressed the doorbell. Nothing. I knocked. Silence again.

I was about to go when I heard it. Weeping. Whining. A high-pitched note that I felt, in my spine, could easily be a girl, bound and gagged, too weak to scream after hanging in a closet for days. I tried the door. It was unlocked.

"Hello?" I yelled. "Is anyone here?"

I stepped inside. "Hello? Sorry to intrude. Hello?" I stood still, thinking maybe I was wrong, and then it came again: low, high, tearful, a moan from behind a door down the hall. Fear raced through me, an irrational desire to forsake the mission, to get in the car and drive home and hide in my room. Instead I knocked.

"Are you in there? Do you need help?"

Now it came louder, a whimper, a yelp. I opened the door, leaping a foot high in terror as a fuzzy white kitten shot through my legs and disappeared into the house.

Holy shit. I caught my breath. The door led to a small, empty, harmless bedroom. The window was up, no doubt how the cat got in, though why it was too stupid to jump back out, who knows? As my heart rate slowed, shame replaced the fear. In a dusty wall mirror, I regarded my woeful visage in disgust. This whole thing had been a prank. Blkrose was a sad old man or three bored teenagers. Time to listen to the manager and go home. Then I noticed the closet, partially ajar, reflected in the mirror behind me. There was something in there. I opened it. Two mangled hangers hung from the pole. One cheap black stiletto shoe lay in the corner, heel snapped. And scratched into the wall paint, crooked as a child's scrawl: HELP ME.

I left. Sex slave or prankster or child playing hide and seek, there was nothing more I could do. The sun was fading. It was cold but it smelled like spring. There was still old snow caked in the corners, gathering soot in a delicate pattern like dark lace on white thighs, but the big thaw had begun. Two crows hunched on the house across the street, as if they had followed me from the river. One cawed, mockingly, and flapped his torn black wings.

In April the calendar changed to pandas romping and munching bamboo, and Dr. Chang decided I too was ready for the next phase. She suggested a special incense so rare and exotic as to be unknown even in Chinatown. Amy had to get it for me from Queens. You took a slice of the herbs, which came in a tube like sausage, and sandwiched it between a slice of some stuff called moxa, which burned slowly like punk, and one of ginger, then pinned it all together with a needle and set it on the lower belly, in a spot that I found by measuring from my navel. Then you lit up and relaxed.

The healing process was becoming increasingly abstract and unbelievable in direct proportion to its effectiveness: The herbal pills were just medicine after all, the needles poked something somehow, the cups at least touched my skin, but this? How would smoke passing near to my body help? Yet dismissing something that worked just because I didn't understand it seemed as foolish as believing in nonsense.

So I tried it at home, lying on the floor beside my bed, just to see the results. First, it stunk. Next, I felt a warm tingling sensation that I thought might be the magic working. Then the tingling became painful and the warmth became really quite hot, but I'd been told to let it burn out to ash, so I gritted my teeth. Finally, when I checked, there was a small blister on my skin.

Dr. Chang seemed bemused. It turned out I had shoved the pin too far, through the ginger, which was meant to protect my skin. As it was, the metal heated and scorched me.

"You burned yourself? Why?" she asked.

"I didn't realize it was burning me. I thought it was working."

She shook her head — clearly I was hopeless — and showed me again. But when I got home I found a note from the landlord demanding that I stop cooking whatever I was making in the house, so I decided to try the park. It was the first really fine day.

I found a shady sheltered spot near the river and lay down. I prepped the little sliced treats precisely as instructed, got my old cigarette lighter going, and set it on my belly like an especially delightful hors d'oeuvre. It was nice. In the trees above me, tiny sparrows chirped and chortled in a constant bubbling stream, flitting among young leaves and twinning branches, like a happy tapestry weaving itself in the sun. The perfume wafted over my face and blew away, leaving my skull pleasantly filled. I shut my eyes, and the little jewels beneath my lids began to float and weave, just like the tree above. I felt I too might drift away, like smoke, if weren't for the grass under my hands.

"Excuse me, sir."

Returning to earth, I opened an eye. "Huh?" A circle of police faces peered down at me. I sat up in panic, toppling my little tower. "What is it?"

"Sorry to disturb you, sir," one older cop said. He was a ruddy blond fellow. "What are you doing exactly?"

"It's this Chinese herb my doctor gave me. You can take it away if you want. It just cost like five dollars in Chinatown," I lied slightly to simplify things. "It's supposed to help me quit smoking. To be honest, I couldn't think of what law I'd be breaking."

"You're not actually," the cop agreed, then frowned sheepishly and leaned closer. "Some of the tourists complained." I looked around. I had failed to notice a large nearby structure, some kind of vague monument of wood and stone and steps. Tourists were snapping photos of each other with the Statue of Liberty in the background. Also, they had an excellent view of my belly. The cop shrugged. "They think you're smoking pot."

Ridiculous, I thought, if anything it looks like I'm smoking hash. Instead, I just said, "Oh, sorry. I'll stop."

"No, that's OK," he said. "You relax and enjoy your herbs. Have a good day, sir."

"Thanks, Officer!"

He leaned in deeper as his comrades wandered off. "Is it working?"

"Sorry?"

"With the smoking. Is it helping? I'd do anything to quit."

"I kind of think it is," I told him. "I know it sounds nutty. You should try it."

I was too self-conscious to light up again, so I stamped out my stuff and went home. It was just as well. There was a sudden snow flurry that afternoon, white confetti tumbling down like an overstuffed cloud had burst, freeing a flock of flowers. It didn't stick, though, melting on arrival like sugar on a tongue. That was the end of winter.

I finally met sweetsally, the diet-and-exercise slave. She came in on the train from Princeton, where she was in grad school, and where she lived with her fiancé, a wonderful guy who didn't understand her need to be treated like a dirty slut. I didn't understand it either, but I was willing to oblige. As soon as I opened the door, however, I knew I'd made a terrible mistake. Sweetsally was fat. Very fat. Obese.

I smiled stiffly while she told me that she had put on a few pounds and slipped up on her diet since the picture she'd sent. I laughed it off and mixed her a drink from the bottles of rum and Diet Coke she'd brought. She explained how she needed to be spanked, whipped, abused by older men, and how, since high school, she'd sought this out, cheating on her boyfriends compulsively. In fact, her fiancé texted while she sat on my couch explaining this. She casually texted back that she was in the library. He was in Philadelphia at a conference, doing postdoctoral work, and was going to be a shrink, of course. Then she stood and grabbed her overnight bag. Where should she change?

I fretted while she was in the bathroom, but escape was hopeless. I considered fleeing and leaving her in my own apartment, hiding around the corner till she left. I thought about calling 911 and reporting a fire or faking a heart attack. Honesty was out of the question. I was no postdoc in psychology, but I somehow grasped that whipping her enormous ass (it was like a love seat cushion) while calling her a fat pig was somehow OK but declining to whip it, however politely, was cruel.

She emerged in a bustier, garter belt, stockings, and heels, an outfit that had sounded exciting when she described it in writing but wasn't quite what I had envisioned. I now saw myself bouncing on her vast belly like a waterbed, catching my neck between her huge breasts, and slowly blacking out. Still I screwed my courage to the sticking place.

I did what I had promised. I did not disappoint. I spanked her huge ass red. I slapped the big tits till they flopped and flew. I fitted her with the collar and leash she'd brought and ordered her to beg and roll over. God help me, I stuck a carrot in her ass and a cucumber in her pussy, made her crawl till they fell out and then take a bite, to teach her proper nutrition. I tied her to the bed and pounded away until I was exhausted and came all over her tits. I toweled the sweat from my eyes, and as my vision cleared, I realized she was quietly weeping.

"What's wrong? What's wrong?" I blurted, jumping up. I tried to wipe her tears with my sweaty towel but just smeared makeup across her face. She shook her head and kept crying.

"I'm sorry, I'm sorry," I kept repeating as I untied her with trembling hands. She hustled into the bathroom, and I heard the shower start up.

I dressed quickly, pacing and wringing my hands as I rehearsed my apology. The shower stopped. The toilet flushed. She emerged, wrapped in a towel.

"How do you feel?" I asked, carefully, keeping my distance across the room.

"Great," she chirped. Her eyes sparkled. Her skin and hair shone clean. "What a release. How about you?"

"Me?" I asked. "Terrific! Thanks."

She had another rum and Coke and smoked a cigarette, which stunk like death, but which I was too polite to complain about polluting my room. She offered to stay and have another session, but I said she had overwhelmed me. I was spent. When was her train?

The second she left I showered and climbed into bed, curled on my side, gripping myself like I was someone else, another person whom I cared for and who desperately needed to be held.

Later she sent a thank-you email and tried to make more plans, but I demurred and finally she left me alone. In fact,

I was so upset that at first I didn't really take in the obvious: I had performed manfully. I was cured.

The weather got warmer, I went out more, and after a while I began talking to real-time, off-line girls again, in shops, in elevators, on the street. They gave me the brush-off, of course, but some did it nicely, with a smile or a bit of banter, and I realized they acknowledged me as human, and not some basement-dwelling monster. Then one girl didn't dismiss me, she sat on the stoop and talked and gave me her number, and soon we were spending our nights together and planning a trip for summer.

The bad news was I lost my insurance and couldn't keep seeing Dr. Chang. But she said it was OK, checking my pulses and peering at my tongue one last time. I was better, she said. I was free to go. She shook my hand, and Amy waved from where she stood, sleeves rolled as at a workbench, applying suction cups to an old lady's back. The calendar showed a hillside covered in cherry blossoms. It was May.

In spring the snow melted, and the tiger came down from the frozen mountain to hunt in the greener valley below, freed from the prison of winter to wander, alone, into the great cage beyond.

Literature I Gave You Everything and Now What Am I?

I

Writing is a desperate act. Like tucking a scribbled note into a bottle and tossing it onto the waves, it is a last resort, a hopeless gesture, a howl and a flare. Even worse if you write fiction — the urgent news about imaginary people. A story is savage, childish magic: toy dolls and invisible arrows. A vain stab at the hearts of strangers.

Little wonder then that so many writers, engaged in such a fatally frivolous pursuit, take up extreme or irrational strategies. Really, why not wear a lucky writing hat or eat a ritual tuna sandwich at the same time every day? They say Joseph Conrad had his wife lock him, stripped, in a room like a kicking junkie and withhold food and clothing till he produced something. Balzac supposedly kept himself in a constant state of sexual arousal, working up to the point of orgasm without crossing it while simultaneously consuming vast quantities of strong coffee, fueling fourteen-hour writing sessions that resulted in more than ninety novels and death at the age of fifty-one.

The Balzac approach has much to recommend it. It keeps

234

one sharp, honing the instincts and mobilizing those dark forces upon which all creation depends: hostility, anxiety, craven desire, yearning loneliness, self-loathing, and itchy discomfort. On the other hand, it can be highly counterproductive. You've unlocked the lowest self now, after all, and Cousin Id, released from the basement, does not want to sit still, thinking about verbs and perfect tenses.

Fledgling authors, sick with desire and unable to focus, might well be tempted to ease their vigilance and "unwind" before setting to work. Relax and release the tension is the idea here. But that is precisely the problem with this method: lack of tension. Now you want to nap, not write. The postorgasmic writer is content, and contented, peaceful souls do not produce great literature. The blank page is like an empty bed — those fields of crumpled white — where the desperate meet at midnight to make a final stand.

Hence the most important question facing any young writer may well be: How often should I masturbate and when? (It also brings up the second most important question: How much coffee should I drink? But here the answer is clear: As much as you can without dying.)

That's why I spend my days at the Hungarian Pastry Shop, which I chose precisely because it has no Internet service, endless bitter coffee, and a staff who frown on removing your pants. Sit there long enough and you pretty much have to write something, if only a love letter to the beautiful Albanian and Ethiopian waitresses who move among us lowly, seated folk like queens, dispensing éclairs and hot chocolates atremble with cream. The downside of café life, however, is the fact that they let in other people, practically anyone who can afford a cup of coffee. Now, I'm not saying all other people should be banned from cafés. That's unrealistic. And I really don't mind the readers, the thinkers, the studiers or the dreamers, as long as they stay away from my favorite spot in the back corner. With most other writers I maintain an uneasy truce. We nod in greeting, pass the sugar, chat when signaled with a smile that it's safe to approach, and most important of all, ignore one another completely when we show signs of writing, such as staring at an empty screen, practicing a spoon-twirling trick, or just pacing the sidewalk out front, muttering and shaking our fists, enraged.

It's the talkers I can't stand. For Christ's sake, talk at home, not in public. Though to be fair, it's not all talkers. Murmurers I can live with, holding hands under the table, sharing a guidebook. Foreigners in general are fine, the foreigner the better. The soothing babble of languages I don't understand is like Muzak to my ears. It's the loudmouths I want to murder, the pontificators and raconteurs, the sad seducers reheating the same stale anecdotes for a rotating cast of girls, the screechy girls screaming their secrets: These I long to silence forever with a butter knife through the heart. And the worst of all, my nemesis, my temptress and my torture, dark lady of this humble tale: a relentlessly loud talker who talked and talked incessantly — about writing.

Her name was Jasmine. And the reason she kept making so much noise about such an offensive topic was that she not only wrote but also led a whole gang of aspiring writers in some sort of self-help program. Right there. In my café.

. . .

Let me be clear: This was not, as you might reasonably imagine, a program to help them quit writing, like other afflicteds gathered to cease smoking or shopping. That would make sense. I might even ask for a brochure. No, The Writer's Way was designed to take perfectly ordinary citizens, normal, healthy people with no reason to write anything but emails and texts and checks, and turn them into writers, mostly memoirists of course, and spoken-word slammers, but also novelists, short story writers, even poets.

Nor was she actually teaching them anything, certainly not, for example, how to write a grammatically correct sentence or a clear paragraph. Those dreary tasks sound suspiciously like work. Instead, she loudly recommended everyone focus on "thinking like a writer." This consisted of "freeing up the creative flow" and "discovering our true voices," which were not, apparently, the false ones that had ordered their cappuccinos. She was, in essence, a paid muse, and her followers came to her not for knowledge but inspiration. They lacked purpose. This was their problem. They wanted to "be writers," yet they had nothing to write.

Nothing to write! Yet still wanting to be a writer! The mind boggled. It was like converting to Judaism, joining the marines, or leaving a rent-controlled apartment — I couldn't grasp why anyone except a maniac would do such a thing. Voluntarily. If you had a choice. If you could simply not. How wonderful to wake up in the morning with nothing at all to write. You'd be free. Free to go outside and enjoy the nice day, have brunch, like your ex-girlfriends all begged you to, brunch apparently being an extra sort of meal that regular people have, one so leisurely and abundant that it crosses in a wide and sunny bridge from morning to afternoon, touching two meals and relaxing between them, perhaps on the balcony of a nice but casual restaurant. You could walk dogs, install shelves, practice yoga, learn how to play tennis, and bake your own bread. You could have a life. A full, useful life. And offered a life, who would willingly choose to write a book instead? Because you can't have both, you know that. And you know too that a book, even a very good book, is in the end only a small thing, an odd, dubious, essentially useless thing. And your book isn't even very good now, is it?

2

It was not an attractive group. I don't mean they were ugly; on the whole they were average, with several members above (I am no doll myself, being just the sort of troll you imagine lurking in the rear of a café every day), but they didn't feel inviting, like a happy family around a turkey or friends jousting easily over drinks. You didn't want to wander over and sit down. You wanted to get under your table and hide, or accidentally bump an African princess passing by with a tray of scalding drinks.

I didn't, of course. I listened, while trying desperately not to. I wasn't giving up the cherished spot (corner table, decent light) that I shared, most days, with a diminutive, pale blond woman who sported thick glasses, chapped lips, noise-reducing earphones, and a huge plastic file box that she carried in a pack on her small bent shoulders like a snail. We never spoke, just nodding hello or scraping our chairs forward to let each other pass to the toilet, though I once caught her eyeing my own stack of color-coded and numbered index cards as I shuffled and dealt them, hoping to read the fortune of a doomed novel, and she looked impressed.

But unlike my table partner and I, who studiously ignored each other's work, the knights of the round table declaimed theirs aloud, then offered critiques consisting of exuberant praise, mainly in the form of "relating," which is to say finding a way to make talking about another's writing into yet another chance to talk about oneself. Circling clockwise they were: Clyde (Note: The group members' names have been made up because I don't know or care what they are), gay, sad, and largely deaf—I use these adjectives not to be flippant but because this was the topic of his memoir, *Silent Tears;* Maureen, a former temp on disability, whose 9/11 memoir, *Almost There,* purported to relate her struggle with PTSD after potentially being at work in lower Manhattan that day, except she was home with a strained coccyx, but the sections I heard were all from a long chapter devoted to some rich douchebag she slept with once who never called; Sonya, whose memoir, *My Name is Sonya,* described recovery from passive-aggression, sugar addiction, and S issues, which I eventually found out meant sex; and Pat (*Listening to My Self*) who struggled with an emotionally unsupportive work environment, motion sickness, and gluten abuse. Then there were the fiction writers: Frank, a retired accountant writing a series of mystery novels about a retired accountant who solved murders using his accounting know-how; Norman, a dental lab technician writing a series of mystery novels about a dental lab technician who solved crimes using dental lab techniques; and Mohammed, a Palestinian cabdriver working on a multigenerational epic about a Palestinian cabdriver who falls in love with a rich American-Israeli fare in his cab. (He was stuck on chapter two and considering working in a murder mystery angle.)

I knew all this not because I wanted to but because I had to. It was the opposite of eavesdropping: Eaves-talking? Eave-stalking! Forcing your neighbors to listen to you sound off about bullshit no one wanted to know.

And then there was Jasmine. I don't know what it was about her, but when she was in the room, I couldn't keep my eyes or ears away. I found her hypnotically, overwhelmingly, even char-ismatically annoying. She was long-lined and dark, with long black hair, long black nails, a tight black tank top and gypsy skirt, a clatter of bracelets on her thin, waving arms, and a hip-pie clutter of coins and rocks and the scarves of enemy na-tions warring about her shoulders. Dark, kooky, kohl-lined eyes blinked and gooed in a thin face with a hatchet nose, a high forehead, and red lips that smacked and chewed each word as it filled her mouth.

"Clyde," she'd murmur, "read the part where your step-uncle shamed you."

And poor Clyde would nod, red with fresh shame, take out his thatch of pages, and begin: "Meeeeeeee ... ooooncle ... wuzzzz ... nod ... reeely ... meeeee ... ooncle ... ," bleating and blurting in the off-key honks of the deaf. Why couldn't Clyde sign his text, like when I saw his brilliant hands flash and dance about a friend or boyfriend on the corner one evening, fingers sculpting air into elegant hieroglyphs? Why couldn't he have someone else read it for him? Or, since he lip-read their comments anyway, at least have them mouth-mime, sparing me the agony of hearing them?

Because Jasmine insisted. He had to "own" his text. It was

essential to his deeper process. So she tormented him, smiling blissfully while he struggled, baying and hooting: "I . . . haaad . . . toooo . . . sit . . . onn . . . heees . . . laaap."

Then came the insights. Maureen, patting his hand and enunciating into his face: "I loved it, Clyde. I really related to the uncle because it reminded me of the part in my memoir when, while I'm attending my cousin-in-law's bachelorette party in the Meatpacking District, a handsome dashing stranger sends a bottle of champagne to our table. He was so charming and proper, I agreed to visit his Tribeca loft to give him my opinion on some fabric swatches. He seemed like a true gentleman, and offered me use of his guest room since he didn't feel comfortable with me driving home. Next thing I knew I was swept away in passionate lovemaking. Only the next morning when I looked through his wallet and briefcase did I realize he was CEO of a major salted snack company that you would all recognize if I was legally permitted to say the name out loud. But the part your memoir reminds me of most is six months later when, after he hadn't returned any of my calls or emails, I decided to take the high road and showed up at his office with a picnic lunch. When security escorted me out, it retriggered my trauma, and I flashed back to that moment on 9-11, when I realized that, if my temp agency had booked me to work at a firm in the towers, I would be dead now."

"I agree with Maureen," Sonya put in, tonguing whipped cream from her lips. She'd traded her sex issues for food issues, and her belly, sprinkled with crumbs, no longer let her close enough to the table to properly assault her wedge of Black Forest cake. "The shame and the saltiness reminded me of the first time I fellated a stranger . . ."

At this point I fled, circling the block and gulping big portions of cold, clear New York air. On my return, I got more coffee and a napkin, which I began to ball up and stuff in my ears while Jasmine inspired the group, who sat with eyes closed, except for Clyde, of course, who eagerly watched his guru's lips. Sonya's softly chewed.

"Breathe out," Jasmine intoned. "Exhale fear, doubt, and judgment. Now breathe in creativity, abundance, and light. Invite your higher self to take you by the hand. Can you see it? Your spirit guide?" Everyone nodded. "Good. Name it."

"A golden angel . . ."

"Friendly elf . . ."

"A tiger who can speak and also turns invisible . . ."

"A dragon I can ride . . ."

"An Indian warrior, I mean native person . . ."

"A flock of magical wonderful birds . . ."

"Elloophann!"

"Excellent," Jasmine said. "To name the thing is to create it, to call it forth! This reactivates the primal power of words. God speaks and so let it be thus. We too partake of the divine when we create. But be careful of this power, friends. Use it wisely. As writers we truly change the world."

They all nodded, pleased yet sobered by their awesome gifts. She went on: "That's why each morning I dedicate my practice to the goddess within. I meditate, light incense, then write my morning thoughts in a special book with my favorite pen before breakfasting quite simply on green tea and fresh fruit.

"I never edit my work or block my flow. That is the ego speaking, the controlling male principle. I keep my sacred channel free and let my goddess flow directly through my opening, as though she were speaking, moving my lips while I merely transcribe. I am but the instrument. Hers is the beauty and wisdom. In the evening I chant my thanks and light a candle. I express any question or creative complexity I might have, I do not say 'problem' because there are no problems, only learning opportunities, and what you call block is merely a clog in your channel. Usually, I dream the answer. I meet my characters in the dream, and they tell me what they need from me. Sometimes I even wake up with the answers jotted in the notebook I keep by the bed. It's like having your book write itself!"

The group bubbled over at the idea of eliminating the tedious writing part of the writing process. I meanwhile had been working for six hours that day. I had written one sentence. Then I had crossed it out.

Why did everyone find my work so easy except me? I readily admitted I could never do theirs. No lawyer, baker, auto mechanic, or social worker would suggest I just show up at his job tomorrow and take over. Nevertheless, at weddings and bar mitzvahs, HR executives and architects forcibly pitched me their life stories, without ever once asking for my input on labor policy or building design. An oncologist cornered me at a Christmas party, demanding to know where writers gathered to "swap ideas." I longed to tell him I'd had some thoughts about cancer in the shower that morning. Could I swing by the spot where doctors hung out, the lab or medical conference, and make them all sit and listen? Instead, I told the truth: Writers don't hang out. We sit and grind our teeth, and the only ideas we swap are about how to obtain insurance. We came to this café because it had light and heat and a working toilet, things that might not be true at home. I myself was cat-sitting for another, more successful writer while she was out of town on a magazine assignment. My plans for next week were to move to a friend's couch. After that I could camp in the park and roast weenies over my unpublished drafts. But meanwhile, as long as I had two dollars, I had a home.

Then something beautiful happened. As I sealed my ears with wads of napkin I'd dipped in my water glass, my silent tablemate removed her headphones. Staring bashfully at the crumbs on the table, she whispered to me softly: "I hate her too."

It was a sweet moment. I wanted to take her hand under the table, but I was afraid to scare her off. It had taken months just to reach this stage. Really, we had Jasmine to thank. Nothing brings people together like hate.

Meanwhile, Jasmine's students all took their notebooks out and began scribbling away like five-year-olds, letting their consciousnesses stream. She peered about through slitted eyes. "Sorry, everyone, but I feel bad vibes from somewhere. Don't let them invade your sacred space."

At this we both giggled, the tablemate and I, like students caught whispering during quiet time. Jasmine shot us a dirty look and we faced away, trying to swallow our mirth, which as we all know just makes it mirthier. It was wonderful. We snorted and snarked, peeking at each other from behind fingers and bangs, falling in love right under Jasmine's glare. I hid my smiley face behind a newspaper. My girl tried to settle herself with a sip of tea, but she sprayed it all over her meticulous notes, which made me laugh even harder. Then she started coughing. Then choking. I looked over and her eyes bulged. Her face was red.

"Hey, are you OK?" I asked as she gurgled, trying to remember if I was supposed to pat her back or do a Heimlich. Then she fell out of her chair. Her teacup shattered on the floor. She curled on her side, shaking, as the waitress ran over. Someone yelled for 911. I helped turn her over. Blood streamed from her nose.

She managed to stand, clutching a bloody napkin to her face. I trailed uselessly as the waitress rushed her to the hospital down the street. Shaken up, I knelt to gather her papers, the careful microprint now stained with tea and blood, when I felt something like a cold finger tracing my name on the back of my neck. I shuddered and looked up. Jasmine was staring right at me, eyes aflame. She smiled.

3

When I got to the pastry shop the following afternoon, my tablemate had not returned. The waitress, bringing my coffee and cheese Danish, said she was fine, and I left it at that; I had an important sentence to tackle that day, and as soon as I read the newspaper and failed to complete the crossword, I was going to get right on it. I savaged my Danish. I got more coffee. I went to the bathroom, just in case, as if prepping for a long flight. I didn't want to be interrupted once I got going. I rolled my sleeves up. I decided I was chilly. I rolled them back down. I opened my document. I took a sip of coffee. I began to type:

When I first met Samantha Jane, she seemed like any
other ordinary veterinarian. What I didn't know, nor
did I then suspect

I did not then know, nor did I yet suspect
Knowing not nor having had suspeculated
Suspicious. Was I? No.
I should never then have thought
I shouldn'st. I shan't.
Oh, I shan't, shan't I?
You darens't!
FUCKFUCKFUCKFUCkFUCKFUCKFUCK

My fingers ground to a halt. I could not go on. It had been a rough day. I stood to stretch my back. Jasmine was in session across the room. Her acolytes were all writing with their eyes shut now, using their nondominant (submissive?) hands, to free up their chi or some such.

"Creativity is a gift from the universe. We are but humble servants." She was speaking with her own eyes closed, palms up, offering invisible fruits. "The story chooses the teller. Who knows why it comes or whence it goes? Why does the moon come and go? Both are mysteries. The readiness, that's all."

I know. Preposterous nonsense. But meanwhile there they were, churning the words out like mad organ virtuosos, hands aflap like frenzied doves. Their faces shone ecstatically. They heard the inner song. Their hearts were open fountains, gushing forth. My heart was a dry socket. A clogged drain. A corroded pipe packed with dust and hair and tears. I had not written a usable word that day, nor finished a sentence in weeks. It had been months since I filled a page without destroying it immediately. Honestly, when was the last time I had written anything worth reading? Years? This was my shameful dirty

secret: I had sacrificed everything to a calling that no longer returned my calls. I had refused to quit writing, but writing had
quit me: I was blocked.

As Jasmine's gang continued to cover page after page in
spastic scribbles — Who cared if it was illegible nonsense?
They were writing! They couldn't stop! — something in me
snapped — Fuck it! — and as if to degrade myself even further,
to grind myself under the boot heel of my mind, I shut my
eyes and typed blind, letting the spirit move my fingers across
the keys. I have to admit, it did sort of cheer me up. I smiled,
craning my head in a tribute to Ray Charles, and playing the
chords to "Hit the Road Jack." Then I opened one eye and saw
Jasmine. She was looking right at me. Our gazes crossed. She
smiled slyly. There was lipstick on her teeth. Scowling, I shut
my laptop and hurried out.

That night I had trouble sleeping. I ate a huge bowl of ice cream
(vanilla chocolate chip with salted peanuts on top), watched
TV till I was bleary (back and forth between *Law & Order: CI*
and *House* marathons), and finally, floating on my back, caught
a wave. But it was one of those sleeps so light they barely cover
the darkness. You hear every car cough and drunken mumble,
each toilet flush and stairwell sigh: our neighbors, the ghosts of
New York. Finally, around four, I got up and decided to e-pay
some bills. I opened my laptop and there it was, my blinded
brick of text.

It was, as expected, mostly mush, a sloppy sauce of gibberish
spiked with the occasional morsel of digestible language, but
not much nutrition:

qerewlrweljdlksjldjlkclkxnckxcnxbitchkd;kd;skd;asj\kds
a;kd;sakd;afkdskdfskj;skdnvnoa"34pjfj;4kjijpndlvkdanfs
sssss;kkf;sdfk;sdfk;ss;k;sdkf;skf;sendorphinskeiodijvnrg
derds

You get the idea. It ran on like that for a couple of pages. Certainly no novels were getting written like this. Still, with the
buzzing hyperawareness of insomnia, I noticed the random
words thrown up like driftwood here and there and collected
them in a pile, ignoring as unsporting one-letter words like "I"
and "a." Here they are, transcribed:

bitch endorphins lose it ernie vacuum engine moon evening biotech estuary lard incontinence extra vein early
morning evil battles endeavor lilies include each vaca-
tion earwax motion escape

I did make out one semicoherent sentence, if you can call it a
sentence, scattered words staggering like lost drunks through a
cloud of typographical burps and stutters:

But every leaf is ever veering every moment evermore.

I poked around for other nuggets, without luck, but I did notice a pattern. The words began with many of the same letters,
repeating like a rhythm that coursed through the run of type:
"BELIEVEMEBELIEVEMEBELIEVEMEBELIEVEME."
I mumbled them over, barefoot at my desk, as if sounding out a
strange tongue: "Believe me."

4

By morning the small chill of my discovery had faded. OK, so my left (right?) brain had spit up an alphabetic pattern, or code, or whatever, and beamed it across the dark hemispheres to my right (left?). So what? Hardly a breakthrough. It wasn't even a decent avant-garde poem.

I shrugged it off and trudged to the pastry shop, as if turning up for my shift. I would have been better off donning an apron and grabbing a tray — at least there'd be tips — but I wasn't pretty and I couldn't steam milk. As it was, I was more like a file clerk, a minor functionary in a distant suboffice of the vast and crumbling English department, itself teetering on collapse.

My table was taken so I sat nearby, glaring, until the inter-lopers left. Then I opened my laptop and got ready to get down to business. But my courage faltered before the blank screen, and I found myself dawdling again over the accidental sentence I'd discovered the night before.

"But every leaf is ever veering every moment evermore." Really it was not too bad. It had a certain ring to it. I got more coffee and read it over a few more times. I jotted it down acrostic-wise on my scratch pad — "B.E.L.I.E.V.E.M.E." — and doodled it out in script. Believe me. Believe me. Believe me.

"Do you?"

The voice was a whisper, soft and female, tickling my left ear. I jumped as if stung, but there was no one. I was tucked up alone in my corner. Could it be a next-door neighbor? A mouse in the wall? Then I noticed Jasmine. She had joined her tribe while my back was turned and was busy exhorting them to release the inner beast. While they growled and whimpered around her, her eyes found mine, and though her lips kept forming the words of her monologue, her voice, in my ear, whispered only to me, asking: "Do you? Do you believe me now?" And at least for a moment, I did.

That moment passed. Our eyes unlocked, the sound came back, and her normal, grating tone returned. "You are a vibrant animal in touch with the inner fire of creativity. The flame of your goddess burns bright!" I shook it off. The clamor of the café closed back over me, and I told myself, Don't worry. You are merely hallucinating. Get back to work. Enough nonsense. I had a real sentence about an imaginary veterinarian to finish.

I was determined to get some sleep that night, but when I got home, or rather got back to my friend the art critic's home, I discovered that Princess had wet the bed. Princess, I hasten to add, was the cat I was sitting, tiny and imperious, narrow as my wrist and lithe as a ballerina in a black leotard, with fuzzy white legwarmers on her agile limbs. Her tail, long as her whole body, was like a separate being, swanning and aloof.

I locked the little bitch in the kitchen and stripped the bed. I scrubbed the mattress furiously with some fabric cleanser I found under the sink. As a result, the bed was now even wetter, plus it smelled like toxic chemicals mixed with urine. I brought a fresh blanket to the couch and lit the scented candles on the coffee table. Then I got out a legal pad and my last good pen, figuring my own writing would put me to sleep faster than any book.

But as soon as I lay down, my thoughts circled back to that minor attack of schizophrenia in the café. Is this what happens when you spend your life thinking about make-believe characters — they start to talk? I knew madness was an occupational hazard, but I couldn't afford insanity; I wasn't covered. Still, crazy as it sounds, I'd often daydreamed about being crazy. There was a residential facility up the street from the pastry shop, and some of the patients stopped in. They were genial folk, though they had to be reminded not to smoke indoors and sometimes blocked the aisles with their rolling suitcases full of paper. The only people who carry around more paper than writers are nutjobs.

I'd actually found myself envying their lot: a clean room on a high floor that the government paid for and someone else cleaned. Warm, starchy meals and basic cable. In-house shrinks and free dental. Why couldn't I just retire from the life of the mind? If writing is not a regular career, then it begs the question: How do you quit?

I focused on the candle flames, dancing in space like three sprites, Sage, Vanilla, and Original, who smelled like shampoo. Perhaps an answer would come, or at least a decent night's sleep. I breathed. I shut my eyes. My brain slowly loosened its grip.

And then, in the darkness, I heard it. A broken, keening cry. I shivered as the shadows of the flames leapt across the walls — but this was no muse or madness come to call. Princess was whining in the kitchen. I even saw a paw slide under the door, like a tiny burglar's white-gloved hand. Knowing I'd never get to sleep this way, I released her, though I made a point of snubbing her too. Of course she turned loving and contrite. She leapt up and purred in a circle, settling on the legal pad I held in my lap, and with that soft bundle warming my belly, I passed out at last.

I don't know if it was the cat or the candles, the crippling couch or the urine in the air, but I had a wild dream. I was flying a pyramid through outer space, wearing one of those retro spacesuits, a tight white one-piece with a fishbowl helmet, sitting at a vast control panel covered in dials and plugs and a row of piano keys that blinked rainbow colors when pressed. I don't really know how to play music, and if I did, it would not be electronic dance music, but that is what emerged from my fingers as I steered my craft across the galaxies. Then I crashed. Crawling through my wrecked ship, dragging myself toward a crack of light, I realized: This was the womb, the air hose attached to my belly was an umbilical cord, and I was about to be born. My journey had been through the darkness of time, not space!

I forced my helmet through the opening, and it broke like an eggshell as I wriggled from my suit. I was naked now, creeping through the warm mud of some stinky, primeval jungle. Somehow the disco still throbbed all around, a house beat with a heavy bottom. I hate that kind of music. Birds and lizards screeched along, thunder boomed, and forks of lightning set the trees aflame. Finally I arrived at a temple, thirsty, hungry, exhausted. A maze of steps, it rose from the muck to the sun. And there, at the top, stood Jasmine, resplendent in a leopard bikini, glitter all over her body, necklaces now chunked with diamonds, emeralds, and rubies. A peacock-feather headdress shimmered like a waterfall to her ass. Her right hand wielded a golden sword, while her left lofted a tray crowded with bright pastries and steaming drinks. She sang out to the roaring music, as though we were in a nightclub, "Who ordered the decaf mocha latte?"

. . .

I woke with a start. The candles were out, and I sat up, knocking Princess to the floor with my crumpled pad as I fumbled for the lamp. She screeched and gave me a dirty look, then turned her tail. The downstairs neighbors were either having a party or sex, or both, as the disco pumping through the floor was accompanied by the occasional cry or grunt. Then I noticed the pad. I didn't recall writing a word before I fell asleep, but there, in my very own lefty handwriting, it said:

Jasmine
601 W 113 St. 5A
Come now

5

I went. What else could I do? I didn't understand what was happening to me, but whether I was insane, or psychic, or still dreaming, or caught in a magic spell, what was the difference? I still saw only two options: go to her or go to the hospital. I might as well try her first. Worst case, she called the cops and I got a free ride to the nuthouse. Either way, I was done for. Why turn back now?

Three a.m., and frigid, Broadway was at peace. The reds, greens, and yellows unraveled in strings as cabs swam by in silence. Here and there, a drunk wove home, a homeless shadow huddled. Above the violet streetlights and the mountains of brick and stone, heaven's cold vault darkly gleamed, a blackness pierced with pure light from the future or the past. I walked fast, in a rush to do this before I lost my nerve or the cold air woke me.

I found her building. I buzzed, rehearsing my apologetic speech — how could I even explain who I was, the surly guy from the coffee shop? She didn't know my name! — but she buzzed me in immediately, without a word, as if she had been waiting, and indeed, when the elevator arrived at her floor, she was there, in her robe, at her door.

"I ... I ... I ..." I didn't know what to say. But she put a finger to her lips, beckoning me on, and as I entered her tiny lamp-lit studio, she stepped back and let her robe fall open. Just as in my dream, her sleep-scented pajamas were covered in a leopard print, and on her narrow, unmade bed, the sheets and pillowcases bore a peacock-feather design, a hundred aquamarine eyes regarding me serenely.

"I'm sorry," I choked and began to sob. "I'm so sorry." But she pressed a finger to my lips and led me to the bed, where she held me tight until I fell into a sweet and dreamless sleep.

When I woke up late the next morning, my mind was clear, and even through closed eyes, I perceived the truth: I'd been a fool. There was never any struggle, any failure, except in my own head. What did it matter if I was published or not, read or not? Perhaps my whole purpose was to write one sentence that one soul would find tomorrow or a thousand years from now, long after the name on my gravestone was worn smooth. What did it matter if I filled a dozen pages today or wrote a single word? Doing, to the best of one's ability, what one has been sent here to do: This is the definition of happiness.

Happily, my eyes opened, and I realized Jasmine was gone. On her pillow was an open notebook, with the place held by a pen. "Good morning," the note said, "I have done my morning writing and gone to meet a client. Green tea and fruit in the kitchen. Help yourself! XO —J"

Humming, I went to the closet of a kitchen. I'm not really a breakfast person, and I prefer coffee to tea, but it was all about being open to change, so I put the kettle on and took a bite of apple. Not bad! Then, while I waited for the water to boil, I got curious. I had never yet read her own writing. Was it wrong to peek at her notebook? I'd never been a snoop, but surely she didn't mind if she'd left it open with a note to me inside.

I turned back to her entry for that day. It was numbers, just numbers, arranged in rows across the ruled lines, adorned with exclamations points and question marks, splattered with green tea. Confused, I flipped back, page after page. One was all *X*s, one just the words "Sample Sale" over and over. Most were gibberish, random letters, making less sense even than my blind typing, not words at all but pure nonsense neatly printed in block capitals, running on, line after line. Yet it was all carefully and cleanly inscribed. It had to have taken many hours, even days of concentration. Panic seized me as I gazed around the room. It had been dim in there the night before, and it was only now, in the light of day, that I realized: The whole wall was covered in shelves, and each shelf was packed tight with these notebooks. Swallowing hard, I pulled one out and opened it. Both sides of every page were filled with nothing but the alphabet, endlessly repeated. I grabbed another: unpronounceable nonsense in dialogue form, like a play performed by babies for a hundred pages. The next was more numbers, one long algebraic equation, adding up to total madness. I opened book after book, growing more and more frightened as the avalanche of letters and numbers and meaningless words overwhelmed me.

Three filing cabinets crowded the wall between the kitchen and the door. I slid one open and found more chaos: cleanly typed manuscripts covered in perfect rows of pointless babble, files stuffed with papers filled with cursive Zs and Ys, notepads covered in zeros. I began a frantic search, tearing the place apart, like a thief or a cop with a search warrant, seeking a clue, a key. But there was nothing. All I found was a wilderness of writing, typed, scribbled, or painstakingly printed in her clear, pretty hand.

The kettle began to whistle, but I didn't answer. I got to my knees. I shut my eyes. I prayed. GOD PLEASE JUST LET ME DO ONE BEAUTIFUL THING BEFORE I DIE.

Perhaps one night I might save a child from a burning house. If not, then let it be a story or a poem. Not this one. It's too late for this one now, I know. But maybe the next one, tomorrow.

Then I turned the stove off and I left, locking the door behind me. And I never went back to that fucking pastry shop again.

The Amateur

It was in Paris, in the Luxembourg Gardens, talking with two friends in the outdoor café, that I met the strange American. I didn't notice him at first — though perhaps I registered him subconsciously, a figure on the periphery, the older fellow in a flat cap and belted tweed jacket, a sun-browned face, sketch pad tilted against his metal table, thick fingers black with charcoal — but as it turned out, he had been listening to us the whole time.

We were discussing love and art and such things, or they were, my friends, for my benefit. Usually we discussed hair, movies, and what to eat next. My friend X was an important scarf designer; a new job had brought her to Paris. Y was on a fellowship in Berlin and had come to eat and drink for the weekend. I was the poor relation, staying with X, dining with Y, all as a distraction from my latest broken heart: As if I could leave that busted pump behind in New York, drop it off at the junkyard, and fly away with only a receipt in my wallet. Instead I carried it in my breast pocket like a pet, feeding it crumbs of cheese and chocolate, trying to soothe it, drug it, drown it in beauty really — the blazing purplepinks of the flower beds, the patterned carpet of steps and splitting paths, statues of pale gods and angels seeming to vibrate in the warm air, the silver trees, the rain-colored roof slates and stone streets, the smooth-shouldered girls in printed frocks and office boys in white shirts and striped ties in the windows across from my room who laughed and waved when I realized they could see me, hair damp from the shower, emerging from the bathroom in my towel.

We finished our coffees. My friends had to go. They were busy. I was not. So I stayed, ordering a mint soda — they taste like toothpaste, but I love them — and wrestled with desire, toying with the single Gauloise I'd bummed from my friend: I hadn't smoked in a year. That was when the older fellow appeared, or made himself known, I should say.

"Excuse me." He spoke American English, with a profound New York accent. "Do you need a light?"

"Sure," I answered. "Thanks." Fate had decided. He leaned over and flicked a gold lighter. I breathed in deep. It tasted like car exhaust.

"Sorry, but I couldn't help overhearing your conversation. That's how it is over here. Your ear just zooms in on English."

"Sure," I repeated, not sure what he was getting at. I wanted to stub out the cigarette, my body had turned on them, like an old love grown toxic, but I felt awkward, so I held it in the air away from me, bent-elbowed, like an existentialist. "Have you been here long?"

"Two years," he said, "but I can't pick up the lingo. It's fucking hard, French. But whatever. It sounds fucking beautiful. I just walk around and listen. But when I heard youse guys, I had to say hi. It's my only chance to talk to somebody."

It was indeed a pleasure to hear him speak. His accent was true old-school New York, as pure in its way as any Parisian's precious French, and more rare. So when he asked, "Mind if I join yuh?" I said "Sure" and dropped my cigarette in the raked sand. He shut his sketch pad, scooted his metal tube chair around, and waved for the waiter.

"Cawfee." The waiter nodded and asked if he wanted milk. "Nah," he told me. "How do you say 'espresso'?"

"*Deux expressos, s'il vous-plaît,*" I told the waiter, who nodded and was gone. He shrugged and lit a Marlboro. "I can't get used to French cigarettes," he said. "Like smoking dried dog shit. My name's Eddie by the way." He reached to shake, then realized his hands were filthy with charcoal and tried wiping them on a napkin. I noted his sapphire pinkie ring, his chunky gold bracelet, his fat, expensive watch. "Fuck it," he concluded. "Whaddaya gunna do?"

The coffees came. He sipped his, sat back, breathed in smoke, and squinted his black eyes over the gamboling kids, the trees in spare rows, the flowers drenched in yellow and blue, the perfectly clouded sky. "Life," he declared, "is fookin bootiful." Then he shrugged: "But I godda tellya, kid. It can't always be peaches and herbs. What? Whaddaya laughing at? Fine. Gahead. What do I care? Go fuck yerself. I enjoy life every day. Having a coffee, drawing, goofing on people. Painting in the morning. Walking to the park in the afternoon. Stopping at the bakery for one of those apple things. Fuck it. I didn't come to Paris to be a miserable cocksucker."

Since that seemed to be precisely why I did come to Paris, I couldn't help but ask, "Why did you come? You said you paint? Are you an artist?"

"Nah," he said. "Just an amateur."

Two years prior, back in New Jersey, he'd actually been in art school, though not as an aspiring professional, rather as a dabbling auditor, living in a quiet suburban town that hosted a small liberal arts college. Before that, he'd never even finished high school. What was the point? But now he was retired, he had this nice house, free time, plenty of dough in the bank. So what the fuck, why not? He signed up for a class, Beginner's Drawing. Then Painting I. He was the oldest student, by double at least. Triple maybe. And he was the worst. By like a hundred. A hundred what? Times, years, percents.

The thing of it was not just that he sucked, though. After all, you didn't expect to hit a homer the first day of Little League or cook like one of these French guys as soon as you crack an egg. Even Picasso had to start somewhere, right? The thing of it was that he sucked and never got any better. He just kept on sucking, harder and harder.

And when he said "suck," he meant serious ass. He tried to draw a woman and it looked like a house. He tried to draw a man and it looked like a really old house. He tried to draw a house and it looked like a fucked-up cow. As for painting, he just made a total mess. Everything ended up brown. He couldn't even stay in the lines. His swing was so off that he accidently splattered other people's canvases or dripped on the teacher's shoes when he was trying to help Eddie follow the smooth curve of an apple with his wrist loose, feeling the ripeness of the fruit. The other students were confused or amused. The teacher was in despair. But Eddie didn't give a fuck. He was happy. He loved to paint.

In particular he loved painting Doreen. She was his muse, like. A performance art major minoring in philosophy, she worked as a nude model to make extra money and also, one sensed, because she just liked getting naked in front of people. In fact, he suspected that her performance art consisted mainly of nude posing as well, plus talking or playing a CD of some weird music. In class, however, she simply held whatever position the teacher, a homo but a great drawer, put her in, then pulled on a kimono to smoke and send text messages during breaks.

Doreen was his type: big boobs with a narrow waist and thin arms, high hips, round ass, narrow ankles, pretty feet. The kind where her breasts (naturals, he specified) stuck out like a balcony over her rib cage. Long black hair she tied up but that hung halfway down her back when she let it. Pale skin, blue eyes, pink nipples. Kind of a weird nose that was tricky to draw. Shaved her puss, which he was not a fan of, he was old-school '70s and liked hair on his pie, but that's what they were all into these days, and anyway it was good for the sake of art. You could really see what was going on there. Not that it mattered, the way Eddie painted it. His painting of her lying back with spread thighs looked like a house, a little fairy house with a narrow pink door, nestled between two bony white mountains.

Eddie liked painting Doreen so much, he even paid her to model for him privately. There was nothing shady about it. He was too old for her and this wasn't a strip club and anyway she only liked girls and had a girlfriend. She made all this quite clear when he broached the subject after class one day while she was smoking in her kimono. He understood completely, he just needed more time to finish the oil portrait he was doing of her — head and supine torso this time, another pink-doored house with blue windows above two pink-tipped snow-white hills and hair like black chimney smoke streaming into a canvas sky. He offered her double what the school paid and she said yes.

It was nice. He turned the living/dining room into a studio, since he ate in the kitchen anyhow and hung out and watched TV in the family room. He'd paint her, or when she wasn't there he'd paint Felix, his cat, and when Felix wasn't available he'd paint flowers he bought from the deli or a still life of apples or just the tree outside his window. He'd play music while he worked, classic rock or regular classical, or Ella and Frank, or else he let Doreen put on some of that hippity-hop indie pop or whatever they listened to now. He'd cook sausage and peppers or lasagna. And they'd talk. She'd talk mostly, he had to concentrate, painting is fucking hard, and anyway he preferred to listen to her, stretched out there naked, petting Felix or eating his still life apples and talking about herself, maybe with the gas fire on to keep her and Felix warm while the cold rain tore leaves from the tree outside. He didn't step out of line. He didn't lay a finger on her. Did he want to? Sure. But it wasn't the main thing. He was older, mellower, he guessed. Once in a while he'd drive over to the massage place and let one of those Romanian girls take care of him, but even then he took it easy. Bad heart. Really the thing was just to be there, painting and hanging out with someone young and alive and beautiful. Was he in love with her? Maybe a little, but so what? Fuck it.

Of course, he understood perfectly well that she didn't love him back, and only came around for the money. He knew it was just a hustle when she gave him a whole song and dance about tuition or rent. He knew the money went to the junkie girlfriend, some tall harsh blond Viking-looking chick with dope fiend written all over her. He knew the deal. He wasn't a chump. Or, OK, he was. But he knew it. He just didn't care. He'd rather be a happy chump. Isn't that what love is, after all? What else do you call a grown man writing poems and trying to dance like a fruit, or a dignified old gent on his knees playing dolls with his granddaughter, or a woman carrying a dog in a designer bag even though the fucking mutt has four good legs, except someone who has found a good reason to act like a fool? Everyone is a chump, sooner or later.

So when she didn't show one day, he didn't think too much of it. His expectations were low. He just painted Felix, who also got bored with posing and wandered off, tail in the air. Girls and cats are like that. But when she didn't come to class, and then didn't answer his calls, he got concerned. Then a few nights later, she showed up at the door.

She said she'd come to say good-bye, but he knew it was to hit him up for more money. She said she was taking time off from school because of family stuff, but when he saw her girlfriend waiting in the car, engine running, smoking like a furnace and checking the rearview every ten seconds, he knew it was trouble, drugs most likely. So he gave her a good-luck gift of a hundred bucks traveling money and told her to keep in touch. Then he said good-bye. Sad, sure. But what are you going to do? He figured that was that and let it go. He made some dinner for Felix and himself and worked on his last unfinished portrait of her and then he went to bed.

She was back around five in the morning, with her finger on the buzzer, jolting him out of bed. She was distraught, tear-streaked already, and as soon as he opened the door she started again. He sat her on the couch and asked what the fuck had happened — a car crash, a fight? Her lip was cut and swollen, bruises on her arms, and he figured the junkie girlfriend had been smacking her around again.

Did she hit you, that bitch? She shook her head. No. It wasn't Judith. She's in trouble. My God. She got hysterical again, hyperventilating and hiccupping, so that he thought he might have to slap her himself. Instead he hugged her, like he would a little kid, while she drooled and snotted all over his robe, but it got slightly awkward because she wasn't a kid, she was a fully grown woman, and he could feel her heavy boobs against him and had to be careful when he patted her back not to go too low and touch her ass. Finally she seemed to taper off and he got her some water and Kleenex. She blew her complex nose with a wet honk.

So tell me now, calmly. What happened? Did Judith get busted? That's probably for the best in the long run. They'll detox her, maybe send her to rehab. She shook her head vehemently, and for a second he was afraid the waterworks would start up again but she just blew another lusty blast into a tissue and told him, No, Eddie. That isn't it. It's worse. They took her. Like for ransom. That's why I need your help.

What? Who? What the fuck are you talking about? Finally she calmed down enough to explain. The girlfriend, Judith, had been trying to deal a little bit, coke mostly and some dope, nickel-and-dime stuff, and in classic junkie fuckup style had ended up partying it all away and now didn't have the money to make restitution. What a surprise. That's why they had decided to split, like Bonnie and Clyde. But of course, the supplier had seen that coming. He'd grabbed them, roughed them up, and was holding Judith while Doreen raised the cash. That was why she'd come to him. For a loan. Five grand.

Loans, however, get repaid. Giving money to Doreen was like flushing it down a toilet. Still when she started blubbering again, he caved. But he insisted on bringing the money along himself. He was a sucker, OK, guilty as charged, but not the kind of sucker who trusts a junkie with money or a girl in love with making rational choices, which is pretty much like a junkie anyway, just strung out on hormones and shit. So he told her he'd get the cash as soon as the bank opened in the morning and they'd drive over together, and she had no choice so she agreed.

He got her settled in the guest room he'd never used, with fresh towels and a new toothbrush. Then he went back into his room and lay down, but he couldn't sleep. He kept turning the whole thing over in his head. Then just before dawn, there was a soft scratching at his door. He thought it was the cat. The door swung back, slowly. Eddie? It was her, in the T-shirt he'd lent her to sleep in. Are you awake? she whispered. Yeah, he said, what is it, can't you sleep? She slipped into the blue morning light that swelled from behind the shade and dripped across the window ledge, brushing her dimly. He could barely make her form out in the gloom, his eyes straining for a pale smudge, a curve. She materialized only faintly, then flickered out, like a ghost that had failed to appear. She said, I just thought. I don't know. I feel like I owe you so much. I mean. If you want to. She took off the shirt.

He had seen her naked body many times before of course. This was different. Then he'd pored over every inch. Now he couldn't even see her, but he could touch her if he chose. She was right there. He imagined painting her like this. He'd do her in faded pinks and grays with the door frame white and the dark behind it white and deeper gray. He'd been taught that the goal was to paint just what you saw, not what you imagined you were seeing, but that would mean not painting her at all and instead portraying the air around her, the empty space between their bodies, between her skin and his eyes. But of course it wasn't really empty. It was full of molecules and shit. Of darkness, breath, wind and heat, the scent of her body, of the cat, and of his old man's body too, no doubt. Making all that appear out of nothing. Loading all that onto a brush. That was the trick.

That's OK, he said. Don't worry about it. It's late. Go back to sleep, he told her, like an idiot, and she picked up the T-shirt and went.

In the morning, Doreen was too upset to eat breakfast, but he fed the cat, had his usual oatmeal and fruit, and then they drove to his storage off Route 4. What is this, she asked him as he parked beside the orange warehouse, you said we were going to the bank? This is my bank, he told her, wait here, and found the small space he rented, like a walk-in closet, with cartons of old papers and knickknacks filling the shelves on one side and a workbench on the other. He lifted a small locker onto the bench and brushed away the dust before opening the padlock. Inside were bundles of cash, various documents. He peeled off the five grand, then locked everything back up. All set, he said, climbing back into the car. She was smoking furiously and biting her nails at the same time. He lowered the windows and patted her knee. Don't worry, he said.

The dealer's place was a few towns away, in a working-class neighborhood that had slowly decompressed into ghetto while the surrounding suburbs bloated into affluence. This was where the maids and gardeners of the wealthy lived, where their kids went to buy their drugs. It had been a decade or more since he'd even taken this exit or passed through these streets, Pine, Ash, Maple, and barely a green leaf in sight. He had to let Doreen direct him. It all looked the same to Eddie. The house itself was nondescript — weathered siding, dying yard — but the tightly sealed blank windows and the high-end cars in the drive were tip-offs, a sleek Lexus and a fat Denali, both with shining rims. Eddie gave Doreen's shoulder a reassuring squeeze before he pressed the buzzer, which didn't work. So he knocked.

A classic dirtbag opened the door, long greasy hair, vaginal whiskers around cracked wet lips, crazy eyes, tattoos up his arms like the funny papers, wifebeater and baggy jeans. Doreen said, Hi, Dirk, this is Eddie. We brought the money, let us in. And Dirk scowled but stepped aside, ostentatiously stroking the butt of the .45 automatic he had stuck down his pants. Eddie kept his hands loose in plain sight. A guido with stiff hair and tan muscles in a pink polo shirt and expensive jeans, and another dirtbag, covered in ink and piercings like a sideshow freak, were hanging out on the crappy modular couch inside. There was a coffee table heaped with bottles, ashtrays, pizza cartons. A big-screen TV ran ads on the wall. Doreen made the introductions. Eddie, this is Richie and Renard. Renard the freak nodded amiably — Sup? — but the guido leapt to his feet. What the fuck? Who's this? I said come alone. Obviously tweaked and waving a Glock. Doreen trembled and moaned. No, Richie, don't. Eddie stepped in front of her, hands out, palms up. Hey, hey, take it easy. For Christ's sake put the gun down.

Who the fuck are you? Richie asked, still menacing but a little less sure, gun hand drooping.

Eddie said, I'm the only person she knows with five grand.

Richie considered this, then tucked the gun in the back of his jeans and quickly checked his hair in the mirror across the room. OK. Whatever. Just hand over the cash.

It's in the car, Eddie told him. I want to see the girl first. Go get her, we all walk out, put them in the car and get the dough. Then we drive away. Nice and simple.

What the fuck are you trying to pull? Richie's back was up again. The dirtbags stirred and growled.

Hey, Eddie said. For all I know Doreen was setting me up. This chick is always hitting me up for money. Doreen scowled, fear shifting to annoyance. Hey, that's not fair, she said, though her hands remained in the air, as if she'd forgotten them there. Look, Eddie went on. You can see I'm not packing. He turned around, like he was modeling his button-up shirt and slacks. You got three armed guys. I got bupkis. What am I gonna do? Pull a Starsky and Hutch?

Who? Richie looked confused now.

It's a movie, Doreen explained. Starsky and Hutch.

Then who's Bupkis? Dirk asked suspiciously.

OK, OK, whatever, Richie said. Retard, go get the bitch. Dirk, keep an eye on them. Renard rose slowly, with the unsteady bearing of someone who's been on the couch a long time. Dirk massaged his gun handle. Richie, pleased now that he'd reassumed command, found a box of Marlboros on the table and lit up. Can I get one of those? Eddie asked him. Sure, he said, why not? I'll toss it in no charge. Everyone laughed and the tension eased. Doreen took one too. Dirk fished a Newport from his shirt pocket. They all smoked.

Then Renard yelled from the bedroom. Holy shit, what the fuck! Richie dashed into the next room with Dirk sprinting behind him. Eddie told Doreen to wait here, but she followed right on his heels. Judith had been bound to the bed hand and foot with duct tape. Her eyes bulged and foam drooled down her chin where the tape had been pulled from her mouth. Eddie understood immediately what had happened but said nothing, a hand on Doreen's arm. Renard was shaking her shoulder. Wake up, bitch! She passed out or something. Richie leaned over her, setting his gun on the night table. Judith! He yelled into her empty face as if down a well. Wake up! Time to go! With a cry, Doreen shook Eddie off and rushed the bed, pushing Richie aside. She lifted Judith, hugging her close and rocking her like a baby as more liquid leaked from her slack mouth. Doreen wailed. Dirk wailed too. Oh fuck, she pulled a fucking Hendrix.

Enraged, Doreen turned on Richie. You killed her, you fucking killed her! I didn't, he yelled. It was Retard. He shouted at Renard, You're the one who fucking taped her. But you told me to, he whined, pulling his hair. Doreen began punching and slapping Richie, and he just cowered, beside himself with panic. She cried and moaned. Call an ambulance. Eddie, please.

Those words seemed to electrify Richie, who was starting to realize how much trouble he was in. Come on, let's get out of here, Eddie whispered, reaching for Doreen, but it was too late.

Richie screamed, Nobody's going nowhere, hold them, Dirk, and as Dirk stepped forward, reaching for his gun, Eddie saw where this was going. Three dead bodies to dispose of, however awkward, was better than two live witnesses. So instead of backing away from Dirk he moved toward him, closing the gap between their bodies fast and putting Dirk between himself and the others. With his left hand he grabbed Dirk's right wrist and twisted hard, grinding the small bones painfully. Dirk winced and hesitated, just a moment but enough. With his right hand Eddie pulled the .45 from Dirk's waistband and, pushing the barrel into his abdomen, shot him twice through the gut.

The force of the blast propelled Dirk back and Eddie shoved him into Renard, who was fumbling for his own gun. Richie and Doreen were both still turning to look, stunned by the deafening bangs, barely grasping what had just happened. Dirk fell dying against Renard, and Eddie leaned over and carefully shot Renard through the thigh. He whimpered as the hole in his jeans filled with blood and crumpled to the floor with Dirk's corpse slumped over him. Eddie wheeled left, bouncing Doreen roughly onto the bed, and made for Richie, who was just that moment remembering that his gun was on the night table, a foot or two away. Eddie pressed the hot barrel of the pistol to Richie's forehead. Don't move, he said. Nobody fucking move.

Richie froze with his mouth open, like a fish, blinking spasmodically as his eyes tried to focus on the gun between them. Eddie spoke calmly. Tell Renard not to fucking move or I will blow your brains out. Richie said, Don't fucking move, Retard. I can't fucking move, Renard whined from the floor. He shot me.

Doreen, Eddie said. She was in shock and looked up vaguely at her name. Doreen, he yelled. She looked at him, seeming to wake up. I need you to go get Renard's gun, honey. Can you do that? She nodded and went, grimacing when she saw the wound and briefly shutting her eyes when she had to roll Dirk's torn corpse to the side, but she held up the 9. Good, Eddie said, now get Richie's gun from the table there. Careful, walk around us slow. She did that too, and showed him the guns in each hand. Don't kill us please, Renard said from the floor, then added, I need a doctor.

Look, Richie said, voice low, quavering, afraid to even work his mouth with the gun pressed to his skull. We can work this out. My uncle can take care of everything. He's a boss. He can help us.

What's his name this uncle? Eddie asked.

Richie. I mean his name is Richie like mine. I mean I'm named after him.

Calm down, Eddie said. What is his last name?

Richie, Richard Caprissi.

Richie Caprice? Eddie asked, unable to contain a small grin. Copcar Richie is your uncle?

Yeah, that's him, you know him?

Since before you were born. He must be very proud. You're Vanessa's kid?

No, my mom is Uncle Richie's cousin. I just call him that. I'm from Lodi.

OK, let's call him, Eddie said, and see if he can help. I'm going to put the gun down and you're going to help Renard into the living room. OK? Richie nodded. OK, let's go, Eddie said, nice and easy. Doreen, you bring the guns.

So they moved like Eddie said, with Richie helping Renard hop to the couch. Eddie had Doreen put the guns in a plastic takeout bag she found lying on the floor, then bind Renard's wound with a towel. Eddie told him he would be OK. The bullet had passed cleanly through the meat of the thigh without hitting any arteries. If you were going to die you'd have done it by now, Eddie said, and let him snort a line of dope off the coffee table, which seemed to quiet him down. He sniffled, nibbling at some pills that were mixed in with potato chip crumbs and ashes. Meanwhile Richie called the uncle and bashfully explained the problem. You could hear the old man cursing through the phone. Richie winced. Let me talk to him, Eddie said, and took the phone. Hey, Richie, he said, guess who? It's Eddie. Eddie-Eddie, from the old days. Yeah, Deadly Eddly. He laughed. Fuck, I haven't heard that one in ages. He listened awhile, chuckling occasionally, and Richie and Renard whispered on the couch. Doreen observed all this with a sharpened glance. She seemed to be slowly returning to herself, as if her startled spirit were slipping gingerly back into her body. All right, Eddie was saying into the phone. No problem. He handed it back to Richie. Here. Yes, sir, Richie said into the phone, sitting up straighter on the couch. I understand. He hung up.

First of all, Richie said to Eddie. He started to stand, but sat back as he remembered the gun. First of all, sir, let me apologize. I sincerely meant no disrespect. I didn't realize who you were.

Eddie shrugged. Now you know. He switched gun hands to shake.

Yes, sir. My uncle talked about you all the time.

And let me add, sir, that it is a real honor to meet you, Renard piped in, pain dissolving in the flow of opiates. His pupils were black pinpricks. Sorry about before.

That's OK, kid. Eddie smiled. No hard feelings.

Damn, Renard whooped. Crazy Eddie! Tell us about the time you capped those three motherfuckers inside that taxi.

No, Richie said. The best is the one about the fork, remember, Retard?

Oh shit, right, Renard said. That is fucking awesome.

My uncle told me about that when I bought myself an Uzi, Richie explained. Sweet little piece, right, but Uncle Richie says, Remember, it's not the biggest gun or the biggest guy who wins. It's the ruthlest motherfucker in the room. Then he says, My old buddy Deadly, he's only five-five — no offence. Eddie shrugged. Deadly is in a diner. Sitting in a booth unarmed eating breakfast. About to sip your coffee when that big mook Jimmy Sausage pulls a fucking Magnum.

I love this part, Renard blurted. Go on. Sorry to interrupt.

So what do you do? Richie asked. Cool as fuck, you splash hot coffee right in his eyes, then grab your fork and stab him in the fucking jugular. Bam, he bled right the fuck out in the booth.

Fuck yeah, Renard yelled, clearly high now.

And then, Richie went on, talking to Renard as if Eddie wasn't there. Then he pays the bill, leaves an extra big tip for the waitress, and says, Sorry for the mess. The two boys laughed appreciatively.

So cool, Renard said.

That's when my uncle said, I'd bet on Eddie with a fork over an Uzi or Magnum any day. You know why?

Eddie shook his head, smiling ruefully. Richie shouted, and Renard joined in happily, Because he's not afraid to fucking stick it in!

They laughed and high-fived, and Eddie snapped his fingers to get their attention. OK, party's over. Let's get moving. You boys can finish sucking my dick in the car. So they took off, Eddie driving, and headed over to this bakery in Ridgefield to see the uncle. Doreen still looked like she was sleepwalking. Had it really been only the afternoon before, still less than twenty-four hours ago, that she and Judith were running away to Florida together? Had it only been a day before that she was in class, a somewhat normal girl leading her somewhat normal life? If everything that had happened in that house had completely turned her mind inside out, the bakery was the final twist. Up front it was an old-style Italian bakery with a ticket machine for taking numbers, a canister of string hanging from the ceiling, and a heavyset mustachioed lady in a hairnet behind a glass case full of wetly gleaming cannolis and éclairs and pignolis and anisette toast with stacks of yellow and brown semolina bread on the shelf behind. In the back was a room with tables and chairs and a waiter in a uniform, but there were no regular customers, no kids or families eating cake, just men sitting around, smoking, drinking espressos, playing cards, who all acted like Eddie was their long-lost hero as soon as they walked in. A skinny older guy in a tracksuit and blue-tinted shades, a fat guy so huge Doreen thought the little metal café chair was going to get wedged in his ass crack when he got up, a couple of younger muscled-up dudes in tight Armani tops, expensive jeans, tattoos, and hair like carved lacquered wood — they all hopped right up to hug Eddie and slap him on the back, as if him shooting two dudes and spanking the nephew was the greatest thing ever. They called him Crazy Eddie, Deadly, Dudley Do-Wrong. They all rushed to light his cigarette and then parted as an even older guy, slope-shouldered with sky-blue golf pants across his round belly and a polo shirt and glasses on a chain, gray hair sprouting like crabgrass from ears and nose and eyebrows but gone from his smooth, shining brown skull, shuffled forward and gave Eddie a big hug and a kiss on the cheek. Eddie introduced her.

Richie, this is Doreen. How do you do, sweetheart, it's a pleasure, the old guy said, squeezing her hand in both of his. I'm so sorry for all the trouble. Have a seat, please. Richie, he told his nephew, take your friend and go with Dominic to the doctor. At this the fat guy got out his keys, and Little Richie and Renard hustled off with more handshakes and apologies for Eddie. Then Richie, meaning old Uncle Richie, ordered cappuccino and cheesecake and some assorted cookies for Doreen before he took Eddie by the hand and led him back into the kitchen. There was a guy in there in an apron mopping up, but he left when he saw them lean on the counter. Richie sighed dramatically and shook his head. What a fucking mess. Family, huh? A real pain in the ass that kid.

Hey, Eddie said. It is what it is. What are you gonna do?

I appreciate that, Eddie. As far as I'm concerned, we can call it even. Hey, who knows? Maybe you scared some sense into the kid. Believe me, it ain't like in our day. Bunch of amateurs now. I could use you. If you ever need a job.

Get the fuck out of here. I'm retired. I just know the girl from around, you know.

Yeah, speaking of. That could be a bit of a problem, Eddie.

Kind of a loose end. I mean you're a rock, we all know that. Richie's dumb, but he's family and the kid they call Retard is his boy. But this girl. Her we don't know.

Yeah, Eddie said. I see your point.

You get me?

Yeah.

I can have one of the guys handle it.

No thanks, Richie. I don't mind.

OK, good. Richie patted his hand. However you're more comfortable. Not around here, though. I can't even fart anymore without the Feds sniffing my shorts. Believe me you're lucky to be out of it. Remember the house in the woods?

The place we went fishing that time?

No, my wife's mother's old place, remember?

On the hill? With the gate?

Yeah. Nanette kept putting off dealing with it, then she got sick and you know. It's for sale but we can use it. Bring her there tonight.

OK, Richie. And listen, I was sorry to hear about Nanette. She was a great lady.

Yeah, thanks, Richie said. We got the flowers. It meant a lot to me. And you're sure you're OK doing this? I understand if you feel sentimental about it, like if you were banging her or whatever.

No, I don't mind.

Richie smiled, showing brown and gold teeth and only the fake ones weirdly white. Same old Eddie. At least some things never change.

Eddie fetched Doreen and they got back in his Caddy. She'd been hungrier than she realized and had devoured all the cake and half the cookies, which she had to admit were all amazingly good, and now as soon as they pulled away she asked him in a rush everything she couldn't before. Eddie had to wait for her to exhaust herself before he could even answer. Yes, he knew these people. Yes, he used to work with them. Yes, the stories they told were true, more or less. Even the one about the fork? Pretty much. But they left out the part about how I ended up in prison for ten years. For that? For a bunch of things. Anyway, that's where I got into painting.

Eddie dropped her at his place. He told her to relax, take a bath, have some wine and try to calm down but not to leave. Everything was going to be fine. She just had to wait till he got back and then they'd talk. She was too freaked to go anywhere anyway. She took a hot shower and then sat on the couch where she used to pose, wrapped in a towel, petting Felix the cat and letting her hair dry.

Eddie drove back to his storage space. He opened the locker again, and this time he lifted the tray full of cash and got out the two pistols he had hidden underneath, one a long-barreled Magnum revolver, one a small semiautomatic that was easier to conceal. He cleaned and loaded both by the single lightbulb in the storage space and put them back in the locker. He took out some of the cash, then relocked the box and put it in his trunk. He threw everything else in the storage in the trash, including the key. Then he drove home. When he came in with the locker, Doreen was still on the couch, although the cat had gotten bored and wandered off to crunch some kibble. Eddie told her to go get dressed, and while she was upstairs he called a cab and stuffed the cash from his pocket into a manila envelope. When she got back he sat her on the couch.

Here, he said, handing her the fattened envelope. That is thirty grand.

What? she asked him. What for? She opened the envelope and started ruffling the bills in amazement.

Listen to me. He pushed the envelope closed. There's a cab coming to take you to the airport. You don't go home. You don't call anyone. Give me your phone. She reluctantly took it from her purse. He smashed it under his shoe.

What the fuck, Eddie, you're scaring me.

Good. You should be scared because this is scary shit. You understand me? This is real life. School is over. You don't go home. You don't pack anything. You have plenty there to buy what you need. You pick a place you always wanted to go. But not somewhere you know anybody. Someplace new. You buy a ticket tonight and you go. And you don't come back. Ever. If you come back, if you stop, if you turn around, you're dead. Do you understand me, Doreen?

The whole time he spoke she had been crying, tears streaming over her cheeks while she shook her head and her fingers gripped at his. He squeezed back now and asked her again, Do you understand me, and she nodded, yes, she did. But what about you?

I'll be fine, he said. I just have to tie up a few loose ends. The cab honked outside. Eddie could see it in the driveway. I mean, she said, can't you come with me? Can't we meet up?

Sure, Eddie said. Later. He scribbled a few words on her envelope. When you get settled in your new spot, you wait a month and then write me at this email. No names no details no location, just hi, how are you. I'll know it's you. If I answer, then it's safe for us to meet. If I don't, wait a month and try again. OK? She nodded. The cab honked again. OK, he said. Let's go. He walked her to the door and she hugged him tight. Thank you, she whispered in his ear. That's OK, kid, he told her. Forget it. She shook her head and said, No, never, and kissed his cheek, but he knew that she was very young and that eventually she would.

When the cab left, Eddie realized how hungry he was and how tired. He cooked a steak that was in the fridge. He ate most of it, gave the rest to Felix, and then went upstairs and took a nap with a loaded gun on the mattress beside him. When he woke up, he got scissors and needle and thread. Sitting at the table in his boxers, glasses on his nose, he slit open the lining of his suitcase and layered in all his cash. He stitched it up and packed his essentials, some clothes, his reflux meds, heart pills, an extra pair of reading glasses. He took a shower, shaved, and got dressed. He went downstairs, it was starting to be sundown now, and gathered up all his work, his paintings, drawings, sketch pads, and burned them in the barbeque out back. He had to hack up the bigger paintings with a hatchet, and some of the oil paint smoked thickly, but the wind was high and he didn't think the neighbors would complain. He put the suitcase in his backseat. He attached a silencer to the automatic and put the guns in the two side pockets of his jacket. He locked up, carrying Felix under his arm. Outside, he took his collar off and set him free. Then he drove out to the country, to Richie's wife's mother's old house.

It was dark now, and when he pulled up to the gate, he flashed his lights once and honked lightly. One of the Armani-wearing muscle dudes from the bakery pulled back the rusty gate and waved him into the drive. The Denali and Lexus were both there too.

Hey, Eddie, Armani said. Where's the girl?

In the trunk. I'll pop it, but you do the lifting. My back is killing me. I'm way too old for this bullshit.

Armani laughed. No problem. Eddie closed his door and followed the kid around to the back, then pressed the button on the key chain. The trunk unlatched and Eddie stepped behind him, pulling out the silenced gun as the kid lifted the lid. Huh, he said curiously, as Eddie shot him in the base of the skull. He fell like a log and Eddie rolled him down the slope of the driveway into the shrubs. The door to the house opened, and the skinny guy in the tracksuit stepped out, peering into the darkness. Eddie hid the gun behind his back and walked quickly toward him.

Hey, Jerry.

Hey, Eddie, where's Paul?

Getting the girl out of the trunk. You better give him a hand. Kid's making a mess of it. Richie inside?

Yeah, watching the game, Jerry said. Hey, Paulie, he yelled. For Christ's sake, how hard can it be? As he walked past, Eddie raised the gun and shot him twice between the shoulder blades, then leaned over and shot him again in the head. The muzzle flash lit the shadows and the woods around him absorbed the pop of the silencer. The air smelled damp. Maybe up here it had rained.

Eddie put the gun back in his side pocket and headed into the house, latching the front door quietly behind him. It was a small old house, mostly dark, with light and noise coming from the den in back where the game was on. But he heard movement in the kitchen and ducked in there first. Fat Dominic was at the counter, making himself a sandwich from a platter of cold cuts and fresh rolls and rye bread. Hey, Eddie, he said. You hungry?

No thanks, Dom. I just ate a rib eye but I could use a beer if you don't mind.

You got it. Dom headed to the fridge and bent over with a sigh to withdraw a beer. Eddie shot him several times through the liver, more or less, it was hard to tell on a body that big. Dominic fell into the fridge and Eddie leaned in and put the last round in his head. The game was on loud, but the crash of Dom's bulk was loud too, so Eddie quickly pulled the Magnum and headed for the den. Little Richie appeared in the door. Eddie? He put a hand up, instinctively, to fend off the huge barrel, and the blast tore most of his fingers away before exploding his head like an egg. The sound was shattering and Eddie's ears rang as he rushed on through the door. Uncle Richie was in the recliner. Renard and the other Armani dude were on the couch. Eddie shot Renard first, in the gut. He looked sad and genuinely surprised, as if he'd thought they were pals. By then Armani Two had his gun out from his ankle holster, but he shot too quickly and the bullet went wide, punching a hole in the paneling. Eddie shot him through the heart. Then he turned the gun on Richie, who hadn't moved. His hands were on the arms of the chair. One held a beer, the other the remote. He muted the game.

Just like I always told them, he said, looking over the corpses. Most ruthless fucker in the room.

Eddie sighed. Sorry about this, Richie. It didn't seem right, about the girl. You know how it is.

Richie nodded. Sure. I understand, Eddie. Do what you got to do. He waved the remote. The whole world's shit anyway. He sat back in the recliner and shut his eyes, as if for a shave, and Eddie shot him in the head. With the gun barrel, he pressed the remote, turning off the TV, then checked the other rooms. Everything was quiet. No sirens or cars approaching. He left, shutting the door and killing the lights behind him and wiping down the knob. He pulled out carefully, avoiding the bodies, and relocked the gates. He drove a ways, then pulled off on a small bridge and wiped down both guns before tossing them in the murky water and heading onto the Turnpike. He took an exit into a nameless industrial patch, parking in a crowded lot behind a strip club. He grabbed his suitcase, leaving his keys in the door, and used the pay phone in the clam house across the way to call a cab to the airport, where he got on the night flight to Paris.

Eddie lit another smoke. The afternoon was edging into evening, with the shadows leaning lower and the tourists mostly gone. The little wind picked a few leaves, then let them drop on the ground. Eddie stood and put a twenty-euro note on the table. "Jeez, I talked your ear off," he said, glancing at his watch. "Guess I really got tired of not speaking English. This is on me."

I protested feebly, but he wouldn't hear of it. "No, forget about it. Anyway, I leave for Rome tomorrow so I've got to get rid of this money."

I reminded him that both countries now used Euros. He laughed. "Oh yeah, I forgot. At least in Italy I'll be able to understand a menu, maybe." He waved his Marlboro at the park. "But Paris sure is fucking beautiful."

I agreed. It sure was. He coughed wetly and pulled a hankie from a back pocket. "Anyway, have fun. And stick with the not smoking. These fucking things are going to kill me."

"Right." I stood to shake his hand. "Bon voyage."

I sat back down and watched him amble off, wondering if anything he'd said was true. Was he just another random bullshitter of the sort one met in bars and cafés worldwide? I didn't even know his last name. I sipped the melted ice left in my soda glass. He was not lying about Paris at least; it was indeed fucking beautiful, impossibly so. Like a vast and perfect work of art — a coral bed or a cathedral — to which countless generations had added their small bones. Then I noticed that he'd left his sketchbook behind. I flipped through. It was nearly full, with dozens of sketches, some quite detailed, in charcoal and pastel and pencil, of Paris's buildings, trees, people, and bridges in different seasons and lights. They were, without a doubt, the worst drawings I'd ever seen in my life.

ACKNOWLEDGMENTS

I would like to thank my editor Ed Park for asking if I had a "cache" of stories he could see and making this collection a reality. I am immensely grateful to him and to everyone at Little A. Thanks especially to Lynn Buckley for another amazing cover. I also continue to have to the world's best agent, Doug Stewart. I am deeply grateful to him and everyone at Sterling Lord Literistic, especially Madeleine Clark. Several of these stories appeared elsewhere, and I am very thankful for all the support my work has received. Most particularly, I wish to thank Lorin Stein at *Paris Review,* who plucked my odd little tale from the heap and made a teenage dream come true, and Nicole Rudick for helping me get it right. Thanks also to the folks at *Fence,* and as always to Rivka Galchen, who continues to be a much better friend and comrade than I deserve. Most of all I want to thank my family, whose love and faith have always been there, and the many friends who have carried me this far.